The moment is rapidly approaching when humanity must choose its future. What appears a simple choice between love and fear is complicated by the desires of two opposing cosmic forces. Artemis Andronikos rushes to discover a message the ancients left in stone ruins around the Earth. Aided by her partner Lucy and the rogue astrophysicist Wolfgang Strang, Artemis assembles a team of brilliant young scientists to decode when, where, and how the choice is to be made.

Convincing the former Harbinger children to grow beyond their Ivy League training and listen to their inner voices is the first step. Preparing them to accept a new version of reality proves more difficult. And Artemis must deal with an existential threat of her own; one that could separate her from her soulmate for eternity.

Theories of consciousness and philosophy battle as the cosmos bears down. How does one select a future when everything one has been taught is wrong? When knowledge fails, only the gods of one's own heart remain.

REVELATIONS

The Artemis Series, Book Three

Mary Eicher

A NineStar Press Publication

www.ninestarpress.com

Revelations

Printed in the USA

ISBN: 978-1-64890-254-3

First Edition, April, 2021

Also available in eBook, ISBN: 978-1-64890-253-6

WARNING:

This book contains sexually explicit content, which may only be suitable for mature readers.

To Rachael, Steve, Kathleen, Robyn, Cherie, and Sue who gifted me with support and encouragement.

"The intuitive mind is a sacred gift, and the rational mind is a faithful servant. We have created a society that honors the servant and has forgotten the gift."

—Albert Einstein

Chapter One

The absence of a single speck of light in the night sky was hardly a catastrophe. Except to Dr. Wolfgang Strang. Mystified, the astrophysicist removed his reading glasses and rubbed his temples. Objects, even unexplained objects, did not simply vanish. Suspicious of the sterile numeric data, Strang set it aside and stepped into the yard to inspect the cosmos with his own eyes. The "great river," as the Inca had called the Milky Way, floated serene and seemingly unchanged in the southern sky. But to Strang the universe was regrettably diminished, and he felt the loss deep in his soul.

"Stargazing, Wolf?"

Strang turned to find a tall, slender figure emerging from the shadows. "No, my dear. I am merely looking for an old friend."

He flashed a self-deprecating smile and accepted an affectionate hug in response. The astrophysicist offered his arm to his companion and noted how well moonlight suited her. The pale rays illuminated Artemis's ebony tresses and lent a violet cast to her pale, intelligent eyes. "What causes your noctambulant wanderings this night, Temmie?"

Artemis closed her fingers about his arm and gently nudged him to walk with her. "You know me, Wolf. I came to commune with the moon as usual."

Strang chuckled. "Ah yes. Artemis and the moon are legendary companions."

Echoing the small laugh, Artemis glanced at her friend, noting how the light deepened the lines at his eyes and accentuated the folds on his bristled cheeks. Strang was looking older of late, as if he were struggling with a burden grown too heavy.

"What is it, Wolf?" she asked, pausing their leisurely stroll.

"The object has vanished." Strang motioned to the lower edge of the Milky Way. There, amid a plethora of unnamed bits of light, a single object had captivated him seventeen years ago. It was the birth star marking the moment the Harbinger had awakened and reality had vaulted into chaos.

Artemis glanced at the familiar stellar formation Strang was indicating and shook her head. "You can't possibly tell just by looking, Wolf. Perhaps it has merely dimmed once again."

Strang patted her arm. "No, no. My darling girl, I realized the object has never been visible to the human eye. I am referring to the latest information from the observatory. I assure you there is no mistake. The object is no longer there."

A chill skittered down Artemis's spine. She had not expected a sign. The question of the Harbinger's purpose had faded over the years. A generation endowed with precognition had reached maturity. Gifted. Blessed. Awakened with the ability to foresee events. To most, the Harbinger was considered an evolutionary gift to the human race. And Artemis had chosen to merely let it be.

Allowing herself to cease the quest to understand the reason behind the Harbinger, she had put away her suspicions for a decade.

She could feel apprehension in Strang as well. He shared her concern, she knew, just as it had been with the Harbinger's mysterious awakening, the object's sudden disappearance presaged an approaching danger.

Artemis closed her eyes and willed a nascent panic to subside. Taking a calming breath, she lifted now darkened eyes to Strang and whispered, "Then it has begun."

*

Lucy scrolled listlessly through page after page of unappealing items for sale, finding nothing remotely suitable for Strang's sixtieth birthday. He was a man of few needs and even fewer wants, content to spend his time exploring distant worlds seeking to understand the purpose of existence.

"Okay, I'm stuck," she told Artemis with a sigh. "What does he like? I mean, I know it's impossible we don't know what he likes. Wolf has been a member of the family for nearly two decades, but I don't think I've ever heard him express a desire for anything."

Artemis plopped a pile of freshly dried clothes on the bed and nodded. "He has everything he needs."

"Which is exactly how many Hawaiian shirts anyway?" Lucy joked, watching her partner walk to the closet. "He has one suit, not that he ever wears it. I can't imagine he'd know what to do with a tie. What would tickle his fancy?"

"I doubt he has a fancy!" Artemis grabbed a handful of hangers and headed back to the bed where Lucy sat fiddling with the laptop.

Lucy groaned. "You know what I mean."

Artemis shrugged. "He once said he used to shop for useless things. Let's get him something useless."

Lucy ran her fingers through her light-brown bangs and threw a smirk at Artemis. "Yeah, that'll work. I'm sure there's a category of useless things just for astrophysicists. There are dozens of knickknacks all over his bungalow. Not! Wolf has his books and his computer and Willa's urn. That's it."

"Maybe we should give him a medal for putting up with us all these years." Artemis offered, voicing the first thing to pop into her head. "Here, go to collectibles." She reached past Lucy and tapped a few keys on the laptop and then returned to folding clothes.

"How about this?" Lucy asked, enlarging an item on the screen. "It only costs a million dollars. Bet they'll take nine hundred thou give or take."

"Hum?" Artemis tossed aside a pair of stonewashed jeans and leaned over Lucy for a better look. "How did you find this?" she asked, rotating the laptop toward her.

"Hey!" Lucy complained. "I didn't find it. It just appeared. You're the one who touched the keyboard, not me."

Artemis picked up the laptop and examined the photograph of a smooth metal disk measuring three inches in diameter with a symbol expertly engraved on its face. "Says it's made of platinum and look here. It was just listed a few seconds ago."

"What's that symbol on it?" Lucy put her chin on Artemis's shoulder and leaned forward for a peek. "Some sort of weird yin-yang?"

Artemis set the laptop on the desk so they could both see it. "It's the Taijitu, part of the supreme polarity. No, wait. This one looks like a version attributed to Zhao Huiqian." She traced the symbol slowly with her eyes. "Actually, it's even older than that. This rendering is quite ancient. It's found in cultures throughout the uni...ah, all over the world."

Lucy caught the abrupt verbal redirection and stared quizzically at her partner. Artemis merely shrugged, leaving Lucy to file the slip of the tongue away with the scores of other unexplained phrases her soulmate had used over the years.

The screen abruptly went blank. Artemis cuffed the laptop on the side to restore the image, but it did not reappear. Scrolling up and down, she could find no indication the item had ever been there. "What the hell?"

Repeating the actions yielded the same result. "That is odd. An item typically stays up even after it's sold, until the transaction is completed. But it couldn't have happened that fast!" She stared at Artemis. "Did you see who posted it?"

Artemis closed her eyes and tried to recall details of what she'd seen on the screen. "No. It said something about a dealer in London. Hanover Street, I think. Here, let me have the laptop. I'll see if I can identify a source."

Lucy handed her the computer and took over the task of folding clothes. "I cannot believe it got sold so fast. Who has a million dollars to spend on something like that?" She poked Artemis in the ribs. "Besides you, that is."

"Uh." Artemis grunted, completely absorbed in following the code she was trying to hack. It was pointless. The item had never appeared, according to the first hack she tried. The disk was worth every penny if it was what she suspected. It was priceless, and it possessed a power capable of unspeakable evil. The dread she had felt with Strang took a giant stride forward.

She turned to Lucy. "We must find that disk."

*

Raphael Berticelli ran his hand down his spotless white cassock and savored the smoothness of the fine wool. He had worn the papal garment for three months since the College of Cardinals had selected him to lead a half a billion Catholics to the Kingdom of Heaven. A perilous journey given the times. Never had heaven seemed quite so distant, with conflict and hatred growing ever more prevalent in the world.

Raphael brushed his fingers along a slumbering rhododendron and envisioned the riot of lavender-blue spring flowers that would bloom in a few weeks. He shared the bush's impatience. Raphael, too, was eager to fulfill his purpose. The seeds of ambition were germinating in his soul. As pope, Raphael had chosen the name Peter, demonstrating a self-importance the earlier pontiffs, indeed he himself, had once eschewed. But the name had appealed to him for a reason. Like the original Peter, Raphael was destined for greatness.

Pope Peter II was blessed beyond normal men. He felt beneath his rochet for the object to which he attributed his heady climb to power.

"There you are!" Raphael grinned at the slender metal disk shimmering in the yellow morning light. He pressed the disk between his hands, finding comfort in the object's warmth. The disk was his constant companion; it centered him in an uncertain world. It guided his thoughts and had brought him to the pinnacle of power.

Hearing the church bells marking the hour, Raphael slipped the disk into a pocket above his heart and headed back to his private chapel to say mass. He took off the pectoral cross and unbuttoned the mozzetta. Then he reached for the heavy vestment that had been laid out for him and hesitated. Retrieving the disk, the pontiff reluctantly set it aside. Pope Peter II considered the object a thing apart from his religious duties and thought it best not to combine the object with the ritual of the transubstantiation. Mystery upon mystery was too much even for a pope to contemplate.

When the mass was completed, Raphael returned to the papal apartment to begin the day's work. The sound of chanting carried up from the courtyard below. Raphael opened a window near his desk, inviting the soothing Gregorian chant into the small room. There had been similar chanting when he'd first encountered the disk, and a memory flooded back.

He recalled seeing it among Benedictus's belongings one evening after serving the pontiff his supper. Raphael, merely a monsignor in service to Pope Benedictus at the time, had found the disk in a drawer. He had picked it up and traced the symbol on its face, enthralled by the disk's smooth, hypnotic feel.

Shortly thereafter, Pope Benedictus had fallen ill. *Could it really be eleven years?* Raphael wondered, remembering the morning he had found Benedictus stricken in bed, his body barely functional and his mind confused. Monsignor Berticelli had spent those years caring for the shell of a man Benedictus had become. He had concealed the depth of the pontiff's mental deterioration, seeing personally to the various documents and decrees the Vatican required. Given the looming scandal, the Vatican was eager to conceal Benedictus's growing incapacitation from the public. What was assumed to be a brief period of convalescence had, however, stretched into years. Trapped by an initial lie no matter how rightly intended, the cardinals kept the secret of Benedictus's condition and permitted Raphael to fill the void. The disk had guided his way.

At its bidding, Raphael had used the opportunity to elevate himself to cardinal. Then the disk had spoken to Raphael again one evening while he bathed the feeble body of the pontiff, listening as the pope prattled on unintelligibly about the Harbinger and the children he had sought once to destroy. Carefully placing Benedictus back in the papal bed, Raphael had gently folded the blankets about the man and waited for him to sleep. Then, moving his arm in blessing, Raphael had taken a pillow and pressed it over Benedictus's wizened face.

Within weeks the disk had made Raphael the new pope as reward for his obedience. Raphael shut the window. The Gregorian chant concluded, he went to his desk and straightened the picture taken the day of his selection. He liked the photograph. It captured his essence. He had been elected on the second ballot by the trapped and undoubtedly wary princes of the Holy Roman Church.

More powerful than a relic and more blessed to him than any ritual he might be called upon to perform, the disk was the new pope's talisman. Now it required him to perform a third task, one very different from the others. The music had come to him as he slept and with it the intention of offering the soothing sounds to the world.

He withdrew a sheaf of paper and began to mark the notes so familiar to his inner ears. Note by note, Raphael recorded the melody he perceived coming from the disk. He would have the choir record them once he had put words to the notes, words that spoke of peace and fraternity and love of the one true messenger of creation.

*

Angela Breem looked at the souvenir and set it aside. She didn't like it. More than that, the cheap aluminum disk made her uncomfortable. The work crew had given it to her in appreciation of her kindness, or so they said. The other archeologists were tougher on the workmen. Angie found such behavior ridiculously shortsighted. The workers labored in the stifling heat day after day, and it had been more than a year since they had found anything to merit praise for their efforts.

Her cell phone chirped, and she smiled, hearing her mother's voice.

"I'm fine, Mom," Angie replied, stepping back into her tent and out of the bright sun. "How are you and Temmie?"

Lucy gave her daughter the whole rundown on Artemis's latest quest. Angie took a few sips of water as she listened and felt something stir in the back of her mind.

"A disk, you say, with a taijitu on it?" Angie put aside the bottle of water. "It was probably a souvenir, Mom. They're all over the place here. My work crew gave me something similar yesterday. It had a different design on. A rather crude yin-yang, not a taijitu, and it was painted, not etched. The back had a blessing written in Arabic. Tell Temmie it's just a trinket and not to pay a million dollars for it. I can get her one for ten bucks." She heard her mother chuckle. "Listen, Mom. I'll tell her myself. Is she there?"

Lucy told her Artemis had gone into town. The pressure in Angie's head ceased. Lucy launched an update on plans for Strang's birthday. Angie hoped Wolf would appreciate the card she'd sent. He was a kind and noble man, and she wanted him to know how much he meant to her. Then Lucy proceeded with the purpose of the call. She described Artemis's agitation and belief someone or something was interfering with humans. Angie closed her eyes as she listened. Lucy sounded very concerned. And Angie wanted to know more, but a knock on the tent frame called her attention. The crew was waiting to be briefed on the day's assignment.

"Ah, hey, Mom, I've got to go. Text me the details and I'll get back to you. Please tell everyone I said hello. And assure Temmie I will help in any way I can."

The last part tumbled out without her consent. The words just asserted themselves unbeckoned. Angie felt a momentary pain in her temples and then the sensation vanished. She put away the phone and went out into the Egyptian heat to give her crew directives for the day. She would send them to a new area, one that had suddenly popped to mind.

*

The universe reveals itself if one listens. Beneath the harsh cacophony of daily life there is a constant to which one clings often without noticing. This was the sound Artemis heard clearly urging her to take the action she alone could perform. The goddess of the hunt, so long satisfied with a life free of conflict, cocooned in the warmth of her lover's arms, knew her time of refuge was over.

The list of candidates had dwindled over the decade since Artemis had created it. She had started with twenty children scoured from the millions who had purchased the game she had converted from the diabolical one the cult had created. The original app had been used to identify children with highly developed precognitive skills and eliminate them. Artemis had done away with the cult. But she had recognized how useful the game would be in identifying the Harbinger children the world would need.

The then-adolescents played a game requiring them to choose between paths and weapons to reach a castle. The game was harmless other than being somewhat addictive. And it had been successful, giving Artemis access to the most talented of the precognitive kids throughout the world.

Once they were identified, Artemis had ensured their development. An unseen benefactor, she had provided scholarships and entry into universities. She had monitored their progress without their knowledge, and she had watched them mature. Some she had had to rescue from circumstances that might have ruined their lives. Several had fallen victim to the vagaries of life despite her best efforts. The majority had disappeared into quiet, normal lives. And a few had failed to live up to their talents. Two had died.

Checking which of the children, now young adults like Lucy's daughter Angie, remained, Artemis found only six suited to her needs. And of those only three or four had studied the subject matter which would be required. She examined the file for each remaining candidate and entered their addresses on the form letters she had prepared.

Each of them would be offered a lucrative job as her assistant. The work would be challenging and important; far beyond what they would find on the open market. Room and board would be provided. Artemis intended those who accepted the position to stay at her mansion where she could participate and encourage them. She could not do the work for them. The gift of the Harbinger, like the decision they would ultimately be called to make, belonged to them. If Artemis was correct about what was about to transpire.

Noting the current situation of each candidate, Artemis prepared supportive letters that would facilitate their ability to accept her offer for an interview. She reviewed her work and drove to town to mail the letters. On her way back, she rehearsed several ways to break the news to Lucy. They were about to forfeit their comfortable, secluded life.

"Lucy's going to freak," she exclaimed when she realized none of the explanations were adequate to the task.

Chapter Two

Strang set his empty dinner plate in the sink and headed to the living room, stopping at the bar on the way to procure a glass of brandy. He had the distinct impression he was going to need it. Lucy had been cheerful enough during dinner, but Artemis had had a thousand-yard stare every time Strang attempted a substantive topic of discussion. The meal had ended up peppered with clichés and seasoned with silence. With a sparkling after-dinner conversation unlikely, a bit of fortification struck the birthday boy as warranted.

He found Artemis standing by the huge window at the front of the room staring at the long shadows forming in the wake of the setting sun. Her arms were folded tightly at her chest, and she appeared lost in the same musing that had possessed her during dinner. Strang cleared his throat and stepped lightly to the seating area in the center of the silent room.

Her pale eyes followed Strang's reflection across the glass. He appeared guarded, his usual ebullience decidedly missing. Perhaps she was projecting her own apprehension on the man, she thought. Relaxing her arms, Artemis brushed an errant strand of ebony hair behind her ear and turned to greet her friend.

Lucy arrived carrying an enormous cake laden with an abundance of candles to note Strang's sixtieth birthday. She flashed a grin as she set the inferno on the coffee table in front of Strang, who responded with a chuckle. Artemis joined them and the pair did a worthy rendition of "Happy Birthday" while the birthday boy beamed in appreciation.

Strang swiped a fingerful of icing and then leaned forward to blow out the bonfire.

"Wait! Make your wish first." Lucy stopped him midbreath. "It took forever to light them. You wouldn't want to make me do it again." She shook her hands, pantomiming exhaustion, causing Strang to chuckle.

"Certainly not," he assured her, rising solemnly to his feet. "Far be it for me to forego tradition. I wish to thank the baker and the candlemaker, both of whom have obviously labored to produce this most marvelous confection." He looked at the two women, appreciation evident in his eyes. "And you, my dear friends, who have blessed this old man with hearth and home these many years."

"That's not a wish, Wolf," Lucy chided. "Come on. There must be something you would like. Although I must admit neither Temmie nor I could think of what that would be."

Strang settled back into his seat and set aside the brandy. "Oh, I see. This is in the nature of an inquisition."

"Not even an interrogation, Wolf," Artemis pointed out with a wink. "Merely a custom laced with curiosity."

Strang thought a moment. "In that case, I wish our oracle were here to share this evening. I miss her. Especially at moments such as this."

"Speaking of which, Angie sent you a card." Lucy handed him an envelope she'd kept tucked away for days.

Strang opened it and read aloud the handwritten message on the interior of the greeting card. "Happy birthday to my beloved father..." His voice cracked. "Oh, my darling girl, how wonderful of you to bestow such a title upon me."

Lucy sat beside him on the sofa. "Well, you have been a father to her in all the ways that matter, Wolf. She's just stating the obvious." She opened the drawer in the coffee table base and handed him a gift box wrapped in Artemis's signature style.

Strang untied the ribbon and tore away the wrapping paper, revealing a bright-red Hawaiian shirt decorated with lacy white unalomes. "How did you know I love island shirts?" he asked with a grin.

"Our stunning powers of observation." Lucy laughed, enfolding him in a fond hug. "Now you'd better put out the fire before the smoke detectors go off," she teased.

Strang leaned down, blew out the candles with an extended breath, and gave a victorious twirl of his hand. Lucy cut a piece of cake for each of them and took a seat on the facing sofa.

"If I have one wish left," he said before sliding his fork into the delicious looking dessert, "it would be for you to tell me what is troubling you, Temmie."

Lucy gave her soulmate a look conveying her own interest in that subject. Artemis had been visibly preoccupied for nearly a week, silently mulling over something, and Lucy had been waiting for an explanation. But none had been forthcoming. If she had to bet on what was going on in her partner's mind, Lucy would put her nickel on another Harbinger related quest. Which was why Lucy had not pressed the issue herself. She found the thought the Harbinger was still capable of intruding on their lives more than a little unsettling.

"All right, you two," Artemis chided half seriously. "Stop looking at me like I'm the after-dinner entertainment. I filed papers creating an LLC this afternoon. Here's another title for you, Wolf. You are now a vice president of Choice Ltd. It's not nearly as endearing as 'father,' but it does mean there is a new mystery for you to resolve."

Strang glanced at Lucy, who was equally taken off-guard. Artemis was impossibly wealthy, hardly in need of a new business venture. They shared the simultaneous realization their quiet, uncomplicated life was about to change.

"May I inquire as to the nature of this surprising new endeavor?" he asked, setting aside the cake and cradling the brandy glass between his hands.

"We are going to save the world," Artemis announced. Only the seriousness with which she said it kept Lucy from laughing out loud.

Strang took a sip from his snifter. "A worthy goal, my dear goddess, but I feel the need to confess I am not aware of any particular threat to this planet at the moment. From what precisely must the world be saved?"

"From itself." Artemis was amused by the blank confusion on her companions' faces. For a moment, she wondered if it would be better to spare them the details of what she feared was approaching.

Lucy shed her shoes, tucked her legs beneath her on the sofa, and cocked her head to one side. "This is about that disk we saw the other day, isn't it?" she asked, remembering Artemis's reaction and attempting to assemble facts decidedly not in evidence.

Artemis nodded. "Yes, the disk is part of it. But it's more than that. Wolf discovered the object near the Great Rift has disappeared. I cannot shake the feeling something has gone terribly wrong."

Turning to Strang, Lucy began a whispered description of the disk Artemis was talking about. She made a circle with her hands to describe the object and started to explain the taijitu.

"I am not familiar with the taijitu. But you aren't proposing this disk is related to the missing celestial object, are you?" Strang asked, taking another sip of brandy.

Lucy started to smile and then caught Artemis nodding. "Wait. Temmie. What? The disk cannot possibly be Strang's missing star."

Artemis sighed. "No, of course not. But they are related, Lucy. To each other and to the Harbinger."

Strang took a final sip of brandy. "My darling girl, we have always speculated the Harbinger was associated with the object. But do you have evidence the Harbinger effect has similarly been diminished?"

"Not specifically," Artemis admitted, but the growing feeling of something being amiss was evidence enough. She frowned. "It's just a feeling."

Sprang looked wistfully at his empty brandy glass. He had learned long ago not to dismiss Artemis's instincts particularly when it came to the Harbinger. The woman's extraordinary talents had been proven a myriad of times. But the scientist in him needed something more substantial if he were to play along. "You once told me 'the universe is a thought, and we are the ones who think it.' I remember your words exactly. Has something changed?"

Artemis ran her tongue along her lips. "Something is interfering. Just as the ancients warned. I believe mankind is at a crossroad between two futures. We are going to help ensure the correct choice is made."

"The symbol on the disk." Lucy ventured. She looked at Strang with unconcealed pride in her eyes. "Which one do you think is right? The yin or the yang?"

"Ah! My dear Lucinda." Strang fixed his gaze on Artemis. "Therein must lay the rub."

*

General de División Maria Isabel Vergara had broken all the rules. At thirty-seven, Vergara, the stocky, dark-eyed daughter of a manual laborer, was in command of the sixth division of the Chilean army. The position required one to serve a minimum of thirty years in the military. She had served for half that. And she was a woman with no physical or sexual charisma. It was as if her ascendance through the ranks had been guided by a higher power.

Politicians feared her, and the soldiers respected her for the ruthlessness with which she had bested her rivals. A quick temper and clever ambition served in place of a formal education or a claim to aristocracy. She had attended military training where she proved a marginal student at best. But then, Vergara's skills were innate, honed in the harsh surrounds of Chile's Near North countryside between the Atacama Desert and the fertile central zone. Maria had learned how to make her way.

Vergara mounted her horse, a handsome three-year-old black stallion, a gift from Minister of National Defense Ariana at her promotion six months before. Taking the reins, she dug her heels into the horse's sides and sent him into a gallop. The sound of the animal's hooves on the dry terrain echoed toward the mountains, and Maria felt as though she was flying. She could see clearly a road leading to the glory and adoration of millions. A road in which only two obstacles remained.

General de Ejército Ernesto Boras, her current supervisor, was waiting as Maria dismounted and made her way into the large tent which served as the commander of the army's headquarters. He was a patient man, only one of the many traits Maria despised about him. He offered her a coffee and plate of melon quarters. She declined, taking a seat at the table where Boras had set a stack of official-looking papers.

"It amuses me, Maria. You insist on arriving on horseback in this weather"—he made a gesture of wiping sweat from his forehead—"when you could more easily take a vehicle afforded to your rank."

Maria knew Boras was still perturbed by her promotion. His sights had been on a favored cousin to head the sixth division. Only Minister Ariana had afforded Boras no choice in the matter. Boras gave her a quick appraisal. He could see nothing exceptional about the diminutive, unattractive female. Certainly, nothing to explain why a woman, and a young woman at that, would have been such a visible exception to the rule. He settled himself at the table and took a slice of melon from the tray between them, making no attempt to conceal the disapproval on his swarthy features.

Bile rose in the back of Maria's throat. The urge to smash Boras's broad nose made her hands twitch. She shoved them into her pockets, finding the touch of the small silver disk there soothing, and the bile receded. She grimaced at the plate of melon. People were starving throughout Chile, but not this dull, placid man. Famine was not the concern of the military, Boras had said many times. He was a fool.

Maria knew famine was not simply a matter of national security but a powerful weapon. A weapon that could unite all of South America to a single leader. A military leader who would feed her followers and destroy her enemies. The disk shimmied against her fingers, and she felt it murmur approval.

*

The ancients had understood the stars. They knew the connection between living things, and they left their knowledge for future generations in myth and stone. They had warned the gods would return and of a final battle between good and evil. To them, such truths were immutable. And evidence of a coming judgement had been entwined in philosophy throughout mankind's history. Stories foretold of a time when humanity would be weighed and found worthy or wanting.

Strang accepted Artemis's supposition the predictions were coming true. He believed further if humans were to be found worthy, surely the ancients had pointed the way. He rummaged through a stack of files and found the one he wanted. The Chakana. He had not thought of it in the years since he had decoded the Incan clues to a time of turmoil the world would one day face.

"Well, let us assume that day has come," Strang said, pushing dust off the folder and setting it on his desk beside the others he'd selected.

The question at the top of his mind was what else had the ancients intended to reveal? For decades he had searched the universe for patterns to explain the relationship between matter and the forces that created it. Perhaps there was a pattern in the placement of the monolithic constructs the ancients had built.

"As above, so below. As the universe, so the soul." He quoted Hermes Trismegistus and twirled his hand. "Thrice great is a most impressive accomplishment, perhaps we should begin by listening to this fellow." Strang cast a glance at the urn on the mantel. "I think a review of what the ancient gods had to say is in order, Willa."

His wife would have responded in the affirmative, he knew. Willa had always been supportive; one of the things he missed most about her even after all these years. Strang opened a fresh notebook and began the process of building a theory.

The Greek god Hermes was also known as the Egyptian deity Thoth. To the Greeks Hermes was the keeper of the laws by which the universe was conducted. A person who understood these laws could master the planes of existence. Thoth, also a most brilliant god, was considered a demon. Together, they represented intelligence in both its positive and negative forms. Perfect foils for Artemis's approaching choice.

Satisfied the gods represented the duality at hand, Strang moved on to review the hundreds of archeological ruins scientists had unearthed around the world. Was it probable the ancients were aware of this duality? Had they left evidence in the monolithic structures they created? If there was a pattern, Strang determined to find it.

Settling his glasses low on his nose, Strang sifted through the old notes. The sound of rain falling pleasantly against the metal shingles of his home lulled him into a soothing rhythm. And he found the work engrossing until his peaceful concentration was interrupted by a knock at the door.

"Come in," Strang called from the study. He rose stiffly from his desk to find hours had passed and Artemis stood dripping in his living room. "My dear woman, you didn't have to dash out into this weather," he said, hanging her rain slicker on a doorknob. "I have a phone, you know."

Artemis flashed a warm grin. "You live less than a hundred paces from the main house, Wolf. Using a phone seems overly indulgent when I can jog over here in a few seconds. Besides, I much prefer to talk face to face."

Strang preferred to communicate in the flesh as well. "I've been going over my old files, Temmie. Do you remember the Chakana and our discussion about what it revealed?"

"Of course. It shows the path to heaven blocked by underworld denizens. Lucy suggested it implied a war or struggle of some kind." Artemis combed her fingers through her damp hair to provide some semblance of order.

"I believe she was correct." Strang settled in a large chair as he spoke and indicated for his guest to take a seat. "I believe there will be a war. And the Harbinger children are meant to guide us to the winning side."

"So, you have put it together—the two sides, I mean." There was a tenseness in her voice echoed by her eyes.

"I deduce one is led by Ze'us." His mouth twitched into a grin as he examined her wide pale eyes for a reaction. "I assume you are well acquainted with that one. The other is not clear. I suspect if I reexamine the information we've collected from various ruin sites, I may find the answer. So, I've expanded the criteria I am using. We investigated the sites looking for heroes all those years ago. We never searched for demons. If humans are to make an informed decision, it will behoove us to know our enemy."

"And you think the ancients left us CliffsNotes on them as well. My word being insufficient to convince you." Artemis hadn't meant to sound so snippy. "I'm sorry, Wolf. My nerves are getting the best of me lately." She ran her tongue along her lips. "Look. I know what you want me to tell you. I can't give you details about the Others. I have tried to remember. I'm not even sure I ever knew."

Strang listened to her explanation of what she had been taught but never personally experienced. The Others, as she continually referred to them, were a species as opposite from her own as possible. They were outside the collective consciousness. Perhaps they were members of another collective, one rarely spoken of, presumably out of fear. The struggle between her collective and the Others was the source of the physical world. The collision of their thoughts produced energy, and energy was all there really was to physical matter.

"Even dark matter," she noted, mindful of the mystery Strang had spent decades attempting to solve. "The taijitu was the clue, Wolf. Duality, opposite forces. When I saw the symbol on the disk, I knew. And the conflicts increasing around the world are proof. There is a force bearing down on Earth. It is capable of manipulating human minds the way we manipulated bodies. Ze'us intended for humans to join with us. The Others have also staked a claim. There are two vastly different futures possible. That is the choice the Harbinger children are meant to make."

Strang tapped his fingers on his cheek. "There are stories about otherworldly creatures in every culture. Vampires, demons, and truly evil entities who possess the minds and bodies of their victims."

Artemis shrugged. "I credit those stories to human imagination, Wolf. The Others are more likely to influence, not to generate, the very human tendency to violence. Attila, Genghis Khan, Stalin, and Hitler were not alien beings. The Others seek to control behavior, not to take mortal form."

"History is full of despots, my dear. Do you think the Others influenced them all?"

"Not necessarily. They may have tested their ability to influence humans through the eons, but it wasn't until the Harbinger activated that the Others became aggressive. I believe they are directly involved in manipulating the outcome now. The object you detected is not required anymore. I believe the Others are here."

Strang shifted in his chair. "I have a theory of my own about the object, Temmie. Odd as it might sound, I suspect its placement was significant. Are you familiar with Hermes Trismegistus?"

She nodded. "As above, so below."

"Of course, you are." Strang shook his head. Hermes was another of the Greek gods.

"He was a philosopher of some repute. But mainly he was what one would call a stoner today." She winked. "He did so enjoy his stimulants."

"I want to show you something." Strang got up and crossed to his office where he continued his remarks as he shuffled papers on his desk. "I made a list of sites when we were looking into what the ancients might have known. If I can locate the damnable thing. Give me a moment, my dear."

Artemis heard papers being shuffled and sank back into the chair to wait. Strang had been searching for a way to assist her. Knowing Strang, she was hardly surprised.

Artemis had racked her own brain for memories and found them incomplete and of marginal help. But the belief she was meant to assist with the coming choice had only grown stronger.

Strang reappeared wearing a fresh Hawaiian shirt. The dark shirt was a signal he was serious. Artemis had decoded Strang's wardrobe years ago. The darker the shirt, the more significant the discussion. According to this theory, Artemis wondered if they would all be reduced to donning black given what lay ahead.

"Here." Strang handed her a sheaf of yellowed papers with a list of ancient ruin sites extending down both sides. "This is the galaxy of options. Perhaps together we can reduce it to a mere solar system of possibilities."

She stared at him with curious blue eyes. "Why these sites, Wolf? There are thousands of ancient ruins."

Strang descended awkwardly into a chair. "Years ago, I took the liberty of devising a set of criteria to apply to the population of sites across the world. Characteristics starting with those we discovered on our journey to Peru with Angie, what is it, eleven years ago now." He paused and shook his head. "Astonishing how time passes. And to think one philosopher speculated that time does not exist."

Artemis merely smiled. *It doesn't*, she wanted to tell him, but darting off on a tangent regarding time would not serve their current purpose. "What criteria did you use?" she asked.

"Ah, yes. Well, basically, I was looking for similarities. The inclusion of references to astrological objects—temples to the sun and/or moon, that sort of thing. Inclusion of solstice points, references to star configurations such as the Pleiades or Orion. Orientation.

Dimensions. Construction methodologies. And I am working on the mathematical interpretation of distances between sites—the relationship to Earth's circumference. It's 24,892 miles, you know." He paused. "I wish I still had computing privileges at the observatory. Perhaps I can enlist the assistance of...of..."

"Wolf!" Artemis called him back to the point at hand. "Is this the result of your analysis so far?"

He grinned. "Yes, but it's only a beginning. I am intrigued by the idea of mathematical relationships, and I am certain there are quantum dependencies expressed in the azimuthal projections." His eyes were bright with excitement. "I'll add to the criteria I mentioned before, nefarious influences and such. The calculations will be complex, but most assuredly doable."

"I'm sure they are," Artemis said with a thin, charmed smile. "But you cannot possibly do all this alone. There are thousands of sites spanning thousands of years of human history."

He thought a moment, his fingers perched on his chin. "Are you thinking of asking someone else to do the calculations?" His enthusiasm had vanished.

"No, of course not, Wolf." She reached out and touched his knee. "You are irreplaceable. But how would you like an assistant?"

He looked unconvinced. "One of those young geniuses you've been secretly shepherding?"

"You know about that, huh?" Her mouth curled sheepishly.

He waggled his brows. "I must remind you from time to time that I am an investigator, mustn't I? But in answer to your inquiry, yes. I would welcome assistance. The urgency of our situation is written on your lovely face,

Temmie. I will find what the sites tell us. Your quest is once again my solitary purpose."

Strang noted the tension still evident on Artemis's face. "I don't suppose you would consider employing the talents of a few other geniuses in your intellectual harem, would you?"

"As a matter of fact, I plan to do just that." She reached for the papers. "Now let's see if we can narrow down this list of yours."

*

Keegan shoved dirty T-shirts into his kit, eager to be on his way. The proceeds from a night of poker were stuffed in the pockets of his jeans. It was enough to get him from Adelaide to Sydney by bus. He took an ornate wooden box he'd stowed at the back of an empty dresser drawer and opened it. If he could find a buyer, the contents should bring more than enough for a ticket back to the States.

Keegan had offered the previous owner a chance to buy it back right after the game. But the kid said he'd have to ask his father for the cash, and Keegan did not have time to wait. Once the university had severed his contract, Keegan was bound by law to leave Australia. He had been working his way around the country existing on small jobs and poker scams where possible. But he knew time was running out. And he was tired of a country where the weather was upside down and the night sky was an unfamiliar place.

Fresh starts don't always work out. This one had lasted less than six months, although it seemed longer given his meager day-to-day existence. He glanced in the mirror and ran his hands through his straggled light-brown hair. He looked pale and resigned. His big brain as he thought of it was not enough to get him through the world. Two PhDs got him jobs but did not provide the social skills he needed to keep them. There was no question he was brilliant. But Keegan was also irritating. It was his only talent aside from poker and mathematics.

He checked his backpack a final time and began the three-mile trek to the bus depot. He examined the faces of people he passed. They were unreadable to him, masks conveying nothing about the person within. The two years since he'd earned his final degree had been spent amid strangers who neither earned his trust nor offered trust in return. He took out his earphones and selected a song on his iPod. Math and music were friends enough, he thought. The music soothed him. He knew he would find a way home.

Chapter Three

Lucy thumbed the remote, scrolling through a dozen channels before deciding she didn't want to watch the news. Adding the daily dose of calamity and corruption to Artemis's obsession with a coming crisis Lucy barely understood was more than she could deal with.

They had been over Artemis's concerns for days. Consciousness, collectives, creation—it all became a blur after a while. Too complex to her way of thinking. Lucy preferred the simple clarity she'd been taught as a child. A person's soul was judged after death and sent either to heaven or hell.

Artemis had started with the concept of judgement and then enhanced it. Judgement was not about an individual. It was for an entire species. More, even: an entire biosphere. And the judgement was not performed by a sky god. It was decided by the species itself. The human race must decide what it wanted to become. Whether we preferred heaven or hell. Love or hate.

Just the other evening when the three of them had again rehashed the subject, Strang had used the word apocalypse in what had been the briefest pronouncement Lucy had ever heard the scientist make. She'd been stunned enough to challenge. "You mean the one in the Bible?"

Strang had put his arm on the mantel, setting his elbow beside Willa's urn. "That would be the one...the Book of Revelations. There are other names for it. The last judgement. Armageddon. The end of days."

Scary words. Lucy did not believe in an end. Even death was not an end. Life was made of cycles like the turning of the seasons, predictable, familiar. Whatever the choice, Lucy felt confident they would all survive.

The hour was late, and her nerves were on edge. The last thing Lucy wanted was to rehash the discussion. What she did want was to stop feeling afraid. Artemis owed her that much at least. If their lives were going to be invaded by the Harbinger yet again, Lucy deserved to know why— in a way that didn't instill a nameless, incomprehensible fear.

Heading toward the hall, Lucy ran her hand along a row of books once belonging to Artemis's brother. She imagined she could feel his presence. She'd never met Ichabod. Yet she felt his essence lingering in the possessions he had loved. *Nothing ends. What is there to fear?*

She found Artemis in the bedroom, stretched out atop the duvet legs crossed, eyes closed, deep in thought.

"What exactly are we supposed to be afraid of, Temmie?" Lucy asked, her tone serious enough to get a start out of Artemis. "Wolf says Armageddon is coming. That's a little hard to believe. How did we go from a choice to war?"

Artemis sat up and directed pale-blue eyes at her soulmate. "Yes, well, that's what I'm hoping to avoid. The best I can tell you is what we've been talking about—

mankind has a choice between two futures. It depends on what they want."

There it was, Lucy thought. "How could one decide between two futures without knowing more about what those futures are?"

Artemis sat up and moved to the edge of the bed. "Okay. My species came to Earth a very long time ago. We found a primitive race of humanoids and enriched them so they could progress and eventually become part of our shared consciousness."

"Why? Why did you come here in the first place?" Lucy tapped into a well of resentment she hadn't realized she'd harbored. "I mean, it's insulting if you think about it. What gave your species the right to manipulate mine?"

Artemis was surprised by Lucy's agitation. It was a subject they had both tended to avoid, Lucy because it made her feel less than and Artemis for fear it would create a gulf between them. She realized it was a discussion they should have had a long time ago. "Because it's what we do."

"So, you made the choice for us," Lucy blurted out. "You owned us. After all, we are such a primitive species, we humans. Compared to gods."

"I am not a god," Artemis said softly. "The origin of my essence is not what defines me. My heart does. I am human in every way that matters. And I love you."

"Like a person loves a cute puppy?"

"No! Like one soul mated to another. We are connected, Lucy. What is it you don't understand?" She rose from the bed and stood beside it.

"I don't understand what the two possibilities are." Lucy tossed her hand out toward Artemis. She had heard the words a dozen times: heaven versus hell, light or dark.

But they were words. "I have no idea who the bad guys are. Shit, Temmie, I don't really know what you are either. Now you tell me our future depends on a choice. And...and Wolf uses words like Armageddon. I really want to know what I am choosing from."

Artemis sat silently for a moment. If she were honest with herself, she knew she should have expected Lucy to ask the question long before. Now that Lucy had, Artemis realized they could not go further without letting her soulmate understand the truth of who she was.

Artemis stood and removed her clothes until she stood naked in the candlelight. She fixed her gaze and let her essence unfold, creating an aura around her body. No longer the young woman Lucy had met twenty years before, Artemis at nearly fifty was nonetheless still astonishingly beautiful. The angular planes of her face were framed by long strands of rich ebony hair. Pale-blue eyes illuminated her face. The straight, patrician nose rested above full lips. Artemis was tall and slender. Her torso was perfectly proportioned, curving from broad shoulders to a narrow waist and then flaring slightly at the hips. And long, shapely legs descended to the floor. Physically, Artemis was perfect and undeniably human.

But the body was a shell. Within was an extraordinary life force. Lucy began to smile as Artemis released her essence. An inner light radiated from Temmie's core, brighter than the light of the candles sputtering nearby. The glow filled the room as Artemis's aura glistened with golden hues, seeming to quiver and pulse outward from the pale human form. Lucy reached out to touch the light, recognizing instantly it was Artemis's spirit she had always experienced. It was their spirits that joined when their bodies came together in love.

Artemis closed her eyes and refused her pulse its urge to race. She stood absolutely still. Feeling Lucy's gaze travel over her body, Artemis loosed her spirit but held her senses close, making no effort to invade her lover's thoughts. Lucy must choose freely to accept her as she truly was. It was the way of choice. It was what the Harbinger was intended to permit humans to do, to see and ultimately to understand what they could become.

Feeling a touch on her arm, Artemis opened her eyes to find Lucy gazing up at her.

"Before I decide," Lucy grinned. "May I see what the other guys look like?"

Artemis enfolded her. "I've never seen one. But I hear they are exceptionally unpleasant. All thought, no body."

*

"Wars and whispers of war." Beads of sweat formed on Deepak Kamakrisha's temple. He drew out his handkerchief and dabbed it to his forehead. It was all too much. No less than seventeen countries were demanding intervention. Even if the United Nations had sufficient resources to deal with the conflicts, there was little likelihood any of them would be resolved. The world was going mad.

Everyone had a grievance and brought it to his door expecting him to resolve the matter in their favor. Not that doing so was his job. As the Secretary-General, Kamakrisha's role was to preside over meetings of the general assembly. The ambassadors were charged with resolving conflict by talking among themselves. The number of disagreements had made that impossible. Instead, the infrequent sessions had become little more than shouting matches, and the world grew even less united.

To Kamakrisha the state of the world was a morass of famine, conflict, and hatred boiling over borders and consuming the hopes of the common people. His beloved India was rife with the same unrest poisoning even the most modest nation-states. Kamakrisha cared little for the petty squabbles and only one of the larger disputes. The homeland was besieged on all sides. His duties had taken him away for too long, and he was ready for his tenure to be over.

Once again, dabbing the sweat from his face, Kamakrisha waited in the lobby for his guest to arrive. Perhaps this one man could perform the miracle that was called for. Miracles were in the pontiff's job description, and history credited the man's predecessors with having performed them. Kamakrisha had even prayed to the pope's version of God to make it so.

Three vehicles pulled into the circular driveway visible just beyond the modern portico. Men in black robes began emerging from the vehicles, forming a contingent between the middle vehicle and the entrance. Once they were in place, a man in a white cassock stepped from the car and waved to the assembled crowd.

Kamakrisha could hear shouting and applause as the man in white walked slowly to the door surrounded by a phalanx of guards.

"President Kamakrisha," the man said with a pleasant smile, extending a hand of friendship.

The guest was unexpectedly youthful in person. He was tall and clean-shaven and had intelligent eyes filled with just a hint of duplicity common to men who wielded power from a non-military source. The crisp white cassock gave the pope a messianic aura.

"Your eminence," Kamakrisha said, grasping the pontiff's hand. "Welcome to the United Nations. We are most grateful you accepted our invitation and anxious to hear your address." He let go of the hand and motioned to the hallway. "Now if you would follow me, we shall begin your visit with a tour. And I will be honored to answer any questions you may have."

The only question that matters, Peter considered silently as the gathering started down the hall, *is whether the United Nations will agree to follow me.*

*

"What are you called, child?" Ze'us asked the young woman who held Artemis's hand. "I wish to know the name of the one who has bewitched my daughter."

"It is awkward for us to pronounce," Artemis interjected, pulling her companion closer. "I call her Lucia—the light."

Ze'us nodded and raised his gaze to Artemis, his expression dimmed with resignation. "You understand, we may not return."

Artemis winced at the sound of finality in her father's voice. Seeing her anguish, Ze'us relaxed his shoulders and threw off his cloak as leader, becoming a grieving parent stricken to be leaving his child behind. "Once separated from us, you will be subject to the physics of this planet. Your body, like hers, will die." He pointed to the girl standing beside his daughter.

"I can take mortal form as often as I wish. When this body dies, I will make another," Artemis told him, holding back the emotions urging her to fall into her father's forgiving embrace.

Ze'us shook his head. "Yes. But your memories will become less each time you subject your essence to a human form. In time you will remember nothing of me or your true nature." He blew out a long breath, glanced a final time at his daughter, and walked away.

The dream faded as Artemis eased her way carefully from Lucy's embrace. She donned her robe, silently opened the door, and stepped out to the patio. She saw the last light go out in Strang's cottage. He was wont to work late on his research, and she sauntered barefoot into the backyard. The full moon glided behind a row of high clouds, and Artemis folded her arms against her chest to ward off the chilly air.

She picked her way to the center of the yard, stepping cautiously through a patch of weeds, careful to avoid the prickly leaves in the dark. Lifting the hem of the robe, she climbed onto the small stone platform in the center of the yard and waited for the moon to emerge from behind a layer of dark clouds. Sinking to her knees, Artemis raised her arms and turned her palms skyward, freeing her spirit to seek communion with another.

Streaks of moonlight embraced Artemis, highlighting her dark hair and lending a silver glow to her pensive, sculptured features. Her blue eyes were tinged with violet in the moon's light. She thought of the one who could help, one who like Artemis had bound herself to this small planet. One with the gift of prophecy and the ability to see backward in time.

"Your visions should be of the future, Artemis. Like humans you spend too much time trying to accept the past."

Hestia's voice filled her mind. It was not a whisper, but the rich, familiar voice echoing like a balm through her soul.

"Father has not forgotten us, has he?" she asked.

"It has been but a moment in time to him, sister. He grieves, aware of what the Others seek to do." It seemed as if Hestia were standing beside her, the presence was so vivid. "Is that the reason you asked to speak with me?"

Artemis lowered her arms. "Tell me what you see, Hestia. Tell me about the Others."

An image filled her mind. A nebulous form stretched into infinity. The form lacked both shape and texture. It simply was there. A cacophony of thoughts echoing within a single consciousness—interlaced, dark and rigid. The mass surged with intent, ruthless in its communal need for order amid boundless chaos. From its collective center, galaxies gathered matter to them, absorbing the sentient life forms they found.

Artemis opened her eyes, attempting to unsee the horror, her heart racing as she thought of Lucy sucked into such a terrifying future.

She drew a breath. "Please tell me what we must do."

"There is a place already prepared. Once there, the humans must combine their minds in a single purpose just as we do. There can be no deviation. Either love or fear must rule them. The decision once made will be heard. Then it will be done."

"Where is this place?" Artemis's pulse quickened. There was so much more she needed to know. "You can see the future, Hestia. Tell me where we must go."

"I cannot see a decision as yet undetermined. The window is opened now, but the forces are not aligned. And I must warn you, Artemis. We are not permitted to impose our will. The humans must decide their own future. It is a final judgement based on all they have learned. They must use the senses we have given them."

Undetermined! Artemis clung to the word. It sent hope struggling against the dread in her chest even as Hestia's presence faded.

"Temmie!" Lucy's voice carried past her on the wind, and Artemis startled at the sound. "Get in here, this instant. It's freezing."

Spinning about, Artemis saw Lucy standing in their bedroom doorway; hands on her hips and a disapproving look on her pretty face. Artemis got to her feet and hurried across the yard.

"I thought... I mean, you were sleeping so peacefully. Ow!" she stammered. Lucy shook her head as Artemis hopped on one foot and then the other, having found the bristles in the grass.

"I understand why you go baying at the moon, Temmie. That doesn't mean I like it, especially when it's freezing out," Lucy quipped as Artemis reached the doorway and took her in her arms. Lucy cradled her head in the hollow of Artemis's shoulder and caressed her back with the tips of her fingers. Their bodies curled together. A kiss was followed by several more, and Lucy melted into the warmth of Artemis's embrace.

"Much better." Lucy grinned. "I hate waking up alone."

"Next time I'll leave a note," Artemis teased and felt a small chuckle vibrate against her chest.

"Or maybe you should wake me instead of sneaking off," Lucy offered.

Artemis pushed a strand of light-brown hair behind Lucy's ear. "If I wake you, I'd never make it out of the bed," she replied with a sexy grin.

"My point exactly!" Lucy said with a smirk of her own. "Anyway, since we're both up, I want you to know I've made a decision. I'm going to go find your disk for you. I think you're correct about the post coming from Europe. I'm going to have Angie meet me in London and go from there. The seller probably took it to a dealer, and I am certain the whole transaction was very hush-hush."

"Lucy. No. We don't know where the disk is. It could be anywhere. I only traced the listing to England before the trail got undetectable. There's no evidence it's still in Europe." She closed the bedroom door behind them and gave Lucy a dejected look. "I don't want you to go. I promise no more midnight sojourns. I figured out what we need. It's a simple matter of where, how, and when."

Lucy laid her hand gently on Artemis's cheek. "I want to help, Temmie. I can see you're overwhelmed. Let me do this. Where, how, and when, huh. Strang will tell you where. Perhaps the disk will tell us more."

A sick feeling churned in the pit of Artemis's stomach. "I don't want you to go. Not now. We're meant to be together. Wasn't that we what decided?"

Lucy climbed into bed and patted the pillow for Artemis to join her. "I think we agreed we are together...forever. Soulmates. Nothing can separate us. A few weeks apart will allow you to throw yourself into the hunt without having me underfoot. And I will be doing something I'm good at, tracking down a story or, in this case, a disk seller." She eased her body along Artemis's. "You know it's a good idea. Or do I need to convince you?"

"Hum. I could do with a bit of convincing." Artemis put an arm about Lucy's shoulders to pull her closer.

"My pleasure," Lucy murmured, beginning a trail of kisses along her lover's collarbone. "I've studied...your... technique...for winning arguments."

Artemis surrendered with a long, passionate kiss.

*

The huge man had a way of making the furniture look fragile. His six-foot-six frame and muscular build simply wasn't compatible with classroom chairs. He eased sideways into one, wincing at the audible creak it made. He leaned forward, elbows on his knees, and rubbed his face.

All his hard work had come to an end, short of the goal despite his efforts. Stefan looked at his advisor, his violet eyes filled with disappointment.

Professor Lewis instantly saw the misunderstanding. "No. No. Stefan. I have not made myself clear. You are not being dropped from the program. You are being granted your degree early. You are a brilliant student. There is nothing more you need to do. Please, let me be the first to congratulate you, Doctor Stefan Ivanov."

Stefan's violet eyes widened. "But...but I am not finished with my dissertation."

"No arguments, Stefan. You have a fine mind. There is nothing more you need to prove." Lewis extended a hand, and Stefan rose to shake it.

"Then I am free to go?" Stefan asked. He petted his mustache. He had no idea where to go, now that he thought about it. The university was his home, and his modest stipend was just enough to keep him at his studies. He had made no preparation for a job, assuming he had months before he would need one. He glanced at Professor Lewis, uncertainty about his future evident on his face.

"Here," Lewis said, holding an envelope for Stefan. "I believe this will satisfy your concern. It is a most generous job offer. The future is bright for you, Dr. Ivanov. You have earned it."

A smile appeared beneath the mustache as Stefan read Artemis's letter. He would be going to America just as he had dreamed as a young boy. He would be as far away from the coming war as possible. He clutched the letter to his chest and raised his eyes to the heavens.

"For you, Mama."

Chapter Four

"Buki!"

Jamie ran along the beach calling for his dog until the pain in his leg made him stop. He had seen the brown-and-white puppy racing down the beach, headed toward the place where a rocky cliff sloped into the ocean. The young boy waited to catch his breath. Smoke blowing in a stiff onshore wind burned his nostrils as he inhaled. His heart pounded, and his leg was starting to throb.

A terrible roar had awakened him from a nap. He remembered how his bed had bumped and swayed beneath him, and the wall had twisted and tumbled down. Then the motion had stopped, and he had heard nothing until the screaming started.

Jamie had waited for his mother to come. Blood oozed around a little piece of wood stuck in his leg. Jamie had rubbed it, but the injury didn't hurt very much, even when he pulled the splinter out. His mother would wash it and give him a big kiss if he was brave. He wondered where she had gone.

Buki had started barking soon after the shaking stopped. The puppy hopped on the bed and nipped at Jamie's shirt with his teeth. Petting the puppy, he waited for his mother. After a few minutes, the little dog had bolted through the hole in the wall and darted toward the beach. Jamie scrambled to his feet and climbed over the cluttered floor yelling for Buki to stop. But the dog had run off, disappearing around the edge of the big cliff.

"Buki!" Jamie called and began running again. He reached the towering cliff and followed it to the beach, where the water was rushing away. Jamie stopped to watch the scores of fish jumping in the sand. He had never seen them do that and thought how his uncle could just pick them up instead of tossing nets from his fishing boat.

He rounded the lower edge of the lava outcrop and climbed partway up to look for Buki. Everything looked different. Palm trees were lying sideways on the sand, and in several places, parts of the cliff had slid onto the beach. A familiar bark made Jamie look up to find the puppy charging down the slope toward him. Jamie knelt and grabbed Buki, who licked his face and squirmed excitedly. Buki jumped from Jamie's lap and ran up the slope to the crest of the cliff, then back down again, and barked at him.

When Jamie tried to catch him, the dog ran back up the hill, digging his paws into the red earth. Jamie called, but the puppy would not come to him. Buki just kept barking and dancing back and forth along the crest of the ridge. A new sound made Jamie turn to look behind him. The ocean was returning. Jamie watched wide-eyed as a line of tall waves surged toward them. The water flooded over the jumping fish and then rushed the beach and kept sweeping inland toward the burning village. Jamie ran up the hill to Buki. A second wave surged over the beach and roared inland. Smoke from the village stopped rising, and when the waves consumed a stand of candlelight trees, Jamie could see what remained of the village. He watched as his home floated in the churning water, colliding with the other huts swirling like his uncle's boat sometimes did when the water was angry.

An article published by the AP three days later listed Emae as one of the islands in the Shefa Province of Vanuatu destroyed when the earth quaked below the Coral Sea. The subsequent tsunami killed a third of the island's eight hundred residents, Jamie's mother among them. His uncle took Jamie and Buki south to the island of Efate in his fishing boat. The world turned its eyes to the greater tragedies along the western Australian coast.

*

"What we know is there are two competing forces interested in our insignificant planet. Presumably soon, homo sapiens must decide between them." Strang pulled his cap down over his forehead and sank down in the passenger seat, trying not to look at the traffic. Lucy's driving unnerved him, and the topic she had just sprung upon him only heightened his sense of discomfort. "I have deduced our beloved Temmie wishes to communicate said choice from a specific location and..." He shuddered as the car swerved in an aborted attempt to change lanes. "And I am endeavoring to identify the location by examining messages the ancients left."

Lucy tapped the blinker and looked to her right, impatient for the delivery van in her way to either move ahead or slow down and let her into the adjacent lane. When it didn't oblige, she blared her horn and sped up to go around the vehicle. Strang stomped his foot down on a brake he didn't have.

"Lucy, I consider it preferable to forestall our conversation until we have reached your intended destination."

Lucy hit the horn again and swerved to the right and then around a corner in a maneuver that earned her a loud trail of expletives from the van driver.

"Oh, dear God!" Strang whimpered.

Spying an empty spot, she pulled to the curb and parked, leaving the engine idling. Strang released his white-knuckled grip on the armrest.

"My dear woman." He sat up and repositioned the cap that had slid into his eyes. "Have we arrived at some place of interest to you?"

"No. I decided to spare you a heart attack." She smiled innocently. "I just wanted to get you alone out of range from...you know those incredible senses of hers."

The scientist wiped the sheen of sweat from his forehead. "I doubt there is such a distance, but perchance Temmie's attention is currently occupied elsewhere. In any event she has not imposed restrictions on any subject matter I know of. I believe it safe to exchange hypotheses whether she is aware of our communication or not."

Lucy smirked. "She may have been a goddess, Wolf, but she's not omniscient. I want you to keep an eye on her while I'm away. She's going to need a light. You can help her think things through."

Strang removed the cap and studied Lucy's expression. "You didn't want Temmie to go charging off in search of the disk, did you? So, you beat her to the punch as they say. Clever of you, Lucinda. But have you thought of what she might do in your absence?"

Lucy shrugged her shoulders. "I know she's going to select some people to hire. She's not a people person, Wolf. She'll need you to make sure she picks the right ones." She looked at him with puppy dog eyes. "And to make sure she gets the skills we need. She can't just go with her gut on this."

Strang understood precisely what Lucy meant. In her current state, Artemis might be prone to imprudent decisions. He nodded. "I shall do my best to assist her. The appropriateness of the candidates given the import—"

"Hold that thought, Wolf," Lucy interrupted. She jerked the wheel to the left, laid on the horn, and pulled into an onslaught of traffic to complete an ill-advised left turn. Strang clutched the armrest and replaced his cap, this time purposely shielding his eyes.

Lucy grinned. "Relax. I'm just going to use the drive-through at this coffee shop and park again so we can continue our discussion. It's just impossible for me to follow what you're saying and drive without coffee. Safety is important."

Strang managed a weak chuckle. "I had no idea you accepted such a premise. But I am delighted that you do. Now, where was I?"

Lucy ordered and paid for her latte, Strang having declined additional stimulation, and then rolled into a parking stall and turned off the engine. Taking a sip of the hot liquid, she waited for Strang to continue.

"Ah yes. When faced with a choice, it becomes incumbent on one to examine the parameters of each option. We must examine the attendant possibilities and a means to evaluate the various characteristics to arrive at a suitable selection."

"The pros and cons of the two collectives." Lucy boiled it down and took another sip of coffee.

"That's what I said." Strang looked vaguely insulted by her shorthand editing.

"We are not debating a coin toss here, Wolf. We know which collective to choose. My concern is the staff Temmie hires. I believe she has a particular set of individuals in mind."

He rested a hand on his chin and tapped a finger on his lips. "The Harbinger children are adults now. They must be ready...in theory. Of course, now she's about to come face to face with her protégés," Strang mused with a flourish of his hand. "The variables are exponential."

"She might be disappointed." Lucy made a wry smile. "That is why I've asked you to help."

"Do you realize, Lucinda, you are asking me to determine the fate of mankind?" Strang set the cap on his head and flashed a rakish grin. "Assuming we survive the journey home, how could I do aught but accept?"

*

"You have enough cash?" Artemis asked as she unzipped Lucy's bag and checked the contents.

"Yes, Mom," Lucy snarked. "Stay out of that. I know how to pack, Temmie."

Artemis zipped up the bag and raised her hands. "Peace. I just want you to be all right. The world's not a safe place right now. Crazy things are happening. You might need some extra money."

Lucy gave her a peck on the cheek. "I'll call every day. If I need more money, you can wire it. Angie's going to meet me at Heathrow. The trouble you're referring to is the crush of refugees pouring into Europe. I promise not to be mistaken for one. Or are you referring to the earthquakes near Australia?"

Artemis shook her head. "There's more. The news is having trouble keeping up. Don't be surprised by anything that happens."

Lucy smirked. "Oh, I've gotten used to surprises. The world is about to end. My lover is an alien. A star has fallen from the sky and landed smack-dab on Amazon.com. I sincerely doubt anything could surprise me now."

Artemis pulled Lucy into an embrace and kissed her. "There has been a lot, huh?"

"Ya think?" Lucy laughed. "I can't wait to see Angie and experience normal again."

Artemis felt her heart wrench. Lucy's daughter was not what she thought. Swallowing words unready to be said, Artemis hefted the suitcase and walked with Lucy to the door. "Are you sure you don't want me to drive you to the airport?"

Lucy shook her head. "It's easier to say goodbye here. I won't be gone long, Temmie. And I'll call you all the time. You have so much to do you won't even miss me."

Not remotely true! "I miss you already." Artemis folded a strand of light-brown hair behind Lucy's ear. She hoped Lucy would find the disk or, if not the object itself, at least a clue to who possessed it. The answers they were looking for had to be found, and that might be impossible without the disk.

A horn sounded from the edge of the driveway. The rideshare driver waved, and the two women went to meet him. A final kiss and Lucy got into the car. Artemis set the bag in the back and watched the sedan pull away, taking with it what she loved most in the world.

*

The European Union had fallen on hard times. An influx of refugees from the Middle East, where war appeared imminent between India and Pakistan, was straining the resources of the member nations at a time when such expenditure had gone from hardship to impossible. While the money dwindled, the rhetoric did not. Heads of state publicly shouted at each other and produced edict after edict meant to bring a rebellious populace to heel. The EU was collapsing like a stack of blocks, one nation after another, and Pope Peter II was watching with a pious, greedy eye.

Continuing what he had begun with the address to the United Nations, Peter had maneuvered the EU into two options: stand their armies against the belligerent wave of human detritus or beg the pope to step in and create order from the chaos. He folded the Vatican newspaper and set it on the table beside his breakfast tray. What the world saw as disaster befalling the nation-states of Europe, Peter read as very good news indeed. He slid his hand into his cassock pocket and clenched the small silver disk. The assurance of ultimate success surged through him. With Europe in his grasp, Peter would soon be able to concentrate on North America and China.

A hierarchy of authority with the pope at its apex was precisely what was needed to end the turmoil of a world constantly on the verge of war. And it had to be accomplished quickly before the generation who had never known the horrors of war took up the cause against him. The Harbinger children could pose an impediment to his bloodless conquest. He could feel them resisting in the one nation still mulling the offer he had given to the EU.

He drifted to the window and stared out past St Peter's Plaza into the streets of the once-holy city now filled with street vendors and tawdry shops. And he knew the reason his native country was hesitant to submit to the wishes of the church. Buried in the genes of Italians was a deep-seated mistrust of a religion known for its treachery, at once powerful enough to enslave them yet benevolent enough to offer them eternal salvation.

"They must think they have me contained," he speculated with a rueful twist of his mouth. "They are mistaken."

The disk vibrated in his pocket, sending perceptible warmth through his chest. Peter returned to his desk and penned a reply to the president of the European Union. The missive reiterated the pope's vow to establish a system of relief throughout Europe and foster the three cardinal virtues of faith, hope, and charity. Resources would be required including buildings and personnel according to Peter's instructions. Most significantly, the pope would begin immediately to feed and clothe the influx of refugees pouring into southern Europe. The missive was concluded with the demand Italy be brought into agreement.

The pope sealed the letter and set his mark upon the envelope, certain the offer would be accepted. His conquest did not depend on tanks or bombs. Refugees were his weapon. His soldiers. The teeming masses of hopeless, wretched people displaced from their homelands by hunger and fear were his army. With them he would overrun the governments of the nation-states. He would feed them and mold them into a force that politicians would be unable to crush. Peter sipped a bit of coffee and savored the thought—the universal church would rise to the pinnacle of power, and the world would once again kneel before a righteous God and his appointed servant.

Chapter Five

Sunlight drifted across the carpet, forming eddies of light and shadow and highlighting the crisp geometric design. Artemis watched the final applicant saunter through the dappled pools and drop indifferently into a padded armchair. She had reserved her highest expectations for this particular candidate, but the casual manner in which the young man conducted himself tempered her optimism. He was slender, trending to gaunt, with longish, dirty-blond hair and the pale complexion of a youth with a penchant for indoor pursuits. He looked at her with bored brown eyes and made no effort to stifle a disinterested yawn.

Keegan Montock was the final interviewee of a promising day, the first two having ended well. Anxious for a trifecta, Artemis opened a folder and reread the résumé to make certain there was no mistake, even though she knew there wasn't. According to the résumé, Keegan Montock was a prodigy with PhDs in Mathematics and Physics, an ideal candidate to assist Dr. Strang. Unfortunately, the person seated across from her seemed more a high school dropout, down to his tattered hoodie and dirty jeans. Not a hint of social grace was discernible anywhere in the overly casual young man.

"Who is this?" Keegan asked, pointing at the photograph on her desk. He recognized the infamous Artemis Andronikos immediately, noting the long ebony hair, pale-blue eyes, and the perfectly planed features of her extraordinary face. But the second woman in the photograph was unfamiliar.

Artemis glanced up from the résumé and stared at the young man draped in the hot seat. The second impression was worse than the first; he was decidedly not what she'd expected.

"That's my partner," Artemis replied, leaning forward to assert control of the interview.

Keegan cocked his head. "I assumed you were the sole proprietor of Choice Ltd. Didn't know you have a partner. But then there's no public information about your little LLC. Is your partner going to interview me too?"

"I am the sole proprietor as you put it." Artemis arched an eyebrow. "You just have to deal with me."

Keegan looked back at the photograph. "Uh-huh. Okay. You do look a bit younger there. I get it, no more partner. Where and when was the photograph taken?"

The hair at the back of Artemis's neck bristled. Her optimism was fading. Still, the need for Keegan's talents was great, and time was pressing down on her to find an assistant for Strang. She knitted her fingers together and mentally debated continuing this particular tangential line of inquiry. Keegan gave her an innocent-looking smile, and she decided to put his off-topic curiosity to rest.

"We were in Hawaii, eighteen years ago. We used to live there. Now if you don't mind, I prefer you to answer questions, not ask them."

Keegan threw his leg over the arm of his chair and broke into an insincere grin. He considered it best if

Artemis learned he was annoying at the outset. Irritating people was his special talent aside from the big brain stuff, and there was no point taking a position with someone who couldn't accept that about him. "And the kid?" he asked, still curious.

Artemis stared directly at him, her blue eyes penetrating to the back of his thick skull. "That is our daughter, Angie. She's an adult now like you're supposed to be."

Keegan looked momentarily surprised. "Oh, that kind of partner. I get it. The kid favors the other woman, so you must be the dyke."

Artemis pushed back from her desk and stood up. She tossed the folder into the trash. Keegan lost the smile the moment he realized how tall she was and saw the intimidating look in her now-darkening eyes. He extended the palms of his hand and grimaced.

"S...sorry," he stuttered. "I like to find out where the line is. Makes interacting with people easier for me. Guess I found the line, huh?"

Artemis let her gaze scorch him as she sank back into her chair. And the anger subsided as she finally got a read of the real Keegan Montock. The attitude was a façade. Once Keegan had momentarily emerged from behind it, she'd seen the insecure boy within, understanding instantly he knew too much about the physical world and comprehended too little about the beings who populate it. She knew Strang could handle Keegan's prickly personality, provided the brain it concealed was as exceptional as she expected. She picked up her cell phone and sent Strang a text.

Seeing Artemis busy herself with her phone, Keegan assumed he'd blown the interview and rose to leave.

"Where do you think you're going?" Artemis asked without looking up.

He shrugged. "I can see myself out."

"Am I wrong, or do you need this job?" she asked, returning the phone to her pocket. "You've been out of academia for several years now and failed at five jobs. I'd say we are probably your last chance—unless you prefer flipping burgers as a career."

"No, ma'am." Keegan looked contrite enough to make Artemis suppress a smile.

"Then sit your butt down and wait." She leaned her elbows on her desk and gazed at him, analyzing the insecure boy within. "We need your brain, Keegan. We can teach you manners, that part's easy. Saving the human race is not. You are going to learn a lot of things that may seem unbelievable at first. The world is not at all what you have been led to believe. You are going to be challenged, and I suspect you will enjoy that. The work is exhausting, and it will take someone with your abilities to perform it."

The office door flew open, and Strang, dressed in denim shorts and a gaudy Hawaiian shirt, strolled in, the slap of his flip-flops thudding along the carpet. He smiled at Artemis and then looked at her disheveled companion and frowned. "This is the aforementioned genius? My darling goddess, are you quite certain?"

Keegan's eyes widened as he turned back to Artemis. She was indeed impressive, especially for an older woman, but the man called her "goddess." He shook his head and dismissed the designation as merely an endearment.

"Dr. Strang, meet Dr. Keegan Montock. He's a handful," Artemis said, walking around her desk to whisper a few comments out of Keegan's hearing.

Strang nodded as he listened. He looked at the scrawny young man and chuckled. Putting the wunderkind through his paces might actually be amusing, he thought. And the confused look on Keegan's face made it seem all the more so. *Ah, youth*, Strang mused, *I really, really do not miss you.* He lifted his arm and twirled his hand. "Come along, son," he instructed his prospective assistant.

"You are Dr. Wolfgang Strang, aren't you?" Keegan asked. "I've heard of you somewhere." He tapped his forehead with his finger. "The Harbinger. That's it. You're the guy who solved the Harbinger. I remember reading about you when I was a kid."

Strang chuckled. "That was the accomplishment of our dear Miss Andronikos. I am merely the man who held her coat, as they say." He turned to Artemis. "I will let you know if this young genius is up to the task, Temmie. I take it you endeavor to hire him officially?"

"Either that or execute him," she said, sounding far too serious to Keegan's ear. "Bring him back when you're done. I'll decide then."

*

The antique shop was on the corner of a quiet street at the edge of London's West End. Lucy checked the address with the one Artemis had written down from what she remembered of the brief listing. She had gotten it correct—1414 Hanover Street. The little shop looked older than its elderly proprietor, who emerged from the back when the tinkle of a bell announced Lucy had opened the front door.

"G'day, miss," the man greeted her as he sat on a stool behind a gnarled wood counter. "How may I assist you?"

Lucy flashed a bright smile. "May I look around?"

"Surely."

The shop was filled to overflowing with wondrous things. Pottery and porcelain figures lined two of the many shelves, along with odd machines whose functions were impossible to discern. Lucy held her handbag firmly at her breast as she walked the aisles lest she inadvertently damage something. Along a row at the back were shelves of books, their leather covers faded with age. Lucy thought of Cab's Place, their shop on Maui, and how her mother would have loved this quaint shop.

She went to the counter and gave the man another smile. "Perhaps you can help me," she said, taking a drawing from her purse. "I am interested in this."

The man perched a set of glasses on his nose and examined the drawing of the disk. "Ah, a common trinket." He removed the glasses and gave Lucy a squinty-eyed stare. "You have one you wish to sell?"

"No." Lucy shook her head. She had caught a glint of recognition in the man's eyes, although he tried to conceal it. "I am interested in buying this particular item."

"Oh, I see." The proprietor sagged. "Well, there are plenty of them on the street. They're nothing but cheap souvenirs. People come in here and try to sell them to me, pretending they are made of pure silver and therefore valuable. I suppose there are villains on the street telling the same lie to tourists. You best be careful." His eyes narrowed at the last.

Lucy got the distinct impression the man was the one lying. "I saw this disk for sale on the internet. It gave your address as the contact."

"Impossible!" The man scrunched his nose. "I have no use for trinkets. Nor do I fancy the new style of commerce. I sell right from my shop to customers who seek to purchase an item of quality. Don't know why you believe what's on that deceitful contraption anyway. Nothing true there. Nothing true anywhere anymore." He rolled his eyes. "Nothing is as it seems." He pulled a watch from his vest pocket and checked the time. "You want anything else, madam? I'm ready to close up. Go on west a few blocks. You'll find a vendor with a variety of items, perhaps the very one you're looking for."

Lucy exited the shop and followed the man's suggestion. There were a few souvenir carts at the edge of a pretty park. None of them had a disk of any sort for sale. Hungry, she caught a bus back to the hotel to meet Angie for dinner.

*

Ronan McAndrew was exhausted. He had a thousand things to do. He had to pack and make ready to move by tomorrow. Miss Andronikos wanted him "on premises" as quickly as possible. The expectation had floored him. She had not only given him a job, but a place to live as well. A very nice place, judging from the part of the mansion he had seen during the interview. With four dollars left in his pocket, Ronan was delighted to start being paid.

He rubbed his red-rimmed eyes and then tried again to focus on the page he had already read five times. The letters seemed to slide away, and he decided to let them. Closing the book, Ronan wondered how late it had gotten and caught a glimpse of light breaking over the sill of his apartment's single window. For a moment he wondered what day it was rather than the hour. Then his brain seemed to awaken, and he knew where and when he was.

The smell of bacon wafted in from the apartment above, and he realized he was hungry, very hungry. Ronan couldn't recall the last time he had stopped to eat. He made himself a sandwich, ate it quickly, and washed it down with a bottle of soda. He needed to finish packing, load the car, and make the long drive down to Corona. But first, he wanted to organize his findings. There would be no time to sleep. Impressing his beautiful new boss was foremost on his mind.

The psychologist took a moment to gather his wits and tune his thinking. He could explain the location and purpose of the diffuse network of nerve pathways in the human brainstem. It connected the spinal cord, cerebrum, and cerebellum. Current science attributed the Reticular Activating System, RAS, with mediating the overall level of a person's consciousness. What Ronan wanted to explain to his boss and what she had expressly requested of him was how the RAS accomplished that.

Ronan carried a pickle spear to the window and munched on it while watching the sky slowly lighten. Even at the early hour, the streets were busy. People were beginning to fill the sidewalks, and cars were moving in groups, their progress orchestrated by the turn of lights from green to red and back in a continuous cycle. He saw a delivery truck pull up and unload boxes for the shop across the street. People and cars flowed past the truck, seemingly disinterested and undeterred from their own destinations. Ronan observed the activity for a while and found the answer his textbooks had failed to inspire.

"The RAS organizes the flow of information, directing the important things to the consciousness and relegating unimportant information to side streets. Like a traffic light, the RAS feeds some information to the brain while prohibiting other input to pass."

It wasn't a perfect analogy, but the idea was workable. Ronan felt exhilarated as he opened his laptop and began typing his proliferating thoughts. The RAS was a filter more than a traffic cop. It reacted to a person's focus of interest and selected from the billions of bits of sensory information only the input which fed their focus.

A human brain was subject to a constant flow of sensory stimulation. Most of it we ignored, enabling us to focus on a specific task. The RAS was the mechanism that enabled us to do that. And it was not an act of concentration. It was a built-in capability. It was precisely the mechanism that Artemis challenged him to find.

Exhilaration having replaced exhaustion, Ronan headed in for a shower. He stepped out of his clothes and banged his knee against the bathroom cabinet as he climbed into the shower. Ignoring the sharp sensation, Ronan lathered his reddish crewcut and began humming a jaunty Irish ditty.

*

Paolo stooped over the campfire and picked at the logs with a stick. The two strangers had been in the leader's tent for more than an hour. Paolo was uncomfortable with what the meeting meant for his future. He was a volunteer with no intention of staying with the ragtag band of soldiers. He had not enlisted in the Chilean army. He merely wanted to find food for his family.

One of the visitors was a woman in a general's uniform. Paolo had heard the rumors about a woman officer high up in the chain of command. The visitors were obviously from the government with their expensive weapons and shiny boots. Paolo stood and gave the stick to the flames, glancing once again at the tent. He could not be certain, but he thought he caught the name General Vergara drift out from the conversation. Paolo hoped it was true. General Vergara was said to be the one hope for Chile in a world that was growing meaner every day. Perhaps this woman was this general, he considered.

Paolo rubbed his stomach and told his body to be patient. The whole world was hungry as far as he could tell, except for the visitors who looked well-fed enough to test the buttons of their shirts. Sniffing the cool, evening air, Paolo caught the scent of something cooking, and his mouth watered. Uncaring what manner of meal the villagers were making, his stomach ached at the savory aroma.

The little band of men he was with had been observing the village in the valley below for two days. Nothing suspicious had occurred, and the self-described soldiers were certain they had not been detected. They had seen the strips of meat hanging from drying frames. The famine that had driven Paolo from his own village was not yet devastating the border area. Paolo stared down at the peaceful village and frowned. He had become famine itself.

Due to relieve one of the sentries in twenty minutes, Paolo was reluctant to leave without knowing what the visitors had wanted. In his heart, Paolo hoped it would not mean a purge for the peasants in the valley below. He was a peasant himself, and while eager to defend his homeland, Paolo had no desire to make war on innocent people.

He looked at his watch and back at the tent. He would be late if he didn't head to his post now; even running through the brush would barely get him to his post on time. He slung the battered rifle over his shoulder and started to trot up the sloping hillside. Looking back, he saw the visitors exit the tent and climb into their Humvee. Paolo's heart sank as he knew at that moment the next day would be filled with the sound of women and children screaming as their menfolk were murdered and their village burned. Their only crime was being on the wrong side of the border separating hungry people from those who were starving.

The sound of music drifted up from the officers' tent. It was a new song with Spanish lyrics issuing forth in a deep baritone voice. But it was the melody that wafted through him, and his apprehension dissipated as he listened. Paolo leaned against a tree and looked down at the lights in the village, no longer feeling any hesitation about what they would do in the morning.

Chapter Six

Dr. Wolfgang Strang erupted from his chair, sending it clattering loudly to the tiled floor. He whipped off his glasses with a shaky hand and tossed them to the desk.

"By the gods!" The rangy astrophysicist stared at the map, amazed at what he was seeing. *Impossible!* And yet there it was. Perfect in its simplicity. Strang ran his hands through his hair and heard the echo of Willa's voice. *Breathe, Wolfgang.*

Strang took that breath and felt himself begin to calm. His first impulse was to reach for the phone and summon Artemis to come share his discovery. Seeing the lateness of the hour, he decided to wait until morning, although he half expected Artemis to appear at his door if only to inquire about the midnight clatter. Standing motionless, he willed the pounding in his head to lessen. He closed his eyes and listened to the sound of crickets chattering in the yard and felt the cool breeze slipping through the small open window.

Once his composure returned, Strang found himself pleased to be alone with his discovery. The time to share it would come soon enough, but for the present it belonged to him alone.

Strang leaned forward, setting his hands on either side of the open atlas. His eyes traced the bright-yellow line he had drawn. The locations of more than a dozen ancient ruins formed a sine wave across the surface of the map. The astonishing significance of the wave had taken him to his feet. The epiphany had been like a burst of light exploding in the center of his staid, logical brain. Ten thousand years of human endeavor had not been random. It couldn't have been random. The labors of the ancients had been intentional, coordinated, and undeniably purposeful.

Righting his chair, Strang sat down at the desk to recheck his calculations and revel further at the astonishing discovery. He confirmed the longitude and latitude of each of the sites Artemis had asked him to research. The seven sites she had selected were within a single degree of latitude of the wave: the Easter Island, Nazca, Machu Picchu, the Great Pyramid, Mohenjo-daro, Preah Vihear and Anatom Island. *A string of pearls!*

A handful of other structures fell within several degrees of deviation from the line. And there were others, so many others, situated near the wave as it slithered across the map: Petra, Puma Punku, and Gobekli Tepe were too close to the line to be randomly constructed. Strang had marked them all, one by one, with careful precision. When the map was completed, he had set the atlas vertically on the desk. Somewhere, staring back at him, was the destination Artemis had charged him to discover.

The wave was actually a distortion caused by rendering the Earth into a flat, two-dimensional surface. It began at the Equator, rose to the Tropic of Cancer, and then descended to the Tropic of Capricorn and returned to the point where it began.

Transferred to a sphere, the ancient sites would form a single continuous line that circumnavigated the center of the planet. To the jubilant scientist who had spent a lifetime exploring undecipherable objects vast distances from Earth, the simple wave line was a thing of beauty. It was knowable and mathematically perfect, possessed of qualities he had rarely encountered in the vast emptiness of space.

Strang refreshed his grin. The alignment could not be coincidence, not that his mind had ever accepted such a concept. The sites were bound in a ring around the center of the Earth. And by a host of similarities: the precision of the monolithic stones, their exact orientation to cardinal points and astrological configurations. These were facts, not anomalies.

He set the atlas flat on the desk and smoothed the front of his shirt. There were variants he would need to understand. The dates attributed to the sites spanned millennia in no perceivable pattern. Although as he thought about it, dating a site was often argued, and scientific theory was constantly updated. Nor was he capable of determining the relative importance of the sites without additional insight from Artemis.

Strang opened his laptop and performed mathematical comparisons similar to the computations he used in his research of cosmic objects. He loaded the orientation of each site and other information that might prove important to Artemis. The more he worked, the more fascinated he became until his mind began to rebel against the rush of possibilities. It would take hours, possibly days, of concentrated calculations to determine the precise relationships between the sites. Keegan would have to help with the work. And it would keep the irritating young man out from under foot.

Strang leaned back in his chair and rubbed the bridge of his nose. The adrenaline rush had receded, leaving him physically drained. It was more than he could deal with in one night. Everywhere he looked, the relationship between the major sites took on profound dimensions and meaning. The laptop seemed anxious to continue the game, urging him to enter more data so that it could reveal additional surprises. With a weary sigh, Strang gently closed the laptop, reluctantly deciding to leave further computation for Keegan. Exhausted, he got slowly to his feet and meandered toward his bedroom, pausing by the pretty urn on the mantel.

"Saving the world is a complex business, Willa," he said in a tender voice, placing his hand on the urn. "Time to give the brain a rest." Nostalgia enveloped him as he remembered his wife's voice speaking those exact words. Emitting a little chuckle, the weary scientist pressed his fingers to his lips and then to the urn before continuing to his solitary bed.

*

"No, Lucy. I don't like the idea at all!" Artemis clicked the phone, transferring the call from speaker to the privacy of her ear. "I want Angie to stay with you, especially if you intend on going east. Something is erupting in Cambodia..."

"Angie's already on her way home, Temmie. She's excited to see you." Lucy made an extra effort to sound cheerful. "My flight to Paris is leaving in a few minutes. I just wanted to keep you updated. London was a dead end. Although I did finally find some of the souvenirs the shopkeeper was talking about. They are coming from the east. I sent some back with Angie. Listen, I've got to go. Love you."

"No, wait. Lucy?"

The line was dead. *Damn. Damn. Damn it!* Artemis paced around the bedroom twice before heading to her office. Seeing it was only seven thirty, she doubted Strang was awake yet. He had been up late into the night working on who knows what. Artemis resolved to let him sleep before preparing him for Angie's return.

Lucy's daughter had gone off to university six years before and never really returned. Armed with a PhD in Anthropology, Angie had fled to Europe ostensibly to begin her career. In truth, Angie was not the simple young woman her mother presumed. Both Strang and Artemis had known the real reason for Angie's long absence. Her human body belonged to a far more ancient soul. *Athena!* Artemis's imperious sister, one of the three alien goddesses who had remained bound to Earth thousands of years ago, had taken mortal form once again. The collective had abandoned its interest in humans, but Artemis, Athena, and Hestia had devoted themselves to the evolution of the primitive race. And, as Artemis had recently realized, to ensure their collective was the one the humans chose to join.

Each of the goddesses had her own reason for becoming earthbound. Artemis had fallen in love with the curious, playful human species. Hestia had been enchanted with the planet's exceptional beauty. And Athena had wanted to rule. Each had taken human form many times, using their godly powers among the various early cultures. They were teachers who nudged humans toward a predetermined destiny when they would become their peers. They provided knowledge and order and law.

All the while encouraging humans to the better angels of their nature.

Eventually, Hestia had retreated to her islands, rarely taking human form, content to watch over her paradise and its beautiful people as the spirit Pele. Athena, too, had not reincarnated for more than a millennium, although her reasons were less idyllic. Humans disappointed Athena, never rising above petty squabbles or greed. Athena had tried even more than her sisters to vanquish avarice and advance the human condition. Eventually, she admitted too few would follow and stayed, like Hestia, watchful from the ethereal plane.

Until now. Artemis sat at her desk, trying to push the anger aside. Athena's choice of human host was an unforgivable intrusion into Artemis's happiness. Lucy would not accept the loss of her daughter to a goddess who was the antithesis of the pleasant young woman Lucy expected Angie to become. Asking her soulmate to accept the presence of yet another alien being so close to her heart was something Artemis could not bring herself to do. And she had remained silent about the Angie/Athena reality for a decade with only Strang the wiser.

"Have you a moment?" Stefan tapped on the jamb to catch Artemis's attention.

"Two if you need them," Artemis replied, setting her musings aside and giving him an easy smile. Stefan was the favorite among the three scientists she'd selected. The juxtaposition of his large, intimidating physicality with his understated sense of irony resulted in an adorable persona. And Artemis enjoyed their frequent conversations.

Stefan lumbered into the office and dropped into the side chair at Artemis's overflowing desk. Uttering a rumbling sigh, he leaned forward and plopped huge hands on equally huge knees.

"I wish to know our deadline." He twitched his mustache. "I work better with a deadline. Without a gun on my head, my ideas wander away, and I make no progress."

Artemis contained a chuckle that wanted to break though. "I see. A deadline helps you focus. Is that it?"

"Well, many things give me focus," Stefan said seriously. "Hunger, curiosity. At the moment, looking at a most beautiful face." He cleared his throat when he saw her eyebrow arch. "But these things do not help me work. I need a deadline for that."

He cocked his head to one side. The uncombed dark brown hair and the dancing mustache gave Artemis the impression she was looking at an inquisitive bear. She lifted a hand to hide the smile refusing to be stifled.

"Okay," she said. "There is urgency to our work, but no definite date by which it must be completed. What if I give you thirty days to finish your work?"

Stefan was taken by surprise. "Thirty days?" He stared at her. "I have thirty days to determine how to manipulate perception? To...to...develop a methodology for communicating a specific message in an undefined situation?"

Artemis settled back into her ergonomic chair and crossed her legs. "Too long?"

Stefan blinked. "Yes."

It was Artemis's turn to be surprised. She sat up and folded her hands on her desk. "Then tell me how long you do need?"

"For a miracle, no time at all." He grinned. "Only I do not perform miracles, Miss Andronikos. What happens if I am not ready in thirty days?"

Artemis finally let the laugh escape. "Then I will have to give you thirty more. But you are right to question how much time we have, Stefan. In truth, I don't know."

The banter continued for a while until, faced with a final opportunity to bring up the real reason for the visit, Stefan lost his courage. A premonition was nothing new; he had experienced scores of them even as a child. And the last thing Stefan wanted was to trouble his captivating boss with the terrible visions he experienced in his sleep.

*

The river was high and running much stronger than Minya had hoped. It would be difficult to cross, especially at night when she would not be able to see any obstacles rushing toward them once they were in the water. But the only hope of safety was on the other side of the river.

She checked the knot at her shoulder, making sure the cloth was secure, and heard her baby fussing at being held so tightly against her back. She eased back into the foliage along the bank and found a sheltered spot to let little Rama nurse. The sound of heavy trucks rumbling along the roads on the highway behind her was unnerving, and the young mother searched the sky for the helicopter she feared had seen the group she was with an hour earlier. She had fled down the embankment before the soldiers came, and she had watched several of her unlucky companions being loaded into trucks and driven back to the camp from which they escaped.

Sheltered in the lee of a small copse of Narra trees, the young woman felt suddenly very alone. She and the infant were in a strange and dangerous place. At the sound of trucks stopping nearby, she cupped Rama's face closer to her breast, waiting anxiously for the noise of military activity to fade. Cooing soothingly, she smiled at the sweet little face of her child smiling up at her. He would have a good life, a safe life once they crossed the river. Suddenly, the air was torn with the rattle of guns firing too many shots to count, like a storm of rapid explosions making the baby cry. Amid the gunfire, Minya could hear people screaming, and she knew her companions were dying.

They should have believed the stories newcomers to the camp had told them. The authorities were killing those who tried to escape. Kam, the man who had arranged their escape, should have believed the stories. But he did not. He should have known the river would be too high. But he did not. Minya rocked her baby and stared at the shore across the river. Kam had said they would be safe there. Tears stung her eyes. Maybe they would not.

Once the terrible sounds had ended, Minya put the baby in the blanket and tied it tightly to her back. She was a good swimmer, and the river sounded like the flow was strong but steady. It would carry them downstream a way, but she felt sure she could reach the other shore if she stayed calm and didn't fight the current in panic. The baby's head was right behind her own. Being so high on her back had to be uncomfortable for him, and Minya told him she was sorry. His little heels flexed against her slender back.

Listening for a sound that might mean the authorities were nearby, Minya waded into the water and then leaned forward and began the long swim with strong, slow strokes of her arms. Rama cried out when the cold water rose over them, and she heard him sputter, but she maintained her steady breaststroke and felt the water take her downstream. She could see dim lights on the shore, probably fires chanced by other refugees who had crossed the water to what they believed would be a better life.

The current carried her past the fires and on down the river, gripping her in an ebony darkness that churned and frequently filled her mouth. The water drained all warmth from her body, and the baby fussed on her back. A jetty of land stuck out from the shore ahead, and Minya used all her strength to swim toward it. The current swirled her toward an eddy, and Minya's feet struck rocks as the river shallowed.

She tried to walk, but the current made swimming more productive, and she moved through the water until she reached the edges of a sandy finger of land. Shivering in the cool night air, Minya crawled onto the shore and passed into a grove of trees. She undid the knots in the blanket and pulled little Rama into her arms. He was cold and silent, and her heart startled with fear. She rubbed his limbs and held the small body close, sharing her warmth with him.

When she could hold back a shriek of despair no longer, the child stirred, and water dribbled from his lips. Minya enfolded him in her arms and rocked her baby, tears of joy rolling down her cheeks. She whispered to him about the good life awaiting them now, and she thanked Allah for his kindness in letting them live. She never even heard the shot that penetrated Rama's chest and came to a stop in his mother's heart.

*

It had taken more time than Ronan had imagined. The move into the main house was the easy part. Completing a professional presentation amid the chaos of resettling had proven more than a simple box/unbox procedure.

There was the constant distraction of meeting his teammates, adjusting to a schedule he didn't control, and being a team member after living alone. In the end, it had all been to the good. Sharing a bedroom with a huge man named Stefan was less than ideal but infinitely better than the claustrophobic apartment had been. Stefan was affable despite his intimidating size. They shared a challenging assignment. How to prepare a mechanism by which some undefined, all-encompassing decision could be synchronized and communicated simultaneously by several people. Ronan was focused on determining how choice occurred. Stefan was to figure out how to synchronize and transmit it. The nature of the choice and the transmission recipients were yet to be revealed to either of them.

Radiating pride for the progress made so far, Ronan summoned his colleagues to participate in the presentation he'd prepared for Artemis. Stefan, Keegan, Strang, and their boss assembled in the library which had become the conference area for the team, the large room's intellectual atmosphere and plush chairs more than adequate to the purpose. Smiling broadly, Ronan tapped the controller, and the words "Reticular Activating System" appeared on the screen.

"Focus is an automatic cerebral function." Ronan started his presentation with the bottom line. "One does not need to augment it artificially."

Keegan stood up, ready to return to his own work. "So, we're done here then?"

The others turned to see if Artemis agreed. Her lips pressed into a thin line, Artemis gave no such indication. "Wait." She glanced at Keegan. "We're going to hear Ronan out."

Ronan cleared his throat. "The Reticular Activating System, otherwise known as the RAS, is a network of nerve pathways in the brainstem. It sits where the spinal cord adjoins the brain proper. Its function is to organize information, permitting the important stuff to get through. It mediates consciousness."

"The primary thing mediating your consciousness is the crush you have on Artemis," Keegan quipped, sitting back down.

"You're such an asshole," Ronan retorted, his face a deeper red than his crew cut. "When a person focuses on a goal, the RAS emphasizes the information and opportunities available to achieve it." He forced himself to look at Artemis. "The ability to enhance focus is hardwired. There is no need to develop a separate system."

Like the Harbinger? Artemis pondered the similarities between the two. She wondered if the two processes worked in concert, and if they did, would it be possible to synchronize the processes between people?

"I think the boy-o is correct." Stefan came to his colleague's aid. "It's obvious. There is a constant flow of input to our brains. Somehow we manage to discern important code from rubbish." The burly young scientist swiveled his chair and stared at Artemis, who had her eyes closed, apparently oblivious to the conversation. "Or ignore inputs completely. Yes? Like our lovely boss."

A ripple of laughter jarred Artemis from her thoughts. She gave them a sheepish grin and motioned for Ronan to continue. He set aside the controller and prepared to use his hands as he spoke off the cuff.

"Have you ever been to a party where everyone was talking loudly, and music was blaring in your ears? And suddenly amid the din, you heard your name called,"

Ronan queried the group. "How did you hear that one sound from all the others? Because you were focused on looking for someone, and when they spoke your name, the RAS let the input pass into your consciousness while diverting all the distractions around you. You were expecting to hear it. So, you did."

Heads nodded, but not the one with long dark hair. Strang set his thumb on his chin and stroked his cheek with a finger. "On the one hand, this is a beneficial function. Once a goal is specified, this activating system enhances one's ability to achieve it. But on the other hand, might not this structure be seen as essentially wish fulfillment? I mean, information contrary to the goal is discarded even if such data is relevant to, say, a larger objective."

"Makes good sense," Stefan acknowledged. "If I create a picture in my mind, RAS directs input to that routine. 'Tis a basic concept to a programmer. Generate the code and let it do its work. Of course, if the code is wrong, the information gets corrupted."

"Perhaps." Artemis finally voiced an opinion. She set clear blue eyes on the stricken Ronan and gave him a consoling grin. The concept felt right to her. And if accurate, the RAS could facilitate not only the making of the choice but the wherewithal to communicate it. "This is certainly worth additional study. You and Stefan need to flesh out the whole process including the output." She flashed a grin. "Good work so far."

Flush with a feeling of success, Ronan gathered up his notes and made ready to leave. Then Artemis asked a final question.

"So, let's say a person had to choose between situation A and situation B. Does this RAS network you're describing treat information about each option equally?"

Ronan nodded. "If the goal is to make a decision, then in theory information on both A and B would be let through. I think. Actually, I'm pretty sure. But once the decision is made, the RAS reinforces it, shutting down information about the other option."

Strang grasped what Artemis was contemplating. "Your hypothesis is the RAS collaborates with the Harbinger, enabling our indecisive chooser to perceive the future consequence of the two situations, thus making the choice all the more clear."

"Um, okay. You have a workable hypothesis, so are we done here now?" Keegan asked, hoisting himself to his feet.

Artemis nodded, and the young men filed out. Keegan and Stefan gave Ronan a congratulatory pat on the back. Strang lingered for a word with Artemis. "I see you found Ronan's information thought-provoking. He could use a tip or two on how to present it better. But he did explain how the mind works."

Artemis smiled. "How the brain works. While all those neurons are chugging back and forth, the mind is translating them into what it wants to do."

Strang shook a finger at her. "You want to tip the scales, to employ an overused cliché, in favor of the collective we were intended to prefer, don't you, my dear? You want a mechanism to overwhelm the information aligned with the other, dare I say, nefarious option."

"Precisely!" Artemis ran her hands along her arms and sighed. "There is a countercurrent running. Just look at what's happening in the world, Wolf. I wish Lucy was on her way home."

"There is indeed an abundance of discord. Do you believe it is by design, Temmie?" Strang asked.

Artemis's eyes darkened. "I am certain it is. There is a pressure bearing down on us. I can feel it. It's paralyzing the Harbinger. You can see how undirected our three geniuses are, Wolf. And they are the most gifted of their generation. They would make the better choice if given a chance. But until they perceive how and when..." She closed her eyes.

"I cannot help with those particular matters, my dear girl." Strang puffed out his chest. "But just wait until you see what I've discovered regarding where."

Chapter Seven

The woman was amazing, not as tall as Artemis, but tall nonetheless, light-haired like Lucy with an abundance of curls surrounding classic features and unmistakably graceful in the way she moved. Stefan was the first to see Angie as she stepped into the foyer. He did a double take, setting the books he was carrying absentmindedly on a nearby table; a smile of appreciation spread beneath his ample mustache. He knew instantly the woman was the often-mentioned Angela Breem. She was precisely what the daughter of the exquisite Artemis Andronikos and the charming Lucinda Breem had to be. Seeing Angie, Stefan dismissed the minor requirement of male participation in her creation. Before him stood the exception to the rule.

He watched as she set down her travel bag and took a deep breath of home. As far as Stefan could tell, the vision had not noticed him staring at her. He cleared his throat and started to approach, only to stop when she engulfed Stefan in a hazel-eyed stare that made his heart skip. He stepped back, managing merely to raise his hand in a small gesture of greeting. Angie inclined her head slightly and then walked off leaving him to ponder what he should have done.

"*Ma olen!*" he muttered, slapping his forehead with the palm of his hand. "I am in the home of beautiful women, and I am a fool."

He turned to see Ronan standing transfixed behind him and realized his own reaction was paltry compared to that of his friend. Stefan punched Ronan's shoulder.

"So, boy-o," Stefan chuckled. "I see your crush on our lovely woman boss is cured. Such fickle affection you have. But this new woman will ne'er spare you the time of day."

"She is gorgeous!" Ronan found his voice. "I mean Artemis is gorgeous too. But this one is perfect."

Stefan nodded. "Ah, the blonde hair and not as matured as the other. Yes, these can be important matters to the libido." He laughed and slapped Ronan's shoulder once again. "And this one has no partner. The probability of success is gone from zero to one, boy-o. Cruel fortune is—the scale is infinite not binary."

*

Strang listened to Keegan prattle on about the latest calculations and wondered how someone so intelligent could be so pedestrian in their reasoning. The young scientist's commitment to casual attire evidently extended to his superficial critical thinking as well.

"Everything you say is factual, Keegan. But your facts are bland. Can you not see beyond them?" Strang tapped a key to enlarge the image on the screen. "Can't you sense it? There is among these sites the one the ancients meant us to discover. It is speaking to us. Listen!"

"No." Keegan mocked. "These places are rather far from me at the moment. Anyway, I don't commune with inanimate objects."

More's the pity. Strang reached out and pulled the earbud from his assistant's ear. "Maybe you should listen to something beside that dreadful music in which you insist on bathing your brain cells."

"Easy, old man." Keegan glared. He retreated a step and carefully slipped the listening device into his shirt pocket. "At least I haven't wasted twenty years pursuing some pointless theory. There is nothing in the math to indicate any particular destination. Maybe you should go see them for yourself."

Strang counted to ten in Greek. "Perform the calculations again."

Keegan folded his arms in a pout.

"What, you have a date or something, Dr. Montock?" Strang looked angrier than he felt. "I intend to present this to Artemis tomorrow. Your work had better be accurate."

"It is." The young scientist reinserted the earbud and turned up his iPod. He took his seat to once again check the information he had validated twice already. There was nothing new to learn. He was bored with the work. Distances between the sites fell into consistent percentages of the Earth's circumference. Several sites were in apposition, while others formed a connection referred to as the Golden Section. Keegan had explored the idea of Vesica Piscis and found several possible mandorla expressed in the azimuthal projections. But there was nothing there in the math to set any one location apart from the others.

Keegan listened to the music wafting through his head. Even if there were, he didn't care.

*

Angie took a bowl of cherries from the counter and set it on the table. "OMG, I haven't had these in years, Temmie." She popped one in her mouth and moaned. "Delicious."

Artemis looked amused. "Bumper crop this year. These are the last of the season. You should have been here a month ago." She began filling glasses with a crisp, light wine. "How goes the research?"

"Research inevitably goes slow," Angie said while munching. "I brought back a few of those disks you wanted. They give me the creeps. I can't believe you actually like them."

"I don't like them," Artemis assured her. "I just have a feeling about them. The real disk, not the replicas. The disk we saw on the internet is the one I'm after." She paused and studied Angie's demeanor, looking for any sign of Athena. "Does the symbol Lucy told you about seem familiar to you?"

Angie spit a cherry pit into a napkin. "The taijitu. Yes, it is rather unsettling. I get that too." She popped another cherry in her mouth. "But the souvenirs are very popular even if they are poorly crafted. Maybe the Daoists are out to rule the world."

"Everyone else has tried." Artemis chuckled.

There was no hint of Athena in Angie. Artemis studied every action, every word and saw only the essence of the girl she and Lucy had raised. Perhaps the goddess had not yet awakened. It had taken Artemis until her late twenties and Ichabod's death to regain some memories of her true self. They had slipped into place, bit by bit, returning from wherever they were restrained during the process of taking on a mortal body.

Relieved, Artemis allowed herself to delight in the reunion with Angie after the long absence. And yet part of her was disappointed not to be confronted by Athena. Athena's wisdom would be a great help in resolving the challenge they faced.

"May I see the souvenirs?"

Angie licked cherry juice off her fingers and reached for her carry-on bag. "Sure. Here, this is the best one. My crew gave it to me just before I left. It most closely resembles the drawing Mom showed me. I have others for you to look at. There's one made of porcelain and several of wood. Most are just cheap tin or aluminum knock-offs."

Artemis examined them and sighed. "Yeah. Nothing here. Do you have any idea why they are suddenly so popular?"

"Not really. There's a song going around. It's in Italian, but it mentions a circle of love." She eyed Artemis as she selected another cherry. "Hasn't hit the US yet, huh?"

"I never listen to popular music, so I have no idea." Artemis shrugged. "Now if they made an opera, I'm there."

Angie laughed and then felt the shadow stir at the back of her mind. *Oh God, not now.*

*

The drizzle took the edge off the heat. It had beat down on Lucy all day as she strolled the Champs-Élysées and marveled at the beauty of the City of Lights. She walked along the Seine watching the bateaux float by with their quirky cargo of tourists. The hulk of Notre-Dame sagged forlornly on the island, still magnificent even in its shame.

The phone jingled, and she smiled at the sound of Artemis's voice.

"It's glorious here," Lucy gushed. "Well, there is a bit of rain, but it cooled everything down. I wish you were here."

"I wish you were here," Artemis retorted. "Please come home. Now. Today. Please."

Lucy laughed. "Word is the new pope is coming to Paris tomorrow. You wouldn't want me to miss that, would you?"

"Sure I would. You've seen one pope, you've seen them all."

"Temmie," Lucy chided. "Sometimes I wonder how you aren't struck by a thunderbolt."

"Thor is a myth, Lucy."

A groan sputtered out of Lucy at that. "That's the pot calling the kettle black, Miss Goddess of the Hunt. You should make me a chart. These gods were real, these ones weren't."

"Good point," Artemis admitted. "Now tell me when you're coming home."

Lucy explained she had a few leads to follow first. Her old editor, Jake Durant, had given Lucy a list of shady antique dealers in Paris, and if they didn't pan out, she was thinking of going further east. The taijitu indicated an Asian influence. She swore she could hear Artemis frowning.

"No, you are not going anywhere else. I need you here, Lucy." Artemis sounded lonely. "Your daughter is creating quite a stir. At least two of our three healthy male geniuses are madly in love with her, and we aren't getting a lick of work done. Well, evidently Wolf has news. But seriously, Lucy, come home."

The mournful tone of the last plea made Lucy blush. "Okay. You win. Listening to your voice is making me horny. I will book a flight for the day after tomorrow. Maybe even sooner if I don't find anything other than these stupid souvenirs."

"Have I mentioned I love you?" Artemis sounded vastly relieved.

Lucy made her way to an antique shop Jake had suggested and dodged out of the serious rain that had started up again. She asked the clerk about the disk, showing him the drawing made from the image on the internet. He shook his head.

"*Non, madame*. I have not seen this object." He shook his head and lifted his chin.

"There are souvenirs I've seen, but I am looking for the original disk. It will be very expensive. May I leave my phone number in case you come across it?"

The shop was a disorganized dump and highly unlikely to handle a million-dollar item, but Lucy was using flattery to see if she could pry any additional information from the man.

"*Oui, madame*." The clerk leaned forward and lowered his voice. "You are the second person who has been asking about this disk. A month ago, a man came looking for the same thing."

The clerk rubbed the tips of his fingers together in a not-so-subtle request for money. Lucy handed him the equivalent of fifty dollars.

"*Merci, madame*." The clerk smiled. "The man was not French. He had long, unkempt hair and was stout around the waist. I judged him to be Polynesian. Is that correct? In America you say Polynesian, *oui*?"

"*Oui*, ah, yes." Lucy gave the man her name and phone number and left, lost in thought about why an islander would be interested in a million-dollar disk.

*

Stefan spooned a third measure of sugar into his coffee and stirred with vigor. Then he lifted the cup to his mouth and took a cautious taste. The grimace that followed conveyed the dissatisfactory results to all who were watching. Stefan pushed the cup aside with a burly hand and shook his head.

"T'will not ever replace tea!" He spat out the liquid, his tongue lolling to the side of his generous mouth.

Angie bit her lip and looked down at her plate to hide the grin she couldn't suppress. Stefan was a bear of a man. Taller by six inches than Artemis and sporting an amazing girth, he was the antithesis of a tea drinker. He was from Eastern Europe, she'd learned, one of Artemis's prize finds. A psycho-neuro programmer who looked more like a lumberjack or professional wrestler. Curly dark-brown hair trailed just past the collar of his shirt, and his swarthy complexion matched the deep baritone with which he spoke. The only incongruity was the merriment in his expression.

Angie sat back and observed the hulk sitting across the dining room table. Stefan's pale-violet eyes crinkled, and he smiled back. They were angelic eyes, otherworldly eyes that bespoke innocence and compassion. Seeing them, Angie found Stefan's whole visage was transformed.

"I think they've ordered several varieties of Estonian tea, Stefan," Angie assured him. "The order should be here in a day or two."

He nodded vigorously as he rose to select another drink from the buffet. "That's good to hear." He grinned, and his true youth shone through. He noticed again how beautiful the new arrival was and swallowed hard. "Um, Angie...may I ask your age? It is rude, I'm told, but you have a timeless beauty so a poor man must ask."

Angie grinned. "Twenty-four. How old are you?" Angie asked, taking a final sip of her own cup of coffee.

Stefan resumed his seat and set a large glass of milk where the hated coffee had been. "That depends on what measurement one uses. In days I am 9840. In months I am 328. In years I am twenty-four." Violet eyes twinkled as he added the last. "But in wisdom, I am as old as the universe."

"And twice as modest!" Artemis pointed out as she swept into the room. Passing by Angie, she patted her shoulder in an affectionate gesture and then grabbed a glass of juice and a bagel from the buffet.

Stefan nodded at his boss who took a seat beside Angie at the table. "You sleep in this day. You look good, better than the past days. I am glad you got your rest. This pretty lady here and I were getting acquainted while you were sleeping. I like her. Is she the one I will be working with now?"

Artemis munched on the bagel. "In a way, yes." She swallowed and took a sip of juice. "Angie is the tactician we sorely need to keep things running."

Stefan's face brightened.

"I suspect I will be working more with Wolf." Angie smirked at Artemis. "I am an anthropologist, Temmie. And Wolf is looking at the ancient sites."

Stefan's eyebrows rose as he observed his boss. "Temmie? I like such a name for you. I shall call you Temmie also." He turned to Angie. "And if you get bored looking at old rocks, come see me. I am the future. Much more interesting than rocks."

Angie responded with a thin smile.

"I'm sure Angie will find Keegan anything but boring, Stefan," Artemis said, finishing the bagel with a final bite.

Stefan scowled. "He is irritating, not interesting. Keegan can upset persons in a nanosecond using only his big mouth. He is what you call a dickhead, is he not?"

Artemis choked on a swallow of juice and cleared her throat.

"I can hardly wait to meet him." Angie laughed. "Temmie is known to dispatch dickheads before lunch. How ever has he survived?"

Artemis waved her hand, still unable to speak. Stefan grinned at her and then continued. "Dr. Wolf keeps him out of sight. But I shall keep an eye out...until lunch as you predict."

He rose from his chair and carried his dishes to the sink. Giving the two women a wave of his huge hand, Stefan headed off to begin the day's work.

*

"I can't believe they've sent troops back into the Middle East." Ronan directed his comments to Stefan, who was trying to determine the angle for a tricky masse shot. The huge TV screen dominated the north corner of the rec room. Ronan sat in a tan recliner listening to the eleven o'clock news while Keegan and Stefan were occupied in a titanic game of pool in the room's center.

Tapping his pool cue on the side of the table, Stefan did a few calculations in his head. "Um, the world is always having a fight. The Middle East, Europeans, even my homeland looks to make war. And the Estonians never make war! I do not choose to watch."

Keegan leaned against the edge of the pool table and waited for his opponent to take his shot. "Come on, Stefan. Overthinking won't help. You have no shot. Just get it over with so I can beat your big ass again."

Stefan looked at Ronan, bushy eyebrows twitching high on his forehead. "See what I mean? Obsessed with winning, everyone, everywhere." He stretched over the pool table and sent the cue ball on a complicated journey ending with the ten-ball falling neatly into a side pocket. "Aha!"

"Lucky shot." Keegan sneered. "I still have you unless you really believe you can run the rest of the table."

Accepting the challenge, Stefan did just that. "See." He celebrated when his victory was secured. "I obsess like everyone in this hostile world."

Keegan gave him a grudging high five and then retreated to a chair and donned his earphones, losing himself in the tune he used to block out the world. The lyrics were simple, but he found the melody almost hypnotic. It revved his mind in a pleasing way and filled in the emotional hollows his Asperger syndrome created. He closed his eyes and let the music dance in his brain.

Ronan stood and stretched. "Time for me to hit the sack, fellas. You two can play all night if you want. But I'm done in." He shot a sinister smile at Stefan. "I trust you aren't planning on making any moves in my absence. I mean if Angie happens by, you mind your manners. Get it?"

"She is all yours, boy-o," Stefan assured him. "You have a move in mind, you should make it soon. I will wait to see you flaming out and learn from your mistake." A grin appeared below his mustache. "We Estonians do make love."

With a snort of disagreement, Ronan trailed down the hall, his hopes of winning Angie undeterred.

Chapter Eight

General Maria Vergara fondled the cool disk in her hip pocket. A lesser woman—or man—might have been tempted to take credit for the ease with which her plans were progressing. But Vergara did not consider herself lesser to anyone. She had the blood of the Mapuche in her veins, warriors who had defeated the Inca at the battle of Maule, ending the invasion from the north long ago.

Vergara had begun her conquest at the place the Mapuche had originated, along the Amazon River. Using the power of the disk, Maria had demonstrated the usefulness of famine, and now the presidents of seven nations were firmly in her sway—Brazil being the greatest of them. Ready to step out of her superiors' shadows, Vergara was about to turn her attention south, gathering Paraguay, Bolivia, and Argentina into her fold.

She tucked a riding crop into her uniform belt and strolled into the bright Chilean sunlight. Maria mounted her magnificent black stallion, jerked the reins, and brought the animal to a trot. The thought of riding Destino straight into President Caron's office made her laugh, and she spurred the animal to a gallop.

Caron was a lesser man. The president was petty and vindictive, and his character had earned the politician many enemies throughout the continent of South America and beyond. Worse, Caron was stupid. He had nearly undone the agreement with Colombia by insulting the drug cartels. Vergara had smoothed over the relationship, not eager to yield the territory she had gained. Her attention must remain on the heart of the continent this day and on the elimination of another man standing in her way.

Maria had no expectations the countries had yielded to her personal charm. She had none. What she did have was the ability to instill fear, and she wielded the weapon with great success. Famine had long stalked the poorer nations. Using the disk to wither crops and send forth the *langosta* to devour harvests, Vergara had not needed the army to bend panicked politicians to her will. They had sought her patronage, and now they were in her pocket like the peasants she fed.

Destino trotted along the hills, sensing they were approaching their destination. With Chile's neighbors proclaiming Vergara's leadership and a restless army whispering sedition, President Caron had sought refuge at his family's farm outside Santiago. But Vergara had no intention of disposing of Caron just yet. It was time to remove the man between them. The disk warmed her pant leg. She slowed the horse and surveyed the countryside. It was hers—this beautiful, amazing continent with its history and its resources and 423 million souls to do her bidding.

She crested a low hill and watched a Humvee make its way toward the farm from the north. General Boras had requested the meeting with Caron. And Boras had demanded Vergara attend in person, undoubtedly intending she be relieved of her command by Caron. The fools had no idea how powerful she was.

Destino pawed at the ground and whinnied at the sound of the Humvee engine. Then the horse started, nearly pulling the reins from Maria's hands as a shockwave pushed them back. The Humvee had exploded into a brilliant ball of fire. She smiled. Paolo had done well. He was a clever boy. She had noticed him from the first, plucked him from the little band of scavengers, and groomed him to do these simple tasks the disk suggested.

Spurring her horse, Vergara galloped down the slope to the farmhouse to see if a stricken President Caron would need time for the shock to wear off or promote her immediately to the now-vacant position as head of Chile's six divisions.

*

Strang had his mojo back. He strolled into the conference room wearing the dark-blue shirt emblazoned with white plumeria petals reserved for very special occasions. He laid the atlas in the center of the large table and beckoned Artemis to observe his "string of pearls." There was no need for commentary. The sine wave was self-explanatory, but he could barely contain his excitement as he waited for her reaction.

Artemis leaned forward to examine the map. She followed the sine wave from one end to the other with her eyes and then with her finger. The connection was one she should have figured out herself years ago, given her long fascination with the ancient sites. But the alignment had never occurred to her.

"Huh!" she said, aiming pale-blue eyes directly at Strang.

"That's all you can say? 'Huh!'" Strang repeated, twirling his hand. "My darling girl, I was anticipating a more sagacious response!"

"Sorry." Artemis shrugged.

He dropped into a chair. "I must confess I am confounded by your reaction. Ancient humans built these places with a singular, coordinated purpose. The ancients not only left their progeny a warning just as you presumed, but they were telling us where the gods await our decision."

"Come now, Dr. Strang. I would not expect a scientist of your intellect to leap to conclusions. Are you prepared to name a specific site?" Angie queried from the doorway. Closing the door, she stood and stared at the room's startled occupants. Only it wasn't Angie.

"Athena!" Artemis rose from her chair to acknowledge her sister's presence. "Please, come in."

Strang's chin dropped. He had known the secret for a decade—Angie was not merely Lucy's daughter. She was the goddess Athena reincarnated into human form. Seeing the transformation left him speechless. His mouth went dry, and he looked to Artemis and then back at the woman who had addressed him. Athena seemed nothing like Artemis, and yet she was the same—a superior life form from the depths of an infinite cosmos.

Athena moved to the map on the table and gave it a cursory examination. "Is this ridiculous scribbling all you understand regarding what is about to happen?"

"It is not ridiculous," Artemis replied calmly. "It's excellent work. Thank you, Wolf, I concur with your opinion. The place we need is right in front of our eyes."

"Then name it," Athena commanded, her arms folded against her chest.

Artemis glanced at Strang and saw him purse his lips before responding.

"I haven't determined precisely which of these sites is the one we need to use as of yet."

Athena took a moment to examine the map more closely. The scientist had clearly discovered something interesting. Arching an eyebrow, she glanced at Strang and nodded.

"Here and here." She traced a line on the map, connecting a pair of appositional sites separated by a perfect 180 degrees of longitude. "And look here. There is a second pair of ruins in opposition. These are meaningful. Think! What do these two tracks tell you?"

Artemis considered the questions, realizing sites created in perfect opposition told her quite a lot. "One track leads to the place we need. The second must be a false trail. The question is which one is correct?" She ran her tongue along her lips and asked a question of her own. "Do you know, Athena?"

Athena formed a slight smile. "Ze'us will have left a sign. Like the Harbinger, the meaning of the symbol must be latent in humans. And who better to help them find it than Ar'tem'is, Goddess of the Hunt?" She smirked at Artemis's reaction to hearing her name pronounced in the ancient manner.

"Ar-tem-is!" Strang repeated the curious-sounding pronunciation. "I like that, but I prefer Temmie." He rose and offered his hand to Athena. "I am honored to meet the Goddess of Wisdom. It would seem we are in dire need of wisdom, lest we be abandoned once again."

Athena ignored the hand and looked to Artemis. "Abandoned? What fables have you been telling them, sister? They were not abandoned. They rebelled."

Strang lowered himself into his chair. "Alas, that is not hard to believe. We homo sapiens are a deplorably independent lot. A virtue your collective might appreciate if we decide to choose you, of course."

Artemis wanted to hug the scientist. He had cleverly divined the most successful way to deal with her imperious sister. *That's it. Stake out the high ground, Wolf.* She indicated for Athena to sit with them. They discussed the possibilities the sine wave presented. Athena eliminated the ruins in Europe which she had recently investigated as part of Angie's work. Artemis dismissed the sites in Peru she and Strang had explored a decade ago. Finding reasons to eliminate a few other ruins based on their alignment or deteriorated state, the three agreed the oppositional sites were their best chance of finding where Ze'us would expect them.

Strang noted Athena used the same name as Artemis had for the second collective...The Others. He detected fear in both of them when the subject was approached. It was perhaps the one issue on which the two sisters were in absolute agreement.

"I will leave you to your task," Athena announced when nothing more could be derived from the map. Then, as unexpectedly as she had appeared, Athena stood and abruptly left.

Strang blew out a breath. "I take it the two of you weren't close," he ventured much to Artemis's chagrin.

"Ya think!" Artemis retorted. "Athena is who she is. She doesn't know the answer, or she would have told us. Neither of us has experienced a choice event." She formed a crooked smile. "We are both rather new additions to the collective."

Strang did a quick calculation in his head and then chuckled. "Precisely how old are you, Temmie? Speaking in Earth years of course. How long do...ah..."

"My relatives live?" Artemis completed the question.

Strang smiled. "I so prefer that nomenclature to aliens. I have always accepted you as a goddess, Temmie. There is nothing alien about you. And on second thought, I don't really want to know the answer to that particular question."

Artemis accepted his change of heart. She patted the map and traced the connections Athena had pointed out. "Athena is right about the two paths. One links Easter Island to Mohenjo-daro. The other goes from Nazca to Angkor Vihear just north of Angkor Wat. I am surprised she didn't seem interested in Ikhet, considering she's spent the last two years there."

"Ikhet?

Artemis flashed a grin. "Glorious light. You know it as the Great Pyramid."

"Ah." Strang nodded. "Ikhet is near but not exactly on the alignment wave. I wonder how wide the wave needs to be." He gave Artemis a curious look. "You know, my dear, I am possessed from time to time of an overwhelming urge to confine you in a small room and have you enlighten me with everything you have learned in your long experience of Earth."

"It would be a boring recitation, Wolf." Artemis's eyes were momentarily filled with resignation. "Human history is a story of violence and suffering repeated over and over. Lessons learned slowly if at all."

"And yet you find us...what? Promising? Lovable? Worthy in some way?"

"All of the above. All living beings have a duality to their natures, Wolf. It is their choices that determine what they are destined to become. In a way every choice is between the light and the dark. I see mostly light." *Light; her light—Lucy.*

Strang had a twinkle in his eye. "When you decide which of the four sites each of us is to visit, please remember I have always wanted to visit Easter Island. I don't think I'm up to dealing with all the falderal going on in the East just now."

"Anticipating my next move, eh, Wolf?" Artemis cocked her head to one side. "I am thinking of sending two teams. You and Keegan will follow this line starting at Easter Island." She saw Strang grin. "Lucy and I will tackle Nazca as soon as I can get her back here."

"Ships crossing in the night." Strang drew his hand along the two lines. "When do you anticipate we will leave?"

"As soon as possible. I'll prepare Angie to take charge of the project Ronan and Stefan are collaborating on. She'll get some work out of them." She laughed at the look of amusement on Wolf's face. "Especially if Athena makes an appearance."

Strang slapped his knee and laughed. "Athena would dampen their libidos and result in considerably less flirting. I am not as sure there would be measurably more working. Let's hope Athena doesn't make a public appearance until you and I are safely away." He extended his hand to help Artemis from the chair. "I am puzzled by one thing, Temmie. Unlike you, Athena is not always present. For the most part, Angie is, well, Angie as we have always known her."

Artemis could only venture a guess. "Memory can take time. The more she remembers, the more Angie will become Athena. When she does, Lucy is going to freak."

"That is certain, my dear girl." Strang walked her back to the main house. "Personally, however, I am saving my concern for the two lads who will have to deal with the rather snippy goddess."

*

Lucy's eyes flew open, and she sucked in a deep breath, the dream still vivid in her mind. She sat up and stared into the dim light trying to orient to her surroundings before realizing she was on an aircraft. Beside her or, rather, on the aisle seat with an empty seat between them, a man turned to look at her. The pull-down tray rested on his stomach, and he held a plastic cup filled with what was most likely water, no ice. He gave her a toothy grin and turned his eyes to the screen on the bulwark separating them from first class. Glancing at the screen, Lucy saw she was nearly home.

Her neck stiff, Lucy regretted having slept with her head angled against the window. She yawned and stretched and envied the man his drink. Her mouth was dry. She had experienced enough travel in the past weeks to last a lifetime. It was good to be almost home. She folded the thin airline blanket and set it in the empty seat beside her.

"Are you happy to be coming home?" the man asked as if reading her thoughts. He returned his tray to its cubby hole and shifted in his seat, intent on engaging Lucy in conversation.

"Yeah." Lucy smiled. "I've been away longer than I planned. You?"

He shrugged, causing his abdomen to jiggle. "Me? No. I am far from my home. It may be a long time before I can return."

He had a tattoo above his eyebrow. Noting it, Lucy connected the distinctive hue of his skin and the shiny black hair with the Maori design. He was Polynesian. Many years living in Hawaii had helped her recognize the marking of people from across the Pacific Islands. But the mark was not one she could place.

"Vanuatu?" she asked, guessing.

The man smiled. "A small island very near New Zealand. It is called Waitangi, but I have not been there for many years. I live in New Zealand on the southern island now."

Nothing in his speech betrayed an accent, perhaps slightly British, but very faintly so. Lucy was intrigued. The man was dressed in a business suit. Yet the islands that had bred him were visible even with the modern façade.

He tapped the dark design above his eye. "It is the insignia of an elder. But I was never truly worthy of it. I went to university in Christchurch and eventually worked for the government of Australia. I am retired now."

Lucy nodded. None of that seemed to fit what she assumed about the man. He was young to be retired, and the clothing looked uncomfortable to him. Maybe wearing a business suit on a plane is by definition uncomfortable, she told herself. Maybe it was the man and not the suit she sensed.

"Are you on vacation?"

He laughed. "No, I am searching for an item I lost many months ago." His face was incredibly sad for a moment. "It is most precious. My youngest son took it with him to Australia without my permission. He lost it in a game of fortune even knowing it was not his to lose. Since then, my luck, too, has vanished."

"Sorry to hear about your misfortune," Lucy said sincerely. "I've been looking for something too. My luck has been no better than yours."

The man smiled again, the same wide-lipped toothy smile. "I know."

*

Angie flicked the dust rag to dislodge what it had collected before starting on the bookshelf. It produced a smart snap, and she watched a spray of motes hang weightless in the air. Being back felt wonderful, a feeling renewed with each of the childhood treasures she cleaned. Maybe being home would make the presence lurking within stay in the shadows of her mind. The shadow had let her listen when she confronted Wolf and Artemis over the map. Angie had been shoved back, but the veil had not been dropped, and she had caught every word. And the look on their faces had hurt and excited her all at the same time.

"Athena!"

Artemis entered the bedroom and pinned the occupant with darkened eyes. Catching the seriousness in those eyes, Angie started to ask what was wrong, when she felt the shadow push through and take control of her body, leaving Angie's spirit alone in a silent void.

"Sister." Athena greeted Artemis with a challenging look of her own.

Artemis found the change remarkable. Angie's pretty hazel eyes were brighter, wiser, and her features more finely drawn. Athena even looked taller or perhaps just stood straighter, her shoulders back in the warrior attitude the goddess had always preferred. It had been a thousand years since they had been together on the mortal plane. Despite the complications Athena's presence could cause, Artemis felt a wave of happiness to be with her sister again.

"So, the process is complete?" Artemis asked. She needed to understand what powers Athena retained if they were to work efficiently together. "Have you access to the memories we need?"

Athena tossed the dust rag aside. "There is no process, Artemis. I am not reincarnate in this body. Your precious niece is very much present. I am with her when I want to be. I was the voice in her head when she was a child and the one who spoke to you when you sought whispers in the night. I thought you would have figured all this out by now. Unlike you, I do not enjoy subjecting my essence to the limitation of a human form." She made a scoffing sound in her throat. "Of course, I do not have a pretty soulmate leading me by the nose or other body parts."

Artemis furled her eyebrows at the reference to Lucy and then was struck by what Athena was telling her. "You're not Angie? I mean she is still as she was...in there with you?"

"It would be more accurate to say I am bound with her."

Artemis felt a wave of relief. "You were Angie's angel. The voice in her head when Angie was a child."

"Yes." Athena grimaced. "It was awkward to bind myself to a child's mind."

"Awkward?" Artemis arched a brow. "You nearly killed her. And what that did to me and Lucy..."

"Your precious light does not know about me," Athena assured her sister. "I am not the homewrecker you thought me, sister. I have always been pleased you have a soulmate. And Angie has learned to accept my presence. I have interfered as little as I could. But I have brought us together because the time for us to return is approaching."

Artemis felt a blush creep up her neck. "I do not plan to return. They will choose to join us, Athena. I know they aren't ready, but if we help them—you and I and Hestia. We can finish what Father set in motion."

Athena shot Artemis an impatient look. "Dear sister. You have no idea what you are facing. The Others have claimed this small planet. They are working their foul purpose even now. We cannot possibly stand against them. And once this planet is claimed, it will be too late for us to leave. If humans join themselves to the Others, we will be thrust into the void. Hestia and I are not willing to take such a risk. It is time for us to return to our true home."

Artemis ran her tongue along her lips. "But there must still be time, or you would have left already."

"Temmie?"

Angie looked startled to see Artemis standing in the middle of her room. "Is there something you need?"

Artemis shook her head, astonished by the sudden transformation. "Ah, no, Angie. I just came by to see how you're settling in. The room's just as you left it."

"She was here just now, wasn't she?" Seeing the odd look on Artemis's face, Angie realized what must have taken place.

"Yes." Artemis reached out and took Angie's hand. "You know who she is, don't you?"

Angie squeezed their hands tightly together. "I've known for years. Can't say that I'm happy about it. But the angel in my childhood head has a name. And I...I live with her. Sort of."

She explained about the periods of missing time and the sensation when Athena took control. "She usually lets me know what is happening. This time she closed me off." Angie managed a wan smile. "You and she must have a secret I am not supposed to know."

Artemis merely nodded.

"Mother doesn't know, does she?" Angie asked. Fear of upsetting her mother was the reason she had stayed away since college except for holiday visits.

"No. And she never will." Artemis gave Angie a hug. "Wolf knows Athena is here. I'll have to explain it's not exactly the way we thought. He figures everything out. It's the scientist in him. But he will not hurt your mother by telling her."

Angie retrieved her hand and rubbed her face. "In a way it feels better to have someone know." She grinned. "A little less crazy."

Artemis opened the door. "Come on. Time for lunch. We have a lot of coordinating to do quickly. As soon as your mother gets home, we're leaving for Nazca. Strang is taking Keegan to check out Easter Island. He asked specifically for that chore."

Angie did an imitation of Wolf twirling his arm, making them both laugh. "What do you want me to do?"

"I'm counting on you to get Ronan and Stefan to finish their work on the message and how to transmit it. They need to be ready once we know for sure where the event must occur."

Chapter Nine

Stefan was the last to arrive. Carrying a dainty porcelain teacup in one of his immense hands, he took a seat at the back of the table and wondered at the reaction he always seemed to elicit. He looked at Keegan, who sported an amused grin. "What?"

Keegan rocked back in his chair and laughed. "I'm buying you a manly mug one of these days, Stefan. I really can't stand the incongruity of you and your pretty teacup. It just does not compute."

Stefan emitted a growl from deep in his chest. "I compute." He muttered. "I compute better with tea."

No one dared laugh except for a faint chuckle from Strang as he tapped his laptop and a map appeared on a large screen behind him. His professorial stare brought the gathering to attention. He explained the image and the significance of the sites being centered equidistant from an axis point in southeast Alaska.

Ronan raised his hand. "Wouldn't an axis at the north pole be more significant? I mean, what's special about Alaska?"

Keegan shook his head. "The pole has changed several times. In its current location the pole points to

Polaris. Thirteen thousand years ago, it pointed to Vega, and it will again in another thirteen thousand years. The Earth spins on an axis tilted fourteen degrees. And it takes about twenty-six thousand years to complete the processional cycle."

"Holy Mayan calendar!" Ronan blurted out, feigning astonishment and causing Stefan to choke on his tea.

Responding to a roll of Artemis's pale-blue eyes, Strang rapped his knuckles on the table to quiet the room.

"My dear wunderkinds, if you will permit me to continue." He tapped four spots on the projected map. "Artemis has narrowed our interest to these specific sites: Angkor Vihear, which opposes Nazca here, and Easter Island, which is in opposition to Mohenjo-daro here in Pakistan."

He noted the GPS location of each site and then tapped the laptop again, projecting a new version of the map with the four sites connected into two paths marking the opposing sites. Giving a brief history of each site, Strang settled into a chair.

Everyone assumed Artemis was going to speak next. Heads turned their attention on her. Only she merely stared, focusing laser-like on the three young men one by one. Each shyly looked away, and the silence became uncomfortable. Searching their minds, she abandoned the carefully crafted script she had prepared to educate them about the nature of the universe and the collective consciousness creating it. They already knew. They didn't accept it, but they knew. Stefan was the first one brave enough to break the silence.

"You wish to hear about our visions," he told her. "You have brought us together for what we see, not what we do."

Artemis inclined her head. *Bravo, Dr. Ivanov.*

Keegan felt indignant. "I'm not a fucking mystic! I am a genius."

You are neither, Dr. Montock. Artemis shook her head and turned to the third young man, Ronan, who sat chewing on his lip.

"You are the benefactor. I sensed you when I was a child. The invitation from Oxford, the scholarship...that was you, wasn't it?" A grin spread across his freckled face. "Thank you."

"She saved me from war," Stefan boasted. "I would be in a grave if she had not plucked me from my village." His mustache cavorted as he spoke. "T'was a miracle my mother told me when she packed my two pairs of trousers and sent me off to university." He balled his hands and sent them thudding to the table.

"Big deal. So, beauty saved the beast...again." Keegan scoffed. He settled back in his chair and yawned. "How touching. As for me, the road was not so pleasant. I was in an institution when our dark-haired benefactor found me."

Strang put his hand on Keegan's shoulder. "You were in juvenile hall, and fourteen months later, you were at Harvard dazzling my former colleagues with your brilliance—a brilliance you squandered for several years before Artemis rescued you a second time and brought you here. This time from Australia where you had no money, no job, and no friends." An audible sigh escaped Strang, betraying the ambivalence with which he still regarded Artemis's decision to retain the unpleasant young man. Character could not be taught. "You most of all should find a spring of gratitude in your heart, Keegan."

Stefan felt a swell of admiration for the woman who had saved them all. "The least we can do to repay you is tell you what visions come to us. If the future is for us to decide, then I am willing to face it. I know what choice we are meant to make, Temmie. I know why you selected us."

Angie caught Ronan staring at her again, a shy smile on his hopeful face. Stefan was on board, she thought, frowning back, but Ronan's sense of the future was still on tilt. *You and I are never going to happen.*

Strang gathered himself to his full height and grasped the lapels of his dark-green Hawaiian shirt. He recognized the wisdom of Artemis's approach. He shut off the laptop and cleared his throat. The Harbinger was theirs; it was time they used it. "Now that you know what is expected, gentlemen, shall we begin?"

*

Minister Pindata Sin paced along the corridor waiting to be admitted to President Chatterjee's office. He had watched two men enter in the past few minutes. And now a third man was granted access while Sin continued to be ignored. He fondled the disk in his pocket as he paced, trying to put a name to the third man. *Deepak Kamakrisha!* The name came to him along with a sense of displeasure. Kamakrisha had brought the pope to address the UN, a tactical and philosophical mistake. Sin had been pleased to hear of Kamakrisha's resignation as General Secretary shortly afterward. Infidels were not the answer to what plagued the Middle East. He, Minister Pindata Sin of Cambodia, was.

The door to Chatterjee's office opened, and the president himself motioned for Sin to enter. It was a grand room filled with art and tapestries celebrating the

Hindu culture. Sin breathed in the richness of the setting and made introduction to the other three attendees. Kamakrisha shook his hand, a weak grasp from an insipid man. The Indian Secretary of State and Chatterjee's highest-ranking military leader were more impressive and more open about their curiosity.

"Thank you, Mr. President, for granting me this opportunity to explore what I believe you will find a common objective," Sin began.

Cambodia was a small country situated between other small nations still licking their wounds from decades of war and dominated by giants like India and China. Pindata had come to India in quest of a realignment. His deep Buddhist principles had given him the wisdom to see a wondrous future where Buddhists and Hindus would be as brothers stretching from the China Sea to the Pacific Ocean.

"We have a treaty with your country, Minister Sin," President Chatterjee pointed out. "Is there something more you would wish from us besides fairness in trade?"

"Much more, sir." Pindata bowed slightly. "A partnership joining my country's vision with your country's military strength. I would have us join ourselves in a goal to eradicate the terror of Islamic aggression and bring peace to our region at last."

To his surprise, Pindata found the weakling Deepak Kamakrisha to be his first ally. The man's experience at the United Nations had convinced him war was coming between India and Pakistan. An alliance to the east would strengthen India's position if handled with care. But Kamakrisha's intention was to avoid war; he was dismayed to learn Minister Sin was eager to start one.

*

The woman had exited the car in the driveway of a magnificent house. Paina paid his taxi driver and stood where his view was unobstructed but he would not be noticed by anyone looking down from the house. He had followed Ms. Breem discreetly, leaving his checked bag unclaimed at the airport lest he lose his quarry in the milling crowd of travelers. Paina had gotten in a taxi and asked the driver to pull forward and wait for a moment. Spying the woman walking to a waiting car, he told the cabby to follow the car onto the freeway and then to Corona and up a series of hills. The trip had concluded at an impressive residence.

Paina found the building charming. *American wealth is an admirable thing,* he thought. Unlike the humble native structures of his youth or even the bland government buildings where he had toiled for decades. His instincts had been correct, he reasoned, paying the taxi driver before turning back to the residence on the hill.

He had placed the advertisement on the internet as bait. In a bit of reverse engineering, Paina thought whoever had the disk would know of its special power and be interested in acquiring another. Or at the very least be curious seeing their possession offered for sale by a stranger. No one else would bother with a million-dollar price tag for a mere bauble. Once the listing posted, all he needed to do was wait for a click before deleting the bogus advert. Within moments, his listing had secured the response he'd hoped for. Overjoyed, Paina had headed to London to await the arrival of the interested party.

The shopkeeper whose street address he'd used was unaware of the details of Paina's little subterfuge. But he had been only too pleased to contact Paina as arranged and accept payment for information about the sole inquirer. The man had provided footage from the shop's security camera, and Paina had made short work of discovering the woman's identity and travel plans. He intercepted Miss Breem at De Gaulle International, managed to book passage on the flight she was on, and followed her back to California. Paina was certain the curse of bad luck from having lost the disk was being lifted.

Strolling in a nearby park, Paina stripped away the business jacket and tie. He watched the sun sink below the horizon and thought of his ancestors and the many trials they had suffered. Being a worthy son had been his main ambition. He had tried the modern world, only to find it was the wrong path. He had been punished for permitting the disk to be lost, losing as a penance all he had worked for. And he had gone in search of not merely the disk but his soul. That which had been lost must be returned. He was Mu, the rightful leader of an ancient land which would rise from the waves and welcome him with gifts of honor and power to command the sea.

He knelt to thank Rangi, Father Sky, and Papa, Mother Earth, for their intervention and forgiveness. Then he heard the disk call to him and rose to climb the hill and claim it.

*

"Have you listened to the music Keegan is obsessed with?" Lucy asked, joining Artemis in the bedroom. She had arrived just after dinner and completed the rounds, delighted to see her daughter and Strang were happy and healthy. She had met the three members of Choice Ltd and wasn't particularly surprised to learn they had moved in.

"Once. I made him turn it down. Why?" Artemis set aside her book. It was good to have her partner home. "Was he playing it again when you were talking with Wolf? Our senior astrophysicist is delighted to have you back, by the way. I think he secretly hates it when we're not all here for him to keep an eye on." She pulled Lucy into her lap. "Not as delighted as I am, mind you."

"That so-called music was blaring out into the hall when I left Angie's room. She said she's going to give him an ultimatum." Lucy nestled in the crook of Artemis's shoulder. "You've turned our hermitage into a bed and breakfast while I was gone. I get why, but I'd have been hard pressed to forgive you if someone was bunking in my mother's room."

"Good for Angie. It's a workplace, not a B&B, and I left Claire's room untouched because I knew you'd want me to." Artemis responded to all three trains of thought, her fingers caressing the soft hair at Lucy's temple. "Your apology is accepted." She grinned.

Lucy jumped up. "Okay smarty pants. I was hoping for a little sympathy, not sarcasm." She went to the dresser and rummaged through the bottom drawer. "Where is that T-shirt I love?" She turned and looked suspiciously at Artemis. "Please don't tell me you threw it out while I was gone."

"It's there, just look," Artemis assured her.

"Ah, here it is." Lucy unfolded a blue shirt with the unusual unalome design down the front and frowned. "It is looking a little worse than I remember. Maybe you should get a new one."

Artemis stood and tossed the book aside. "Get myself a shirt for you to wear? That's logical."

Lucy returned the shirt to the drawer and selected a nightshirt. She slipped it over her head and joined her partner on the edge of the bed.

"You don't need that either." Artemis waggled her eyebrows and issued an invitation with her eyes.

Lucy felt herself enfolded in strong arms and melted into her lover's closeness. But her brain was ablaze with questions about the newcomers, and her libido sat idling in reserve.

"The Irish kid is very cute," she said as Artemis began to nibble on her ear. "Do you think Angie is interested in him? I mean, I know it's only been a few days, but with three young men to choose from, I have my hopes."

Artemis loosened her embrace. "Ronan is a nice fella. He's definitely noticed Angie. I've been keeping my eye on Keegan. There's something odd going on with him. The pick of the litter is Stefan, in my opinion." She pulled Lucy close again. Her center was eager for the talking to end so she could demonstrate just how happy she was to have her lover home. "There, does that answer all your questions?"

Lucy smiled sheepishly. "Yes, thank you." She touched Artemis's cheek and then was struck by another thought. "Which one does Angie prefer? I mean..."

Artemis extricated herself from Lucy with an audible sigh. "None. They're not her type."

"You can't know that, Temmie." Lucy scrunched back against the headboard. "In spite of your wondrous perceptive abilities, you don't read the human heart. Angie seemed restless when we were in London. I think a nice little romance would be great for her."

Artemis looked hungrily at Lucy. *Never let it be said that I'm against romance.* "Uh-huh," she muttered, pinning Lucy with a lusty look. "The young men you're asking about spend most of their time imagining very sexy things. All of which involve one beautiful young woman—your daughter." She arched an eyebrow in emphasis. "Trust me, Angie can have any of them she wants. But as far as I can tell she doesn't want."

Lucy cocked her head. "You're kidding, right? You mean I sent my pure little daughter into a den of lecherous jerks? What have you done about this?"

Artemis tightened her lips. She busied herself smoothing the wrinkles from the sheets and climbed back onto the bed. "Not to worry, my love. Angie plans to introduce Stefan and Ronan to the Advaita Vedanta. Arguing whether the self or the soul is real ought to consume their energy. Mystics haven't resolved the issue for five hundred years."

Lucy chuckled. "That's rather cruel."

"Actually, I believe it's a test to see if either of them proves worthy of her time." Artemis retrieved the duvet and settled on her back.

Lucy slipped under the blanket and curled beside her partner. "In my day, girls just kissed the guy...or girl...to see if someone was a keeper."

"And I thought you led a sheltered life." Artemis wrapped her arms around Lucy, who snuggled closer.

"Do you think it's safe for us to leave the three of them alone? I mean what if the guys come to blows?"

"I have no doubt Angie can defend herself, and if she wants to let them kill each other, so be it." She could feel Lucy smile against her shoulder, a gesture that sent a wave of heat coursing through her.

"They might as well join the rest of the world, which is clearly going straight to hell these days." Lucy rose on her elbow. "In fact, aren't you the least bit worried about us traveling right now? There's famine in South America, rumors of war in Pakistan, and hostilities beginning in Africa. The refugee problem is like a plague threatening the Europeans with bankruptcy. It feels as though everyone's got their mad on."

Artemis pulled Lucy back beside her. "The horsemen have been unleashed," she said, only half joking. "Throw in a few more earthquakes and we'll have the whole quartet."

Lucy traced feathery circles on Artemis's abdomen. "I never expected you to quote the Book of Revelations to me in bed, Temmie." She felt the front of her nightshirt being unbuttoned.

"Revelations, you say." Artemis nuzzled Lucy's neck as she worked. "Excellent idea." She nibbled at Lucy's collarbone. "Let's reveal what you have under here."

"Gods, that feels good," Lucy whispered, relishing the warmth of her partner's hands sliding over her skin.

Artemis looked at Lucy, her pale eyes hooded with desire as she freed Lucy from the shirt. "I much prefer this revelation to anything John of Patmos had to say."

Lucy wanted to ask who John of Patmos was, but her mouth was claimed in a kiss, and nothing mattered except the delicious feeling Artemis' attention was eliciting. She shivered, the sensation of warm lips at her breast sending desire through her core. She tangled her fingers in her lover's dark hair and pushed Artemis lower to the place where heat demanded to be served.

Artemis consumed her lover's body and soul. Savoring the taste of Lucy's skin and the scent of her arousal, she slipped her fingers along the slick folds and caressed them as they swelled. She heard Lucy moan, her hips moving to the rhythm of Artemis's touch. Pressing herself against Lucy's thigh, Artemis took her lover completely, bringing them both to mutual release and feeling their souls join in a burst of light exploding in her head.

As their bodies yielded to the exquisite pleasure, a sound tumbled Artemis meanly back to Earth. She sensed malice approaching and leaped from the bed.

"What the hell?" Lucy reacted to the sudden loss; a shock of cold air replaced the warmth of her lover's body pressed atop her. "Temmie?"

Artemis was at the patio door searching the yard with finely tuned attention. She looked at Lucy and motioned for her to stay put. "Stay here," she said using the low voice Lucy knew meant trouble. "I'm going to kill someone. Be right back."

*

Paina didn't resist the tall, naked woman who grabbed him by the collar and dragged him to the center of the portico. He lay curled on his side waiting to see what the demon would do next. The Breem woman brought his attacker a garment and a phone. Rangi and Papa had forsaken him once again. He said nothing even when he was surrounded by four men, one of whom had the build of a Maori warrior. They could not know his purpose, he consoled himself, only to quickly find he was wrong.

The Breem woman related their conversation on the plane. The demon with the ghostly eyes seemed to probe his mind. Then another woman knelt and touched the tattoo on his forehead.

"He wants the disk," Angie said. "Why would he think it was here?"

The four men set him in a chair, and the big man stood behind Paina, his hands firmly on the intruder's shoulders. Paina ignored their questions, his eyes traveling from person to person, his ears filled with their voices, but he focused his mind on studying them. One of the young men, the quiet one with unkempt hair, slipped back into the house. And Paina of a sudden knew his gods had not abandoned him. The disk was here, and the silent young man possessed it.

Chapter Ten

The winds of hell churned the Pacific into mountainous waves, and the laden tanker rode the swells to the top and then raced down into the troughs where the sea battered the ship mercilessly before lifting it again. Captain James gripped the arms of his chair and watched in horror as his ship rolled to one side and hesitated before righting itself amid the crush of water. They were only hours from port if the navigation was accurate, and there was nothing but hope to verify its accuracy. The storm had found them with incredible speed, and with the giant tanker at the mercy of the wind and waves, it was impossible to know for certain where they were or when they would make land.

The captain stared through the windshield as the ship turned down from the apex of a wave and raced into a black hole where it plowed into another towering wave and shuddered. "Jesus have mercy!" James muttered as the ship repeated its relentless course from crest to trough again and again.

Except for the emergency staff, the crew had been ordered to their quarters. Every aspect of the huge vessel that could be secured had been, and yet it seemed the ship wished to tear itself apart. James watched the instrument panel flash, meaningless numbers scrolling past. Only God could preserve the ship if the storm continued its assault. He looked up into the angry sky and prayed. But the ship pitched heavily to port, and James doubted his prayers were heard. In twenty-two years at sea, he had never encountered such a storm.

His children were grown. His wife's financial future was secure. He could leave this life without regret. But as the waves crashed over his ship, Captain James wanted desperately not to leave. And if he lived, he knew he would never return to the sea, selecting instead a life on a high farm or desert ranch where Poseidon could not find him ever again.

A crack rose from deep below his feet, and the ship quivered as it rolled over the top of a wave and then spun to starboard and folded amidship, reaching the trough below and continuing down past the turbulent surface to the peaceful silence of the deep.

*

Santiago de Chile Airport was packed with travelers making the process of going through customs slow and claiming their baggage even slower. The four travel-weary figures stepped outside the terminal to find a sky promising rain, and their hearts sank even further.

"That's not a part of the hurricane the news is talking about, is it?" Lucy asked, moving the strap of her carry-on higher on her shoulder.

"No," Artemis reassured her. "That one is up near Hawaii. This is probably just a local storm. The seasonal rains have started."

A free airport shuttle carted them ten miles to La Quinta, a clean hotel with spacious rooms, and the little band felt their spirits lift a bit after their long journey. Strang and Keegan disappeared into one room. Artemis and Lucy took a room further down the hall.

Artemis wanted them to relax for the rest day before heading to their separate destinations. The border skirmishes between Chile and Peru were increasing, and the military seemed to be everywhere. The locals were openly on edge, and strangers were eyed with suspicion. Lucy had had most of their gear shipped to their final stops, making them more mobile and less chary to the armed patrols Artemis knew would be combing the city.

"How far is it to Nazca?" Lucy asked, flopping backward onto the king-sized bed and uttering an exhausted-sounding moan.

"A day and a half if we drive," Artemis said, selecting her toiletries bag from her carry-on. Hearing Lucy groan, she laughed. "That's why we're flying."

"Oh, thank God." Lucy dug her elbows into the mattress and leaned up. "Not that I'm eager to get back in another airplane. But that beats driving all to hell."

Lucy heard the shower go on in the bathroom and got up to check the amenities of their room. There was a desk with Wi-Fi instructions printed in English, a minibar with the usual colas and a few bottles of what looked like a local wine, and an assortment of chips and sugary pastries. At least they wouldn't starve, she thought, taking a Coke and popping the top.

Searching the contents of Artemis's bag, she found the itineraries for Strang and Keegan. The men would be flying also. Easter Island was over two thousand miles away so their flight would be even worse than the one to

Nazca. She smiled at the thought of Strang having to deal with Keegan on another flight. He had barely survived the flight to Santiago without strangling his insensitive young companion.

"Better Wolf than me," Lucy said, turning to see Artemis folding a towel around her freshly washed hair. "Gods, Temmie. You look ready to go dancing. How do you do it?"

Artemis opened the towel she'd fastened around her torso and arched an eyebrow, eliciting a hungry look from her partner. "I can think of something much better than dancing, Lucy. Go scrub off the travel dust and I'll show you what I mean."

Lucy set the can of soda down and hurried into the bathroom, suddenly not tired at all. After a quick shower, Lucy dried her body and then emerged naked into a dimly lit room. The sound of rain falling hard and steady against the darkened window was the only noise as Lucy eased her way to the bed and felt the warmth of her lover's body waiting for her beneath the sheet.

Artemis pointed the remote to extinguish the muted TV, but before she clicked, a disturbing picture appeared on the screen. Translating in her head, Artemis read the crawl at the bottom of the screen and uttered a moan.

The quake had struck Monkey Mia, Australia at five nineteen in the morning. Centered offshore just north of Cape Inscription, the quake measured 7.3 on the Richter scale and was followed by a four-foot wave that washed over the sparsely populated Peron Peninsula. The disturbance was felt from Perth to Dampier. Artemis watched the video coverage, fond memories of her visit popping in and out of her head.

Artemis had flown to Perth on an impulse after law school and driven seven hundred miles north to visit the dolphins in Monkey Mia on the northern coast. She had even fed the friendly wild dolphins who swam into Shark Bay each day to freeload fish from overjoyed tourists. Seeing the damage the quake and its rather tame tsunami had caused the area, Artemis was dismayed. She had fond memories of the western Australian coast with its rugged beauty and friendly people.

"There's no mention of the dolphins," she commented to Lucy, who was likewise mesmerized by the images.

"You think the dolphins drowned or something?" Lucy asked before thinking. She blew a strand of hair out of her eyes and cocked her head. "Monkey Mia. That's not near us, is it? We were just talking about an earthquake the other day, weren't we?"

"No. No. And yes" was the rapid-fire response. Laughing, Artemis pointed west. "Australia is waaay over there."

Lucy frowned. "Very funny. Hey, I'm still jet-lagged, okay. I don't even know what landmass I'm on anymore."

Artemis gave her a hug. "Sorry. It's just upsetting to see a place I love destroyed like that."

Settled into the crook of her lover's arm, Lucy sighed. "Maybe it wasn't as bad as it looks. I'm sure the dolphins are just fine."

Artemis turned off the TV. "They're gone."

Lucy wasn't expecting that. "The dolphins? You're kidding. Did the quake..."

"Monkey Mia has been closed for years, Lucy. I think the dolphins stopped coming. I heard that the pod leader lost a calf and went into mourning for months. Wouldn't eat, cried a lot, and eventually, she stopped bringing the pod in for the tourists."

"By the gods," Lucy sounded crushed. "Dolphins are that much like us?"

"Better." Artemis gave Lucy a wink. "Far better in many ways. They talk to each other, you know. They communicate with clicks and..." An idea struck her mid-sentence. Dolphins used sound to communicate without words, and yet even humans could understand what the animals meant. Artemis used to listen to them when she was there. "They communicate complex thoughts full of emotion and playfulness...no words but they talk like we do." *Not exactly like we do*, she thought. *One species receiving the thoughts of another.*

"You okay?" Lucy asked, feeling Artemis's heartbeat change its rhythm.

Artemis blinked. "Yeah. I'm good. Just thinking."

*

The military stationed at the exit of Mataveri Airport gave Strang and Keegan instructions to keep moving. Keegan stared back at them until Strang hooked his arm and dragged him forward.

"Humor me," Strang muttered when Keegan attempted to resist. "And I do not refer to those insufferable Chile-sounds-like-chilly jokes. I cannot endure another of those. Let's just get to the hotel and collect our gear without drawing attention."

Keegan hefted his carry-on and followed Strang to a car rental stand not far from the baggage claim area. They procured a rustic-looking jeep adequate to reach every point of interest on the small island. Triangular in shape, Easter Island consisted of sixty-three square miles which spread from the extinct volcano, Rano Kau, in the southwest, fifteen east miles to Poike, also extinct.

Between them the largely flat ground rose 1660 feet to the crater of Terevara, yet another ancient volcano.

Beneath the rolling grassy hills, a network of lava tubes formed by ancient basalt flows crisscrossed the island. Above them rows of huge stone statues called Moai kept sightless watch over palm trees and roving groups of wild horses. Hundreds of the effigies populated the island, standing guard on its inhabitants with only a single row of Moai facing out to sea at Ahu Aki.

A two-lane road circumnavigated the island, although Strang knew a serious investigation of the island would require them to walk more than drive. First, the scientist was eager to get settled and ensure the arrival of the equipment that had been sent ahead.

Keegan took one look at the dilapidated accommodations Artemis had arranged for them and frowned. "Guess we've come down in the world of a sudden." He followed Strang to the office to check in and pick up their gear.

A handwritten sign posted on the door welcomed them to Makupuna Cabins as Keegan gingerly entered the low-slung office building. "Huh!" he sighed, taking in the rustic motif. "No one is going to be looking for us here for sure."

An island woman named Taty processed Strang's credit card and handed him a key to a cabin in the rear Strang selected from a layout of the grounds. She made sure the tall man and his slender "son" knew about the complimentary breakfast served buffet-style on a table in the office and offered them an assortment of tour brochures which Keegan grabbed before heading to their cabin.

Trudging along a gravel strewn path, Strang made a quick visual exploration of their surroundings. There was no sign of the military near the outlying hotel, and Strang let the tension in his shoulders relax. A brief text to Artemis confirmed their safe arrival. Keegan manhandled the two large duffel bags into the cabin and inventoried their contents.

"It's all here," he said, wiping away a bead of sweat from the exertion.

"Excellent." Strang grabbed a camera and the satellite phone and headed to the jeep. Keegan stepped ahead of him and jumped into the driver's seat. "You be the navigator," he told the somewhat surprised older man. "Where do you want to start?"

Strang settled into the passenger seat and unfolded the map. "Well, let me see. Let's play tourists for a few hours and head to Hanga Roa, the main town. We can grab something to eat there and then veer south to inspect Rano Kau, the first of three volcanoes here on the island."

Keegan popped the clutch and then sped down the narrow road, the idea of food foremost in his mind. Halfway to town, a dirty brown sedan casually pulled onto the road behind them.

*

Another charade of after-dinner socializing struck Angie as unbearable. She slipped away while Ronan and Stefan toddled out to the portico with a six-pack of beer. Making her way to the far corner of the backyard, Angie stared up at the darkening sky, finding a quarter moon and the first evening stars emerging. The moon did not hold the attraction for her it did for Artemis, and she turned her attention back to the vast yard. Using the tip of her sandal, Angie traced the edge of the little stone platform she and Artemis had built a decade ago. It was the place where her aunt would kneel and listen to the universe. It was a place of answers, and Angie wondered if the little platform would provide them to her.

Stefan wanted to take her out to dinner. She smiled at the conspiratorial way he had gotten the two of them away from Ronan and the expression when he had asked. She had felt thirteen again and stumbled over a reply. Angie knew it was not a good idea to entertain a relationship with a work colleague, what with the work he and Ronan still had to complete. There was no time for romance now.

Stefan had smiled that silly grin of his, and Angie had found herself agreeing to the date. She had felt the shadow at the back of her mind shudder. That was just too bad, she had thought. Athena might have been a virgin goddess; Angie was not.

She was tired of putting her own needs and wants to the side. She'd gotten a PhD in Ancient Civilizations in part to either verify or put to rest the dreams that had plagued her since the age of five. She had disappointed her mother and taken a fellowship from a university in Egypt after graduation rather than returning home. It was there amid the heat and the sand and the impossibly boring work that Angie had realized Athena had driven her decisions.

Being home again, even with the turmoil and constant state of apprehension to deal with, Angie knew she wanted to stay. She wanted a real life, a full life. Maybe having dinner with the charming Dr. Ivanov would be a first step.

The cell phone in her pocket vibrated, and Angie's body trembled as a powerful force emerged from within and Athena took control.

"Hello, sister." Athena responded to the sound of Artemis's voice. "So good of you to call."

*

The jeep pulled to the curb in front of a small café sporting a red-and-green canopy over a pair of tables which promised the ability for them to eat outside. The sun was hanging low in the west, turning the sky various shades of orange and purple.

"Tomorrow looks to be a fine day," Strang said, appreciating the view. He was enjoying the trip. He was surprised how small his world had become all these years living comfortably with Artemis and Lucy. It was good to be out and about and on an island once again.

Keegan looked quizzically over the top of a paper menu. "Why do you say that?"

"Red skies at night, sailor's delight." Strang quoted an old canard and pointed to the horizon.

Keegan returned to his menu as if he could read it. A chubby man in a stained apron approached the table and wiped it with an energetic swipe of his rag. Keegan and Strang were barely able to remove their arms from the surface in time.

"Hamburger?" Keegan ordered with a question.

The man made a scribble on his notepad and then turned his attention to Strang and repeated the question. "Hamburger?"

Strang added a request for both *agua* and beer. Once the waiter left to fill the order, Strang turned the paper menu over and took a pen from his vest pocket. He drew a rough oval oriented from northwest to southeast and then began adding familiar names: Easter Island, Hawaii, Samoa, Tahiti, and others less familiar to Keegan, who watched the map of a nonexistent continent containing the Pacific island chains take form.

"What's that?" Keegan asked when Strang sat back. "What's Mu?" he queried, reading aloud the name written at the top of the paper.

"The legendary Land of Mu." Strang waggled his eyebrows. "A creative bit of fantasy said to once have occupied a considerable swath of the Pacific Ocean. The concept has fascinated me for years, and here we are standing at the edge of it."

"Argh. Must we discuss another of your nonsensical myths?" Keegan looked over his shoulder to see if drinks were on the way. But there was no sign of their waiter. "Any idea when this Mu supposedly existed?"

"None whatsoever." Strang grinned.

Keegan tilted his head to one side and smirked. "What is with you, man? This obsession you have with ancient ruins and mystical, magical theories. I never heard an astrophysicist talk about stuff like that. Aren't you supposed to be interested in the future? I mean you have the whole universe to figure out. Why do you give a damn about the past?"

"What we see when we peer into the universe is the past, my friend. Each point of light has taken millions perhaps billions of light years to reach even the most sensitive of our instruments. The past is all we have."

The pudgy waiter returned bearing a large tray. He set bottles of water and beer on the table and then placed steaming bowls in front of each of the men. Strang took a fork, stirred whatever was in the bowl a few times, and gave it a taste. Keegan just stared at what had to be the strangest hamburger, if that was what it was, he'd ever seen. He lifted the lettuce and examined the sliced onions and ground meat cooked to near black.

"You're right about one thing, old man; nothing is what it seems these days," Keegan said, reaching for a fork. His hunger outweighed his confusion. It was a hamburger of sorts, he decided, tasting the concoction. All the components were present, including half a toasted bun at the bottom of the bowl. "A bowl of ground beef is still basically a burger, I guess. It all depends on how you look at it."

Strang took a healthy gulp of beer. "Now you are beginning to understand!"

Chilean soldiers strolled past on the street. Their black uniforms acted like repellent as people stepped off the curb to let them pass. Easter Island was claimed by Chile, but it was actually the southern tip of what was known as the Polynesian Triangle, extending north to Hawaii, east to the Nan Madol, and then southwest nearly to New Zealand. Also known as Lemuria, the triangle encompassed the territory ruled by Queen Mu still mentioned in Hawaiian folklore. As far as Strang could see, the Chilean soldiers were conspicuously out of place.

He watched them stop at a vendor stall and engage the red-faced proprietor, who folded his arms and blocked the soldiers' advance. A heated exchange ensued, and the proprietor found himself slammed against a support post while a hard punch was delivered to his gut. The proprietor slumped to the ground, and the soldiers helped themselves to handfuls of dried fruit before continuing their patrol along the street.

Keegan wiped his mouth with the back of his hand. "I see what you mean about being careful. What I don't get is why there's military in the streets. Easter Island has belonged to Chile for decades. Is there a rebellion going on?"

Strang tossed an ample number of Chilean pesos on the table and headed to their jeep. "I doubt eight thousand people could stage a rebellion, Keegan. Those two are the same ones we saw at the airport and again when they followed us into town. They are more of a flag in the ground, I suspect."

"Flags don't follow tourists, Wolf." Keegan took his position behind the wheel.

"No, but they do tell you which way the wind is blowing."

Chapter Eleven

Twenty-seven hours in Nazca had yielded nothing. Lucy trudged along a trail, ignoring the way her boots rubbed against that one painful spot on the ball of her left foot. Even during the cooler seasons, the unforgiving sun made the Nazca plane feel like a griddle. The long, flat surface reflected heat, and there was not a tree or spot of shade to be found. Sweat trickled down Lucy's back.

"It's right around here...somewhere," Artemis said, examining the map of glyphs to orient the ones they were supposedly standing near.

Lucy took a swig from her canteen. "You don't know that. You said the same thing an hour and a half ago."

Artemis shielded her eyes with her hand and scoured the low horizon. "It all looks so different from the air. It's hard to calibrate on the ground. Maybe we should go back for the SUV. Walking isn't cutting it."

Lucy was down with that. She turned on her heel and began the journey back the way they'd come, renewed pep in her step as the silhouette of the rented vehicle came into view. "I thought you could just sense where we needed to go. You know, with your magic senses or something. Or maybe you should just kneel down and ask one of those unseen friends of yours to whisper a hint."

"Nope. It doesn't work that way. I've tried." Artemis paused on the trail, a sudden sense of sadness rolling through her. *What if Ze'us is forbidding the collective to help? Hestia and Athena warned me not to interfere.* She shifted the small pack at her waist and set the doubts aside. The collective had to be out there, watching, waiting to welcome the humans. And if Strang's work had brought them to the right path, she would find a sign.

Artemis climbed into the SUV, started the engine, and cranked up the air conditioning. Moments later, she and Lucy relaxed with cool blasts pouring over them. Artemis retrieved the map. The hummingbird glyph had to be the starting point. Ze'us loved hummingbirds, she explained to Lucy. The iridescence of their feathers was not unlike the clothing he wore on ceremonial days.

"So then follow where the beak points," Lucy suggested, grateful she needed only to lift a finger to follow the map instead of physically trudging up the long trail. "It points northeast directly at a star glyph, then further to what looks like a landing strip next to some sort of bird, and ends at what the legend says is a killer whale." Lucy looked up from the map to see if Artemis was following along. To her surprise, Artemis looked shocked.

"That's it!" Artemis pulled back her ebony hair and bent over the map. "That's not a star—it's a ship. The spiral is the galaxy...this galaxy to be specific. You're correct about the landing strip, but you left out the glyph on the left."

"Says here that's a wing."

"It's a temple; Angkor has towers shaped just like that. And the glyph above it is not a killer whale." Artemis blew out a breath. "It's..."

The sound of gunshots interrupted her. A bullet pinged off the side mirror just outside Lucy's door, and Artemis floored the gas pedal in response. She swiveled her head, looking for the source of the gunfire. There was no vehicle she could see, and the land was flat on three sides, providing a wide area of view. The shooter had to be in the hills just to their right.

"Jeez! Do they shoot people here just for violating the access ban?" Lucy lowered her window and stuck her head out, searching for the source of the gunfire.

Artemis yelled for Lucy to get down just as a volley of bullets caused a shower of dirt behind their SUV.

Ten minutes later, they pulled onto the narrow two-lane highway and made a beeline for their hotel.

*

Strang shuffled through his papers with one hand and held the satellite phone to his ear with the other. Artemis's call was more than disturbing, and his hands shook slightly as he looked for what information he had about the hummingbird glyph.

"Ah, yes, here it is." He shifted the phone to his other hand. "The hummingbird glyph is the very one I thought most significant. The sine wave passes directly over it, and the distance from the glyph to Angkor Vihear is precisely 180 degrees."

"They are antipodal, Wolf, I know." Artemis's voice was tense, urging him to tell her something new. "And I know about the golden section relationship between the sites. That's why we're heading to Cambodia next. Lucy's making arrangements as we speak."

Strang ran a hand through his hair. "I see nothing in the literature or the mathematics that would prompt someone to shoot at you." He heard Artemis sigh. "But you must be on to something significant, or why else would they—whoever they are—bother? Perchance it was just a warning, Temmie. One is not permitted to wander about without permission. You did acquire the requisite permission, didn't you?"

"Umm. Sure," Artemis lied, but she was not convinced the shooting was a warning. "Listen, Wolf. What else do you know that connects the two sites?"

Strang paced as he thought. "Well, both are located on mountains. Nazca dates back two thousand years, Vihear about six hundred. Although I doubt those dates are accurate. Little is known about the ancient Nazca culture. Vihear is thought to be a Hindu temple dedicated to the God Shiva. I honestly have no idea how they are related other than by their mirific placement."

Artemis was silent for a few moments. What explained the alignment to the northeast? The hummingbird glyph pointed to an object called the whale she wanted to know about next. Strang took out a map of the Nazca lines and located the area she was referencing.

"Yes, I see," he told her. "Only on my map the whale you refer to is labeled a shark. Just below the shark glyph there is one named the wing, but it looks like..."

"Like the citadel at Vihear. I saw that too." Artemis appreciated Strang's sharp eye. "Tell me, what does the shark look like to you?"

Strang scratched his chin. "It does bear an aquatic appearance. Shark, whale, either one works. There is a face below it. If one takes that into account, the glyph could be a rendering of a person thinking about a shark."

"I got the same impression, Wolf. But mountains don't have sharks or whales for that matter, so why would this guy be thinking of a shark?" There was a snicker in her voice. "It is a person thinking but not about a fish. The wide-eyed look on that face tells me the guy is thinking about something unpleasant."

Strang squinted at the image, trying to see what Artemis did. "Your hypothesis is plausible, Temmie. But certainly not an obvious interpretation. Whatever's on the fellow's mind, he doesn't seem happy about it. I'll give you that."

*

"What means this?" Stefan leaned over Ronan's shoulder and pointed to a note taped eye-level on the wall behind the desk.

Ronan slid to one side so that Stefan's muscular arm no longer touched him. He glanced at Stefan, who stepped back to give him space. "I thought you spoke five languages."

"These obscure island dialects are not of interest to me." Stefan snorted. "Who speaks such odd sounds but lepers?"

"You mean leprechauns," Ronan sneered, finding leper the greater insult. He picked up the Post-it and read it with a lilting Irish brogue. "*Ar scath a cheile mhaieann na daoine.*"

Stefan frowned. "Ya, so!"

"Under the shelter of each other, people survive." Ronan returned the note to the wall. If the overly muscular Estonian failed to understand the meaning, he didn't care. Stefan was as useless as he was intimidating. The disciplines of psycho-neuro programming or cybernetics were theoretical garbage to Ronan. The textbook definition of Stefan's responsibility was to bring about changes in perception or at least augment them. And if that wasn't particularly clear, according to Artemis, Stefan was quote, unquote responsible for developing a communication strategy along the lines of telepathy for their given situation.

"I am not a patient man anymore, boy-o." Stefan folded his arms and loomed over Ronan. "I came to tell you I am officially a suitor to Angie. You can step to the background now. No hard feelings." He offered his hand, but Ronan simply turned back to his desk and willed Stefan to go away...far, far away.

*

The slap was delivered with surprising force, and Paolo had difficulty holding his head steady. General Maria Vergara shook the sting out of her hand. "You will not fail me again. Is that understood?"

Paolo wasn't certain how he should answer. His wide eyes merely blinked, and Maria saw contrition in them mixed with fear. It was enough. Sending the untrained farmer's son to perform a delicate task had been a mistake she would not make again. The Chilean army had sharpshooters by the hundreds she could have sent to deal with the women in Nazca if she had wanted them killed. All the general wanted was to know why the two had come to Peru posing as tourists. Perhaps to assist the Peruvian government in its outspoken condemnation of Chile's aggression, Maria had speculated. Paolo was to ransack their hotel and follow them, not kill them.

Being too clever by half, Maria had not wanted any hint of the military involved. Peru was not yet in the fold. The murder of a tourist, especially the famous Artemis Andronikos, could have caused a difficult international incident. Her mole in the office of intelligence had flagged the arrival of Andronikos, the reporter, and two scientists. She had known it was not an innocent visit. The disk had reacted, growing hot when Maria read the names. She would have opened a legitimate investigation if it were not for President Caron and his fear of El Norte.

Hiding her ambition behind a man like Caron chafed. His was the name on the treaties. His was the face the peasants and urban centers saw when the food was delivered. His was the face Maria wanted most to slap.

The disk murmured, and the sound cooled her anger. She sent her aide from the room, retrieved a communication envelope from her desk, and opened it. According to the itinerary it contained, the two women were en route to Lima which would place them out of range. But the old man and his companion would land in Santiago within the hour. The disk grew hot, and she took it from her pocket to set it on the desk.

The silver disk rose and circled her. Maria stared in awe. The object had never done that before. She watched it pause for a moment and then begin to spin. She felt mesmerized, not afraid. This wondrous object was alive, creating visions in her head telling her to proceed. The disk came to a sudden stop and drifted slowly to the desk.

Maria knew she was to intercept the two men before they left Chile.

"Ramon, *ven aquí rápido*!" She summoned her aide.

*

Strang picked up his bag and headed to a check-in line, dragging Keegan with him.

"What the hell are you doing?" Keegan complained. "We've got a three-hour layover, and I'm hungry."

"No, we don't," Strang educated him calmly. "Lucy changed our flight. We're leaving in thirty-five minutes. You can eat peanuts on the plane."

Keegan checked the new itinerary Lucy had texted and exploded in an over-the-top string of expletives. "I'm not spending two days hopping planes, Wolf. We had a direct flight. What the fuck?"

Strang gave his companion a stare. "You can ask Lucy when you see her."

Keegan walked away to cool down. He hated being treated like a flunky. Go here, do this, get to work. He was tired of it, and his blood felt like it was boiling.

Strang gave Keegan his space. He wasn't eager to spend an additional day making their way back to California, but he accepted the wisdom of Artemis's tactics, given the trouble in Nazca. He fished the passports out of his bag and prepared to check them in.

Keegan stood at the terminal window and noticed five military vehicles speed past on their way to the adjacent terminal. Men in sleek, black uniforms exited the vehicles and congregated on the sidewalk. He watched, fascinated, as the military police took up positions along the entire front of the building across the roadway. A woman exited the middle vehicle and received a crisp salute. She was shorter by a head than the soldiers, but the men were clearly cowed by her presence. Keegan watched, intrigued, as the woman officer issued orders and the military police moved to block the entrances.

Keegan gasped as the woman turned and glared in his direction, her hand pressing against the weapon at her hip. He slipped behind a pillar, his heart racing. It had felt like looking into the face of a demon. Strang was waving boarding passes at him. Keegan pulled his sweatshirt hood over his head and hurried to follow Strang up the ramp to the boarding docks.

"We aren't going to the terminal for LATAM airlines, are we?" Keegan said as they fell in line at the boarding gate.

"No. We've been changed to an Argentinean carrier for the first leg. We'll be stopping at Guarulhos International, then off to Houston. Tomorrow, we'll make it back to LA."

Keegan nodded. "Okay. Where's Guarulhos?"

Strang handed the boarding passes to the clerk, and he and Keegan made their way down the stairs to the waiting plane. They stowed their bags in the overhead locker and took their seats.

"Brazil," Strang sang out in a deep baritone. "Where hearts were entertaining June. We stood beneath an amber moon."

"What?" Keegan slid back into his seat and cringed. "Have you lost your mind?"

Strang twirled his hand and laughed. "I was answering your question. Guarulhos is in Brazil."

*

The refugee camp gave off an odor that carried for miles on the wind. Pope Peter II stifled a sneeze and rolled up the window of the limousine. Cardinal Planchette chuckled at the finicky gesture, further evidence the pontiff was ill-prepared for the responsibility he had thrust upon the Vatican. It was not a problem the Church could handle. The refugees had overwhelmed the nations they'd invaded by uncountable millions. And with recent events, surely more would soon be adding to the flood of human misery. Planchette straightened his crimson cassock and wondered if even God could stem such a torrent.

Peter studied the faces with their glimmer of unreasoned hope as they passed by the window. But he did not see the misery the cardinal did. Peter saw an army gathering in the service of a mighty God. He would feed the hordes just as Jesus had done, and they would do his bidding when he called them forth.

The limousine came to a rest at a large warehouse converted to a feeding station in the center of the camp. The pope stepped from the vehicle and waved to the shouting crowd, then stepped into the building and watched as a caravan of chartered trucks unloaded crates of food. It was the second stop of the day. Once Peter had dealt with the refugees in France, he would take his food and his message north into the rest of Europe.

When the unloading was completed, cooks brought by the pontiff set to work preparing a lavish evening meal. At precisely seven p.m., Peter himself opened the doors to the feeding station and greeted the hungry people who lined up outside. He shook their hands and touched their faces. He blessed children and held babies wrapped in dirty cloths. And he won them body and soul, telling them salvation was at hand.

Cardinal Planchette answered a text from the president of Spain. All was going well was the message sent. Not for the unwary politician who was losing control, the cardinal knew, but for the clever pontiff who was gathering the power the president didn't even know he'd lost. He set the phone inside the white limousine and turned to watch the pope move among the mass of people. A verse from Revelations filled his mind.

"And, as I watched, there was a white horse. Its rider was holding a bow. He was given a crown, and he went off winning victories, and to win more of them."

Chapter Twelve

Lucy nibbled on a slice of mango and watched the terrain pass by. After the harrowing experience of driving along the coast while constantly looking over their shoulders, they had turned inland to find the area sparsely populated. Even Artemis had stopped checking the rearview mirror every ten seconds to see if they were being followed. But the paranoia was still evident on Artemis's face. They weren't even going to stop halfway to Lima to get something to eat. Artemis insisted they drive straight through and was challenging the predicted time it would take to complete the trip. Eight hours was not in her repertoire. They would make it in six. Lucy stopped herself from opening a bottle of water. Her bladder was barely going to make it as it was.

"I'm thinking of sending Strang and Keegan straight on to Pakistan from Houston instead of having them go all the way home first." Artemis broke the silence they had shared for nearly an hour. "See if you can get any news on this thing."

Lucy fiddled with the radio with no luck. "I'll try my phone. Do you think we're close enough to Lima to get a signal?"

Artemis nodded. "It's worth a try."

Lucy did a web search but didn't find what Artemis wanted. "What was the name of that guy you told me about?"

Artemis thought. "Sin Pindata or something like that. He's Cambodian."

"He's the Minister of Life—whatever that means!" Lucy told her after entering the name. "He gave a speech about how great Hinduism is last week. It didn't sit well with the Muslims. I can't find anything about Pakistan other than India is unhappy with them. The whole world is angry at somebody. Maybe it's better if Strang just goes home and stays there."

Artemis groaned. The sense of urgency grew as the days passed, and they had no answers. "We're running out of time. They ought to go to Mohenjo-daro before things get any worse. Do you want to go home, Lucy? You've traveled a lot, and I can do the next stop myself."

"Oh no, Temmie." Lucy was exhausted physically, but the danger they'd experienced in Nazca served to steel her will. There was no way she'd let Artemis go anywhere without her. "We'll get this done. It will only take us— what, three or four days to get in and out of Cambodia. I'll paint a red circle on my glabella and fit right in. If we find the sign you're looking for, we can concentrate on the other problems."

Artemis took Lucy's hand and entwined their fingers.

"Remind me to call Angie as soon as we get to Lima. We haven't heard from her in two days."

"She's probably burying the bodies," Lucy quipped.

Artemis broke into a full-throated laugh. It felt good. She couldn't remember the last time she had laughed quite that hard. Lucy loved the sound.

*

Stefan sighed as Angie pulled the phone from his hand and took over the conversation before he let slip they had gone on a date. He was hardly surprised. When it came to talking with Artemis—and Artemis only—Angie went into instant bitch mode. She even tended to look slightly different. The beautiful young woman gave way to an imperious stranger as the planes of Angie's face sharpened.

Athena stepped into an adjacent room to continue the conversation in private. "If you're wondering how things are going here, the word is nowhere. Stefan is locked and loaded. It's Ronan who can't get his head out of his whatever and finish the specs. He just stares at me with those moony, puppy dog eyes and fantasizes about me...in highly annoying ways."

Artemis stifled a chuckle and then added a bit of unsolicited advice. "Maybe you should just bed the boy and get it over with. I'm sure his ego would find the experience humiliating enough to cure his adolescent fantasies."

"You're such a bitch, Artemis," Athena sneered in response. "If I was inclined to bed either of these limited males, it would be Stefan. At least he has an adequate... ego." She could hear Artemis laughing. "Besides, Father would disagree. If you recall, it was interspecies sex that got us into trouble in the first place. And since I plan on being with Father soon, I'm not going there."

"Ze'us was angry about the offspring produced, Athena. He didn't want the gene pool polluted once he'd altered human DNA."

Athena remembered quite well. "Okay, you and Lucy were an exception. I admit that. Soulmates, true love and all that, but..."

"No time for a stroll down memory lane, Athena." Artemis moved the conversation back to its original purpose. "I need them to come up with an answer, and I need it soon. I'm certain Angkor Vihear will tell me where. Have you any more information as to when? Read their minds or try and ask Hestia."

Athena lowered the phone and took a few deep breaths. Taking orders was not her forte and she hated taking a backseat to anyone. Artemis was going to fail; she felt it in her soul. The Others would assimilate the humans. Athena's purpose was to convince Artemis to return to the collective with her before being lost to the void. Maybe it was just being connected with Angie and her physicality, but the thought of losing Artemis forever was exceedingly painful to accept. She lifted the phone to give Artemis one last plea.

"Artemis, you don't have to do this."

But there was no one listening.

*

Stefan went to the whiteboard and drew a red circle around the words "vibrational mind."

"The answer is here." He tapped the words with the marker. "We must redirect the input from here...to here." He drew a circle around the word "conscious," his violet eyes targeting Ronan. "All your bullshit ideas keep us here." He drew a large red X on the word "unconscious" and emphasized his frustration by hitting the whiteboard with his other hand.

Ronan squirmed in his chair, uncomfortable with Stefan's tone and Angie's silent observation from the back of the room.

"The unconscious is ninety-seven percent of the brain's function, Stefan. Why do you insist on playing on the edges?" Ronan ran his hand through his reddish crew cut and dodged a glare from Angie. "I am the one who understands these functions, Stefan. Your pathetic guesses are not getting us any closer to finding the mechanism Artemis wants."

"At least Stefan understands we are trying to connect consciousnesses, Ronan." Angie stood and walked around the conference table to take the marker. "We are looking to establish a link between people. That will happen here in the consciousness just as Stefan is telling you. Not in the animal brain. Get your head out of Freud's ass and figure out how to open the RAS to direct input this way."

"Ass versus RAS." Stefan smiled, adding salt to the wound.

Jealousy surged through Ronan at the look Stefan exchanged with Angie. "Hey, I don't even know what the vibrational mind is, okay?"

Angie folded her arms across her ample chest. Ronan was not as obtuse as he pretended. He just resisted validating a concept offered by Stefan. She put her hand on the back of Ronan's chair and spoke in a low, sultry tone. "Consider everything a vibration. Color, light, sound—touch." She ran her hand along the back of his neck. "Everything. Now think of those vibrations hitting the reticular activating system at the base of the brain and sending notes off to the conscious and the subconscious for processing. Now imagine a code word synchronizing the vibrations between people. Get it?"

Ronan dropped his face into his hands. "No."

Maybe Temmie was right, Angie thought. *If I just fuck him silly, it might help.* She gave him a quick appraisal and shook her head. No way. Ronan wasn't thinking with the wrong head; he wasn't thinking at all.

"Okay, let's try this." Angie took a book from Artemis's extensive library and flipped through the pages. "There has been a debate for centuries regarding the soul versus the self. Consider the unconscious to be the self, full of desires and hungers and all those automatic processes that make the body function. Then see the conscious as the soul, the creative process that manifests ideas and makes them real. Let's assume both of them process vibrations that pass through the RAS. Visualize it happening."

Ronan groaned without raising his head. "Now you want me to solve the mystery of the Vedanta. Give me a break, Angie. I'm a psychologist, not a philosopher."

"You are neither, idiot." Stefan sank into a chair opposite his stricken colleague. "You have the vibration level of a slug."

Ronan looked up and balled his fist. "You're just trying to make me look bad in front of her!"

Stefan grinned. "No, boy-o. You do that yourself." He winked at Angie.

Angie lifted a meticulously groomed eyebrow high on her forehead. Looking at the two frustrated young men, she saw they were on the same vibration level on one topic. She arched her back seductively and softened her tone. "Unless you manage to produce the amplification process Artemis has requested, we are doomed. I suggest you lower the testosterone level and work together."

Both men turned bright red. Angie felt a disapproving shudder lurch within her and reacted with a wave of smug determination. *Go to hell, Athena.*

"I see both of you correctly processed that vibrational input," Angie told the two researchers as she opened the door. "I'll be back in two hours to see what you come up with...so to speak."

Stefan picked up the marker and began flowcharting on the whiteboard. Ronan claimed the book Angie had left on the table and began reading as fast as his libido would permit.

*

Maria Vergara sat astride her horse and pointed the disk at a Peruvian field where corn stalks waved gracefully in the wind. Taking the disk in her hand, she aimed it at the field and felt it grow hot. A dark stream emanated from its center, growing larger, filling the cloudless azure sky with black. The cloud swooped down and within minutes devoured the wheat. Then the cloud of locusts soared skyward and dissolved into the wind.

The loss of vegetation would be a terrible blow to the hardscrabble farmers of the Peruvian Altiplano. The soil was difficult to work even with the regenerative methods handed down from their ancestors. Maria did not feel compassion for the sparsely populated region. She had rarely experienced compassion for anyone, certainly not these people at the windswept top of what was becoming her continent. But they were useful. Their suffering would promote their leaders to act.

She leaned back in the saddle and turned her face to the sun. The warmth felt pleasant. The weather was holding, but winter would be upon them soon. She knew she needed to complete the conquest with haste. It was time to bring the remaining holdout to heel. She tightened her grip on the reins and took a final look at the valley, now a brown stain below the towering mountains. With a stroke of her hand, she could restore the devastated plateau, and she might once Peru sent word it was ready to accept her authority.

Destino snorted and pawed the ground. Maria jerked the reins and set off to inform her troops it was time to break camp. She wanted to head south and prepare for one last push. The location for the final battle had come to her in a vision. It was the perfect place. The spirit of her ancestors would be there, and she would fill their eyes with awe at her glory. But first there remained one more task to complete.

*

"So, what's up, fellas? It's like a mausoleum in here." Keegan found Stefan and Ronan in the rec room, their backs turned to each other and a stone-cold attitude hovering like an invisible cloud.

Keegan had put away the luggage by dumping the duffel bags in the hall. He was eager to share details of their hair-raising adventure with the other young men who, according to Keegan, had been enjoying the good life while he was dodging danger at every turn. At least that was the way he intended to portray it.

Seeing Stefan and Ronan in some sort of gloomy stand-off, Keegan put aside his nascent visions of glory.

"Hey!" Ronan nodded at his returning colleague and went back to staring at a muted television screen.

Stefan climbed to his feet and offered Keegan his hand. "Glad you made it back," he said as Keegan shook the offered hand. "I heard you got followed by the military cops?" A smile snuck out below his mustache. "Boy-o nearly cried."

"Shut the fuck up!" Ronan rose from his own chair and glared at the burly Stefan. "I was the one who told you they were not hurt."

"You were the one who crapped your prissy little pants." Stefan chuckled.

Keegan's eyes darted from the sneer on Stefan's face to the angry scowl on Ronan's. "Wow. You two completely fell apart, and we weren't even gone that long."

Sorting relevant information from the torrent of words flung at him as the two belligerents talked over each other, Keegan got the gist. Neither Stefan nor Ronan had made conclusive progress on their mutual assignment—or, and more importantly to each of them, on their individual efforts to win the affection of the fair Angie.

"Well, I'll let you two sort that out." Keegan shook his head. "I'm not entering the competition. Angie struck me as out of our league right from the start. And I favor one-nighters anyway when I can find them."

"You gay?" Ronan asked, unable to contemplate a male not interested in the exquisite Angela Breem.

Keegan sucked on his teeth. "Nope. Just irritating. Doesn't make for long-term relationships."

Stefan broke into a hearty laugh, the sound of which dispelled the tenseness in the air. "Okay, okay. I respect a man who knows his limitations. Come. Sit down and tell us about this terraqueous place named Easter Island."

Keegan unzipped his backpack and began unloading items onto a table looking for the souvenirs he had picked up for his colleagues. Apart from the candy wrappers and shaving kit, he inadvertently set a wooden box aside as he rummaged to the bottom of the pack.

"What's this?" Ronan swooped it up before Keegan realized what he'd done. He opened the box and pulled out a magnificent platinum disk.

Chapter Thirteen

Minister Pindata Sin walked along the line of troops, barely gazing at the stiff, attentive soldiers. His hands were clasped behind his back; his jaw was rigid with anger. Indian President Chatterjee had rejected the offer to unite with Cambodia out of hand and made disrespectful remarks about Buddha. He had laughed when Sin had gathered his pride and walked out of the president's office. The sound of the dismissive cackle still rang in his ears.

Pindata had hoped for more but had failed even to merit respect. The insult churned in his gut. His was the greater vision. Ending the philosophical disagreements that separated Buddhism from Hinduism would join them in a newer, greater truth. And it would create a singularity of mind for a billion faithful who could finally dominate the middle regions.

Pindata spit on the sandy, Indian soil. *Chatterjee is a fool.* India was not prepared for what it was meant to achieve. What Sin was anointed to achieve. The Cambodian minister was from an ancient family and had been given the name Pindata—"wise man" in Sanskrit. A student of the Vedanta, Pindata felt the divinity of his nature, the purpose of his life to achieve worldly progress and rise above duality into eternal reality.

Reaching the end of the line of troops, Pindata turned smartly on his heels and saluted the men he was sending to their deaths. A small contingent of loyal soldiers had accompanied him to Bombay and waited to see if Chatterjee would accept their leader's vision. In a few days, the men would cross the border into Pakistan and commence the struggle they were predestined to win. Pindata had chosen the place the conflict would begin: a plain where India jutted forward into Pakistan near the ancient sites of the Indus Valley where civilization had once flourished. Dressed as Indian military, his men would find it easier to avoid detection. Pride swelled deep within Pindata's chest. He would strike the first blow against a dangerous enemy. India would have no choice but to join his vision then.

The disk in his vest pocket felt warm. Pindata's mind seemed to blur momentarily, and a flood of contravening emotions flooded through him. Once the war began, all the Middle East would join his conflict. He withdrew the disk and studied the etching on the back. It was a map of what he was being given—a quarter of the world. He recognized the ancient shape of Africa, India, and Indonesia as they had been when the Earth was much, much younger, before the vicissitudes of time and the deeds of lesser men had broken the order that was meant to be.

*

The snake slithered along a rocky outcrop, sensed the two women approaching, and raised its hooded head. Artemis pressed her palm against Lucy's chest, bringing her to an instantaneous halt. Focusing her attention on the reptile, Artemis cleared her mind of everything save a sense of complete calm. Its eyes linked with Artemis, the snake flicked its tongue in the air; then it lowered its head and moved away, disappearing into the foliage.

"Was that a...?"

"Monocled cobra. Yep." Artemis eased Lucy forward with a hand on her back. "He's gone off to tell his friends to avoid our path." *And perform a favor.*

Lucy shivered when the warmth of her partner's hand was removed. "Right. Good." She took a shallow breath. "Tell me again why we couldn't stay with the other tourists and are out here in the bushes."

"Because we're not tourists." Artemis assisted Lucy over a difficult knot of tree roots and let them rest for a moment. "And I get the feeling the guards are looking for us."

Lucy adjusted her headscarf and sighed. "Of course. Not. We're creeping around in this...this jungle instead of climbing the nice, if endless, staircase to Preah Vihear because you're paranoid?"

Artemis resisted the urge to correct Lucy's pronunciation. "Only for a few more minutes. I just want to see what the military does when they can't find us in the group."

They turned in unison to observe the activity on the third gopura and watched as a pair of black-clad guards exchanged words and then headed off at a hurry, one dashing up the stairs and the other racing down to the lower levels.

"See that." Artemis pointed as she pulled Lucy forward. "Come on, let's circle around to the top. We can use the side door there and mingle with the large group inside the main building.

Lucy thought about the guards and then the snake and hurried to follow Artemis to the upper entrance to the main temple. They drifted between clusters of people, maintaining a discreet distance between each other, and searched the Sanskrit sayings carved into sandstone pillars. After a while, they reversed their headscarves and used them to cover the lower half of their faces. Artemis kept an eye on the puzzled-looking guards who stared past them into the milling crowd as she and Lucy descended to the second gopura and slipped behind a pillar.

The third gopura was a large courtyard with small structures to each side. Lucy marveled at the Churning Sea of Milk masterpiece on the front wall while Artemis strolled through the Hall of Divinities. They worked their way down to the fourth gopura separately, passing the second guard, who was headed back up the staircase to join his partner.

The guard eyed them as they passed and turned to follow Artemis, his suspicions raised by the woman's unusual height. Minister Pindata had issued a ban on foreign tourists, reserving the temples for the faithful followers of the true religion. The guard froze when the monocled cobra reared up to block his way and screamed as it struck. Pandemonium followed, people scattering and three nearby guards racing to the bitten man's aid.

Taking advantage of the chaos, Artemis and Lucy joined a group of people to pass through the guarded gateway and make their way back to the van that had brought them. The vehicle filled quickly, and a distracted guard waved them on. Lucy breathed a sigh of relief. The next stop was Siem Reap.

"So, what did we learn?" Lucy lowered her scarf to whisper.

"That Shiva has definitely left the building." Artemis frowned, disappointed at the failure to find any sign in the beautiful temple. "Almost everything we saw was in the Banteay Srei style, which was done by Suryavarman and covered over or destroyed the early construction. I was hoping there'd be more."

"Says here we're going to stop at a museum in Krong Preah Vihear." Lucy murdered another pronunciation. "It's about ten minutes from where we just were. Seems like there's a sacred spot around every corner." She placed the hem of her head covering in front of her lips and whispered, "Let's hope there are fewer guards. I'm getting tired of the scarf and dagger routine in this humidity."

"Aw, I was just thinking how sexy it makes your eyes look." Artemis leered, mimicking Lucy's use of the scarf. "I was going to ask you to do a classic Aspara dance for me tonight. You only need the one veil. Everything else is optional."

Lucy wiggled her shoulders. "Took me months to master the hula. Will that do?"

"Oh yes." Artemis grinned, picturing Lucy gyrating her hips.

The Krong museum was little more than a gazebo housing the figure of a man astride a prancing steed. The van driver stopped and opened the door, but no one was intrigued enough to get out, except for the driver who exited to smoke a cigarette.

Artemis settled back in her seat. "Does anything strike you as odd?" she asked in a low voice.

"Other than this is the smallest museum I've ever seen?" Lucy whispered back.

"The statue is Suryavarman. Look closely. He is adorned with a very interesting piece of jewelry. The medallion is inscribed with the word *romchenhcheum* on it." She smiled at Lucy's blank look. "It means 'hummingbird.' And the statue was pointed southwest."

"Nazca!" Lucy made the connection. And then another. "He's telling us to go back to Nazca? No, wait. Does it mean this is where we should have started?" She blinked several times. "Gods, did we get it backwards? I'm confused which of them is the place you're looking for, Temmie?"

Artemis shook her head. "Neither. There has to be another place." She crossed her arms forming an *X*. "The two lines work together, not separately. They must point to a location between them. And my guess is it has to do with an astrological alignment. Strang will know what to look for."

*

The ancient city of Mohenjo-daro lay within the Indus Valley of southern Pakistan. Also known as the Mound of the Dead, Mohenjo-daro dated to 2500 BCE, when the Harappan civilization thrived. It was one of the world's earliest major cities and flourished contemporaneously with ancient Egypt and Mesopotamia.

Strang loaded his bag into the rental car's barely adequate trunk and pocketed the keys. "I am here, Temmie, my dear. You believe this pile of stones actually goes back ten thousand years." He squinted into the afternoon sun. It was hot and promising to get hotter. "Today, I will either prove or reject your hypothesis. Either way, I hope to collect sufficient evidence to justify my blatant countermanding of your request."

He knew Artemis had to have learned by then he had sent Keegan home and caught a flight on his own to

Pakistan to investigate the fourth site. Artemis would not have approved him going alone, so Strang had made a point of not asking. He slipped his phone into his pocket. Artemis had not texted, and even if she had, Strang was not certain he would have replied until accomplishing his goal.

The walls of the ancient settlement appeared like a mirage among the tan-colored rolling hills. Mohenjo-daro had the feel of a medieval town. The remains of a moderate-sized village were outlined by low walls overseen by a citadel looming forty feet above. There were no defensive structures save two towers rising in the south. The entire site was composed of brown bricks indistinguishable from the dirt of the Indus River's surrounding floodplain.

Strang passed through the distinctive blue iron gate and set off at a casual pace to explore the carefully maintained site. Perhaps too carefully, the scientist mused as he entered the clean swept street. Mohenjo-daro was laid out in a grid pattern with narrow avenues lined by the remains of simple brick houses consistent in size and structure. Sanitation gutters channeled down the center of each street, and nearly every house had a well of its own. The more Strang observed, he found the design and utility of the ancient site had an almost modern feel to it. His hopes of finding evidence of a much older culture began to melt in the blistering sun.

There was a conspicuous lack of temples or large ceremonial buildings, which would make his search even more difficult. Having trekked each of the main streets to no avail, Strang climbed the large stone staircase to the citadel looming on the higher level. The building was round with a low dome at its top and a collapsed wall at the back. Strang climbed through the rubble to peer inside.

"Rather sparse in here," he noted, his disappointment mounting. He backed out and sought refuge from the sun in a sliver of shadow. Wiping sweat from his forehead, Strang took a deep breath. The place was wiped clean, leaving an artificial, sterile façade containing no indication of what lay beneath. Giving in to a hunch, he decided to examine the interior of the building.

A figure etched in the far wall caught his attention. Faint but discernible, it was the image of a human figure sitting lotus style amid a collection of animal reliefs. Strang unfolded his glasses and perched them on his nose to get a closer look at the wavy lines emanating from the seated figure's head. "Looks like he's thinking. Or listening," Strang said aloud when the figure brought another to mind. "I believe I've found the cousin of the fellow you saw in Nazca, Temmie. Now if we could just figure out what these two are thinking about."

Strang took several photos of the image. Having no signal on his phone, he knew he would have to wait to send the pictures to Artemis. But he was certain she would be pleased. Foregoing a second circuit through the lower village ruins, his search satisfied, the scientist wended his way back to the car and began the six-hour drive to Karachi for the night. It would be more than pleasant to be out of the desert, he thought, and with luck he might be gifted with a cooling breeze from the Arabian Sea.

He turned southwest onto the main highway and within minutes spied a dust cloud in the distance. The cloud inched slowly closer, and Strang could see a military convoy heading east toward what he knew to be the

Pakistan/India border. Following an impulse, he made a U-turn and headed north to Larkana, where he had spent the previous night. He wanted to get as far from the military action as possible, and Larkana was in the opposite direction from Karachi. He had no way of knowing the real danger lay much closer. Looking down, Strang saw his phone had encountered a signal. He pulled to the side of the road and sent a quick text to Artemis, copying Angie, with the photos he'd taken and an explanation of what he interpreted the image to mean.

He checked to see if he had any waiting messages just as a blinding light filled the car. The flash was followed by a deep, ominous roar.

*

"You want the good news or the bad news first?" Athena asked into the satellite phone when Artemis answered. Not that they were equal, she knew. Not in the same universe of equal, but both pieces of information needed to be delivered.

"Good news," Artemis responded. "I'll tell you mine, and then you can tell me yours. I figured out what we were doing wrong. The site has to be located where the trails cross." She gave a self-deprecating chuckle. "A statue here has a hummingbird medallion. It's much more recent than the glyph in Nazca. I hope Wolf filled you in regarding what we discovered there. And since the place we're looking for has to be closer to where we started, Lucy and I are headed back to South America. I'm making arrangements tonight. But I need Wolf to start working on it. Ask him to look for a relationship between the ruin sites and astrological formations. I'm certain the place we want is somewhere between Nazca and Easter Island."

Artemis expected a pleased response, but Athena was silent. "Are you still there?"

"Yes. I'll take another look myself." Athena sounded somber.

"No, that's okay. You have your hands full with our two geniuses. Let Strang and Keegan do it." Even before she could get the final words out, a sense of dread blossomed in Artemis's chest.

"Artemis. Strang is dead," Athena said sensing her sister's shock. "It happened about twenty minutes ago. You must not have the news on. India exploded a small hydrogen bomb just outside Mohenjo-daro. Strang was there."

Artemis felt her heart squeezed by an invisible fist. "No. No. Maybe he and Keegan are still being rerouted from Chile. I thought they'd be home by now."

"Keegan got in last night. He told me Strang went on to Mohenjo-daro to finish investigating the sites for you. Oh, and we've found the disk."

The hotel room closed in from all sides. Artemis could barely breathe. She disconnected the call and collapsed into a chair. Lucy rushed over to see what was wrong. Tears were streaming down Artemis's face.

"What is it?" Lucy knelt beside her lover. "Please, Temmie. What's happened?"

Artemis's cell phone chirped, and Lucy saw there was a message. Artemis waved the phone away, and Lucy clicked on the icon. She read the message from Strang and showed it to Artemis, who grabbed her sides and moaned before dissolving into sobs.

*

Minister Pindata offered silent prayers for the brave soldiers who had died heroes in his pursuit of a greater good. The small nuclear bomb no larger than a suitcase had had a massive impact. The soldiers had been vaporized, and hundreds of people had died in the single mile of devastation. Pindata considered even the civilians to have been martyrs sent immediately to paradise.

To Pindata's surprise Pakistan had hesitated to retaliate, presumably stunned by an attack that broke the long reticence of both sides to use a nuclear option. President Chatterjee had denied responsibility in an emotional speech less than an hour after the explosion and begged for mediation. Pindata suspected Kamakrisha's influence in the initial response. And Pakistan had forestalled the urgings of an Imam with a reputation for fiery rhetoric insisting Pakistan retaliate a hundredfold. But Pindata knew retaliation was merely a matter of time.

While the world waited, Pindata made a public announcement in support of India before turning his attention to his own border and requesting alliances with Thailand and Vietnam in case war did come. The disk vibrated in his pocket as he thought of the glory that would be heaped on his doorstep when the nation of Islam bowed to the Buddhist/Hindu alliance.

The argument of a thousand years would finally be resolved, he thought. And he would be known as a bodhisattva who finally accomplished peace.

His wife brought him a robe and told him his bath was ready. Ritual bathing was another value Pindata had adopted from the Hindus. The two philosophies would merge into a more perfect whole. He removed his uniform and stepped into the pleasantly cool water. His wife removed her clothing and knelt behind him in the large tub. She scrubbed his back and lathered his hair and then gently poured water over him to complete the cleansing. He could hear her humming as she serviced him, a tune he had heard playing on the radio and in the army quarters he had visited just the other week. The sound calmed him even as it seemed to fill his body with energy.

He turned and brought his wife forward onto his lap. Then he entered her and gave his seed to create a generation that would find a better world once Pindata had achieved the fullness of his ambitions.

Chapter Fourteen

The noise in his head made Pope Peter II nauseated. There was too much to do, and he was just one man. The refugee camps had stormed the Bastille so to speak, and every European leader had acquiesced to Peter's direct control. The middle conquest was complete, and he was sorely tempted to leave it there. He couldn't be in two places at once. The United States was, in a word, alarmed, and Peter wanted to let them stew. They would come begging to him once he voided the trade agreements and demanded resources for his army of refugees. But the thoughts in his head were not the ones he wished. Images of China pressed upon his skull until he begged for the pain to stop.

He withdrew the disk from his cassock and tossed it to the desk. Was it his fault the authorities had banned his music? *No!* Was it his fault there was no civilized religion in China through which Peter could work? *Decidedly not! If the gods wish the Chinese to follow their appointed ruler, then perhaps they should unleash the pale horse.*

"Moses got to impose plagues upon his enemy," Peter shouted. "Surely I should not be made to labor with less."

The disk rose above the desk and approached the astonished pontiff. It had never levitated before, never done anything except quiver in his pocket. He dropped to his knees and begged forgiveness, his hands trembling as he pressed them together in prayer.

Blood dripped from his hands as holes opened in his palms. Peter sniveled as pain surged up his arms. It was an all-too-real reminder of Christ's suffering. And the idea of martyrdom exploded in his head. He was to be a saint if he would find the courage to fulfill his duty. He lifted his eyes to the disk inches before him and vowed his allegiance. There would be a way, he repeated over and over. If he had to strike a billion people dead.

The disk began to fall, and Peter reflexively reached out to catch it. His hands were clean. There was no injury to his palms, and the sound in his head had vanished. It had been a vision. He staggered to his feet and heard voices rising from the Sistine Chapel. Vespers had begun. Peter rushed out of the door to join them.

*

Lucy sat on the luggage and watched Artemis argue with the woman behind the counter. The airlines were in chaos. Chances of getting out of Cambodia were slim. The possibility of getting straight home to California was long gone. Artemis was negotiating for two seats to anywhere in South America. Angie and the others could join them there. If they could get flights, which wasn't a given in the current situation.

Her head pounding, Lucy could see Artemis going rigid with anger. A man approached and introduced himself to Lucy.

"Listen, I don't mean to intrude, but I can tell a fellow American when I see one." The man offered Lucy a warm smile. He was dressed in an expensive suit and looked much less harried than the rest of the people bustling about the airport.

Lucy returned the smile. "No worries. It's nice to hear a friendly voice."

The man nodded toward Artemis, who was still dominating the flight agent. "She's Artemis Andronikos, isn't she?" he observed, amazed how little the woman had changed in eighteen years.

Lucy acknowledged both facts with a nod of her head.

"Well, I'd like to offer you two a flight out of here before it gets even crazier."

Lucy knitted her eyebrows, confused. "Who are you?" she asked.

"Sorry, sorry." The man flashed a quick, self-conscious smile. "I'm Ted Graziani, president of a tech company you've probably never heard of. But I have a private jet waiting for me outside, and I can take you two as far as London where it should be much easier for you to get home."

Lucy whistled, and Artemis turned around, annoyance radiating from her face. Waving her arm excitedly, Lucy motioned for her partner to come over.

"This is Ted Graziani, Temmie," Lucy said when Artemis gave her a quizzical look. "He says you know him, and he has a plane that can get us to London."

Ted cast an admiring look at Artemis. "Wow. You haven't aged at all. You look just like you did at Hemsley's conference. You remain the most beautiful woman I have ever seen." His neck reddened, and he looked at Lucy. "I doubt she remembers me, miss. But I definitely remember her. How could I forget her? Artemis gave me the courage to do what I wanted to do with my life, and here I am. Please let me help you."

Recognizing him, Artemis managed a fleeting smile. "You're the nerd who spoke up at the press conference about the way technology was a double-edged sword." She noted his tailored Italian suit. "You've come a long way, I see."

Lucy tugged on Artemis's sleeve. "He can get us to London, Temmie," she repeated with a pleading face.

"We'd be most grateful for your assistance, Ted," Artemis told him. "It's urgent that we get back to the States as quickly as possible."

"I'll get you there. I owe you that much. My plane will take you to London. Then I'll arrange to get you back to California somehow. You have my word." Their benefactor motioned for a porter to assist the women with their baggage and headed them toward the waiting jet. "Saving the world again, I presume?" he asked after they'd boarded and settled in the comfortable leather seats.

Artemis sighed, the pain of Strang's death clawing at her gut. "Not all of it."

*

"I said don't open it." Ronan snatched the disk out of Stefan's hands and received a solid punch to the chin for doing so. He gripped the disk as tightly as he could and sank to his knees, his head swimming.

"You pissant!" Stefan wanted to kick the man but thought better of it. He reached down and jerked Ronan's wrist backward, freeing the disk and scooping it up. "I have had enough of your jealousy. Stay out of my way."

Stepping over the kneeling Ronan, Stefan went to a desk at the back of the work room. It was unlikely the disk could be opened. He'd been trying to find a seam or even a crevice on the smooth surface. He could hear a faint rattle as if things were moving inside when he shook the disk. But how they got there had been impossible to discover thus far.

"How'd you get this thing again?" Stefan queried Keegan in the adjacent desk.

"Won it in a poker game." Keegan answered the question for at least the third time in an hour.

Stefan chuckled and watched Ronan walk over to his own desk. "You should have gotten money. This trinket is bad news. It makes my skin creep. Ronan likes it, so you know its vibes are bad."

Ronan issued a curse heard clearly at the opposite end of the room. Keegan went back to working on the longitudinal aspects of an area of Bolivia. Angie wanted to know the position of half a dozen celestial bodies as they would present for the next fifteen days. In addition, thousands of calculations were needed to determine the positions of celestial bodies at the times the sites were constructed. If Ronan and Stefan couldn't stop their bickering, he was going to go back to Strang's bungalow to work, regardless of how dreary the place seemed now that Strang was gone.

Ronan rubbed his chin; it still stung. He knew Stefan was going to ruin everything if he damaged the disk. Angie hadn't listened to him, but Ronan knew it. They were going to need it. Artemis would understand if he could keep the big ape from breaking the disk before the boss had a chance to study it. Keeping an eye on Stefan, Ronan nursed his jaw and brought up a file he'd been creating.

He no longer believed any alteration to the RAS was necessary. Music was a better solution. Music influenced the vibrational state of the brain. There was evidence enough of that right in the room. Keegan often used the disgusting music he listened to as an escape from the conversations around him. Ronan had loaded a recording of Keegan's theme song onto his computer and was experimenting with noise cancellation methods. He wanted to find a melody that would block Keegan's music when played. If he was correct, Ronan was certain he had the answers Angie had assigned Stefan to find.

He looked over at his nemesis, who was spinning the disk in one of his gigantic paws. "Eat shit and die!"

*

The bags got dumped in the foyer and left for later. Lucy went to take a shower, hoping to wash off more than the dust from days of travel, although grief did not wash away. Artemis sought Angie, wanting to see the disk right away.

"Keegan told me he obtained the disk from a college friend," Angie said, handing the object to Artemis. "Apparently, your disagreeable protégé is an excellent poker player and won it with an inside straight draw no one else would have dreamed of playing."

Artemis turned the disk in her hands, feeling its coldness and a sense of revulsion. *The pearl of great price.* This small object, whatever its power or purpose, was not worth Strang's life. She traced the taijitu and then the engraving on the back, unable to recognize it with a mind clouded in grief.

"Stefan has been looking for a way to open it," Angie said. "It kind of rattles if you shake it. But if you ask me, it's dead or dormant. Like it's waiting for something."

"Someone," Artemis corrected. "It's meant for a particular person."

Artemis felt as if she'd been punched in the stomach. *How did I miss it?* The man she'd caught outside the house. The one Lucy had said was on the plane with her. He must have been looking for the disk and, somehow, he had known it was here with them.

She bolted from the room and ran down the hall to the recreation room. She stormed in and grabbed Keegan by the throat, wanting to squeeze the life out of him. Ronan and Stefan sat stunned. They had no idea Artemis had gotten home, much less a clue why she was strangling their comrade. Neither could summon the courage to intervene.

Artemis lifted Keegan from the chair and released her grip. "Come with me," she commanded and then turned and walked out of the door, leaving Keegan to catch his breath and hurry behind her.

Athena was waiting for them. She stood with her arms crossed and stared at Keegan while Artemis shoved him into a chair.

"Tell me exactly who you got this from," Artemis hissed. "Then I might let you live."

"I, uh, well, I won it...in a poker game. Filled in a straight flush on the river. Hearts." He kept staring at Athena wondering why Angie looked so different. "In Australia just before I got your invitation to come here."

Artemis wanted to put her hands around his neck again and squeeze until his eyes bugged out. Athena watched Keegan's head swivel back and forth between her and her sister. She could sense he was certain he was about to die.

"Do you know what the image on the back of the disk is?" Athena asked, sounding more controlled than Artemis.

Keegan shook his head. "No, I didn't. Then when we were on Easter Island, Dr. Strang drew a picture on a napkin and started babbling, I mean, talking about how Easter Island was part of the land of Mu and how the Hawaiians still talk about it and..."

"And?"

Keegan squirmed his hands, gripping the arms of his chair. "I got curious. What he'd drawn looked like one of the shapes on the disk. It's called Lemuria on the internet. I figured the other shape might be Australia shaped kind of weird like. When that Polynesian guy got caught checking out the house, I got scared. I didn't want to give it to him. I didn't want you to find out I had it. Lucy said she saw a disk for sale for a cool million. I...I wanted to keep it."

Artemis leaned her forehead against the wall. *I'm so sorry, Wolf. I should have known, but I wasn't listening.*

"You can't listen to voices that do not speak." Athena put her hand gently on her sister's shoulder. "This isn't your fault, Artemis. Things are proceeding as they should. They are not ready. Not even your precious Harbinger children. You tried. It's time for us to go."

*

The first rockets had started to fall two days after the destruction at Mohenjo-daro. Within hours, what was considered a moderate response led to the deployment of troops all along the border between Pakistan and India, war had begun. A stream of refugees headed northwest to join the masses already pressing toward a reeling Europe whose borders were now firmly closed.

An older man shuffled along the crowded streets of Karachi, just one of thousands seeking passage north. He found a store with the item he wanted in the window and checked his wallet. He had money, hopefully enough, and his passport was tucked in his shirt pocket. Combing back his unkempt hair, the man went inside and made a purchase. Then, stepping into an alley, he dialed from memory, praying his memory was correct.

Artemis saw an unknown number flash on her phone and nearly swiped the call away. But her finger disobeyed, and a voice she never thought to hear again spoke.

"My darling goddess," Wolf said with an exhausted chuckle. "I wonder if you could arrange transport so that I may come home."

Chapter Fifteen

"My dear Lucinda, is speed a requirement?" Strang asked, intending to prompt reconsideration on Lucy's part. "I mean is Temmie in dire need of our arrival?"

"Well, she is eager to see you. She's going to check you out and make sure you didn't suffer so much as a hangnail. In fact, you'd best prepare yourself for a mushy welcome home all around. And don't think for a moment she's going to let you rest," Lucy predicted, her foot heavy on the accelerator. "Anyway, everyone is so happy to have you back, Wolf. You gave us quite a scare."

"Frightened myself, I must admit," Strang acknowledged. "It took me days to hitchhike my way to the coast. I was going against the flow with the military rushing into the devastated area I was seeking to depart."

"I wish we had known. Artemis was distraught, or she might have picked up on your essence or whatever she does," Lucy speculated. "I've never seen her so... incapacitated."

A thought struck the scientist. "How did Angie take it?"

Lucy found it a curious question. "Her heart was broken too. We all sort of fell in a hole and didn't even try to climb out. After we got your call, Artemis tried to get back to work. I left her draped over her laptop looking for God knows what to flesh out her latest theory while I came to pick you up."

The road ahead was clear, and Strang loosed his grip on the seatbelt strap and watched the scenery flow by. "I believe Temmie is correct. The site we seek must be located somewhere close to where we started."

Lucy gave him a wide smile. "Temmie's counting on you to find it."

Strang tapped on the dashboard, encouraging Lucy to look where she was going, and issued a heavy sigh. "It will be my pleasure indeed. I toyed with a few possibilities while I was on the plane. But I wonder if you can enlighten me a little more regarding this disk of Keegan's." He felt the car rock in the wake of a passing eighteen-wheeler. "While maintaining a skillful mastery of this vehicle...and the road."

A smile flashed across Lucy's face. "Still not a fan of my driving, eh, Wolf?" She eased the pressure on the gas pedal.

"One brush with death a month is quite sufficient for me," Strang replied, grateful the car returned to the appropriate speed. "Thank you, my dear. Now, you were about to tell me about the latest theories to intrigue our goddess."

Lucy glanced at Strang. "Ever heard of someplace called Lemuria?"

For the first time in a week, Strang heard himself laughing out loud.

*

Athena unfolded a sheet of paper and gave it to Artemis. "There are four. One disk for each of the continents as they were aligned one hundred and thirty million years ago. It would appear we were not the first to discover this little planet."

Artemis set the map beside the disk on her desk. The etching on Keegan's disk matched the outline of what eventually became Polynesia—Hestia's world. A blind person could see how the rest of the ancient land masses aligned with the turmoil afflicting the planet.

"I've uncovered the identities of the people who are most likely to possess the other disks," Athena said. She sounded almost regretful. Artemis was committed to the doomed quest. Athena could feel time was running out and her recent experience with Ronan and Stefan convinced her even the Harbinger was not enough to ensure which collective the humans would select. Her efforts were focused on making Artemis accept the coming failure before it was too late. "But if I tell you, I have no doubt you will continue with this futile pursuit."

Artemis nodded. "I will try to save them even if you don't tell me, Athena. I love them."

"You have forgotten how many species such as these humanoids there are? You cannot fall in love with them all."

"Not all," Artemis said, folding the map. "Just these."

"Ours is a collective of love, Artemis. We nurture species and assist them in reaching their full potential, and when the species is ready, they join with us freely. It is a process as old as the universe itself. You are tempting fate, and even if you avoid being punished for this, you will not succeed in changing the outcome."

Artemis saw Angie in the hazel eyes trained gently on her. Athena was permitting Angie to listen for some reason. Not as a participant but as an observer of the discussion neither of the goddesses could avoid any longer.

"When did you give up on them, Athena? When they stopped worshipping at your temples? When you became irrelevant in human lives?" Artemis was angry with her sister's tepid assistance. "They called you the goddess of wisdom, but you are not so wise as clever. The clever choice is to abandon them, isn't it? Ze'us abandoned them. You made that choice thousands of years ago, retreating to the ethereal plane to avoid being bothered by the troubles of mere humans. You are a coward, not a goddess. You are afraid of the Others."

Athena didn't yield to the anger Artemis's words aroused. "The humans are not ready, Artemis. It may even be our fault they are not ready. If so, it is a fault we cannot correct. The Harbinger did not fulfill its purpose. It is time to accept what cannot be changed."

"No. It is not." Artemis raised her voice. "I know the humans are imperfect. We are all imperfect. The universe itself is seeking perfection. It's why there are two collectives each struggling with the other. Each in opposition to the other, driven to create and learn."

"You are wiser than you were," Athena said with respect. "I thought taking human form so often had diminished you. On the contrary, you have benefitted from being among them. And believe me, dear sister, I know the pain it will cause you to leave them to the Others. It is the very pain I feel when I fear we will lose not only the humans...but you."

Artemis sighed. "If the Others are successful, Lucy will be lost to me forever. She is half of my soul, Athena. Do you really think I would prefer to live in our collective without her? I'd rather go into the void. I prefer oblivion to half a life."

"You think that now, Artemis. You have forgotten what it's like. How our father loves you. We love you. The wound will heal. Please, consider the consequence of what you do."

"It is the one decision I get to make. I cannot decide what future the humans are to have. But I have chosen mine."

They ran their arguments again, discussing the progress humans had made over the course of ten thousand years. Artemis spoke of bravery and sacrifice. Athena spoke of cruelty and greed.

"Maybe it is a good thing they must judge themselves," Athena said, her patience at last exhausted. "It is at its core a choice between love and hate."

Artemis felt the change, a subtle reordering of facts once locked safely in her mind. A revelation. Words she had heard many times before without noting their meaning. And at once she understood the true nature of duality and the purpose for the creative struggle that was the universe. She smiled slightly.

"No, Athena. That is what you do not comprehend. The opposite of love is not hate. The opposite of love is fear. The disks are weapons of fear. They are meant to fill the world with terror. Everything happening right now is being driven by the Others. You say I cannot save them even if I love them. But love is the answer. They don't need to focus. They need to feel what the Harbinger enables them to foresee."

Lucy arrived at the room just as Artemis spoke the last. She looked at the emotion on Artemis's face and the peculiar look on Angie's. Shaking her head, Angie felt the shadow slip into the background.

"Um, hope I'm not interrupting." Lucy paused on her way to the desk. "Stefan said you were looking at the disk and...what is up with you two?"

Angie stepped over and gave Artemis a hug. Artemis was willing to lay down her own existence to save them, all of them, the entire human race. "Mother, do you have any idea how lucky you are?"

Lucy waggled an eyebrow at her soulmate. "Most of the time, yes, I do."

*

"The planet Earth as it was in the Cretaceous Age." Strang tapped his knuckle on the projected image on the back wall of the conference room. "Four distinct areas. Across the northern hemisphere is a land mass encompassing North America, through Europe, and concluded by what today is China. We believe the first of our four disks is in the possession of the pope, who has been quite active in the middle portion of this area."

Ronan recoiled at the suggestion. "You just leaped a hundred million years and made a stop in the Middle Ages."

Strang raised his arm and twirled his hand. "Yes, in a manner of speaking indeed I did. But leaving the timing aside for the moment, this area composed of what would become Africa and the Middle East in that same hundred-million-year leap is where we believe the second disk is being used. An otherwise ceremonial Cambodian leader, namely Minister Sin Pindata, is apparently trying to unite the region under the banner of a Hindu-Buddhist coalition."

Stefan pushed his tea to one side. "You suggest it is a religious war, Wolf? Bombing is not philosophical."

"A fact of which I am most personally aware!" Strang responded. "South America is this part right here, and disk three is apparently assisting an ambitious woman military leader, one General Maria Isabel Vergara, to consolidate the poor and I dare say starving countries of the current continent."

Keegan's stomach tightened. He had seen it in a vision. Locusts devouring the land, but he had not known where. It was merely one of the many visions he found harder and harder to push down. Without the disk and the music Angie had confiscated, it was as if a lid had been removed, and his imagination had gone insane.

Strang tapped his finger on the projected image and drew an invisible circle. "Which brings us to the final alignment of the Cetaceous landmasses—the legendary land of Mu: a string of islands stretching from Australia on the west, north to the Marshalls, east to my beloved Hawaii, and then south to the less than loveable Easter Island." He turned and nodded at Artemis. "I believe you prefer its more common name—Lemuria."

Artemis nodded. "The disk associated with Lemuria is in our possession. Thanks to the Harbinger-assisted poker prowess of our own Dr. Montock."

"I don't think the kid I won it off was intended to rule Polynesia," Keegan defended himself.

"Probably not. But his father, Paina Kauri, was a member of the Australian executive council and a leading candidate for prime minister. Until his son Manaia Kauri stole the disk believing it would bring him luck at cards."

Keegan grinned. "It didn't bring him smarts either. Mani thought I was a student at the University of Melbourne like him. The family had an estate, well, more of a ranch in the midlands, actually. I didn't know he was from New Zealand. He looked more aborigine than European. He left school about the same time you guys saw to it I was brought back to the States. The disk never gave me luck." He reevaluated that statement when he saw the look on their face. "Well, I guess getting this job was lucky, of course. I just, I don't know, liked it. Like my music."

Angie blew out a breath. She had put a stop to the music. There didn't appear to be any way to stop his mouth.

Artemis lifted the object and pressed it between her hands. "The disk associated with Lemuria is in our possession now. Mr. Kauri remains in custody and will be deported back to New Zealand in a few days. So, it would seem all our luck has changed."

*

The animal peered at her from the shadows, its scrawny body tucked back beneath a large bush. Lucy caught the glint of moonlight reflected in two small green eyes. She set the bowls of food and milk on the edge of the decking and called to the animal, certain it was a stray that had adopted them several weeks ago.

The cat was highly skittish, refusing to approach the woman who left her food every night for nearly a week. To Lucy's delight, it emerged from the bush, tail erect, and looked at her with suspicious eyes.

"Oh, dear God." Lucy sighed at the piteous sight. The animal was little more than skin and bones. Its fur was matted and filthy. One of its ears was torn, and when it moved, the cat favored a hind leg, giving it an awkward rocking gait.

Lucy knelt next to the bowls of food and made cooing sounds, encouraging the animal to approach. The tiny cat took two steps and then stopped and stared warily at Lucy.

"I'm going to win you over," Lucy said gently. "I'm going to get you to come to me, I promise."

Of all the horrors going on in the world, here was one creature she could save. She could fix only a small calamity amid a planet of catastrophes but doing so banished the useless feeling in her heart. Taking a small red ball from her pocket, Lucy showed it to the cat and rolled it across the lawn to her. The fuzzy toy stopped inches from its front feet. The cat stood its ground and lifted its head. Lucy couldn't make out the creature's color. Its coat was light, possibly tan or gray. The moonlight gave the fur a silvery tinge, but it was too full of dirt and mud for her to tell the true hue. Lucy inched the bowl of milk forward and murmured to the cat, who merely stood and observed.

"Okay, little one," Lucy relented. "I'll leave so you can come get your meal. But I'll be back tomorrow, and you are going to learn to trust me. Understand?"

Lucy got to her feet, went into the house, and turned out the exterior light, hoping the darkness would embolden the hungry little visitor.

Chapter Sixteen

The room was cluttered with abandoned work product, discarded plates of food, and idling machines. Lucy picked up the empty water bottles and paper plates, resisting the urge to collect the bits of paper lying everywhere. She had no way of determining what was trash and what the scientists would want to keep. Strang's miraculous return had lifted everyone's spirits for a while, but the joy had dissipated, leaving a general malaise in its wake.

Lucy had ceased watching the news. The state of the world was incredibly bad. She felt at times she could hear the collective moan escaping from most of the eight billion humans as they struggled to understand why their lives were being destroyed. She set the plastic bag of trash beside a chair and sank down, able to do little besides draw one breath after another, slowly clearing her head.

"I've become my mother," she admonished herself, realizing she preferred cleaning to wrestling with theories about how the universe worked or what future mankind deserved. She didn't want to think about the four disks, four quadrants of a million-year-old world, or the four horsemen of the apocalypse bringing the world to heel. Lucy wanted it all to go away.

Tears overwhelmed her, running freely down her cheeks until she brushed them aside. What would Angie's life become, she wondered. Her daughter's future had once seemed incredibly bright. Lucy had found herself anxious for grandbabies she and Artemis could spoil. And what would become of her and the woman she loved more than life? Lucy could sense Artemis was deeply worried. She had even seen fear in Artemis's eyes. There was something so frightening her lover would not speak it. In her heart Lucy didn't need to be told. If the wrong choice was made, Lucy knew she would lose Artemis forever.

Her phone chirped. Lucy wiped her face and looked at the alert before clicking it off. She grabbed the bag of trash and headed back to the room where the others were gathered. They were staring in silence at their own devices.

"This cannot be true!" Ronan was the first to speak. "So even if we find the place Artemis says we're supposed to be, there is no way to get there. Well, that's dandy."

The president had closed the borders and grounded nearly all flights in or out of the United States. But the reason was the most incredible part of the alert. China had gone dark, the entire nation. There had been no communication with the country in nearly three hours. The border was said to be impenetrable. A billion and a half human beings were quarantined, the reason for which remained unspecified.

Stefan fondled his mustache. "That's not possible. Even an EMP would not disable an entire country."

"A solar flare could," Keegan ventured. "A direct hit would fry everything electronic."

Artemis got a glimpse of Athena in Angie's quick glance. They both knew the sun had not caused the trouble. Something far more powerful had—the Others.

"Did we just run out of time?" Strang asked, noting the look the women exchanged.

"Not quite." Artemis went to the whiteboard and drew an approximation of the landmasses during the Cretaceous epoch. "It means the pope has extended his control to the east and will move against North America next. We need to leave as soon as we know where to go."

Stefan held up his phone. "The fighting in the Middle East has apparently ceased. Either war is over, or the Cambodian won and is thinking of Africa where hostilities are reported active."

"South America is consolidated except for Peru. I heard yesterday the Chilean president was about to sign a treaty with Bolivia and Argentina," Ronan offered. "If you are right about General Vergara, the president of Chile can kiss his ass goodbye any day now."

"What about the last quadrant?" Lucy asked, looking pale as she sat down at the back of the room. "Hawaii?"

"Lemuria." Angie put away her phone. "There is another immense hurricane forming in the center of the Pacific, and New Zealand reported an earthquake near Christchurch last night."

The four horsemen galloped through Artemis's mind. "Wolf, any progress on finding the site we need? I'd settle for a best guess at this point."

"Puma Punku," Angie said before Strang could answer.

"My thoughts exactly, dear girl." Wolf twirled his hand, impressed.

I know. Athena just read them. Angie smiled, listening to the shadow laugh.

*

"What does it mean this headline 'China has gone dark'?" Maria Vergara questioned her assembled officers.

The men looked nervously around the table, but only one dared to answer. "There is talk of a plague and the country has lost all power. There is no way to communicate with the country. No flights, no phone service, no internet chatter...nothing. There is only silence."

Maria folded the newspaper, covering the three-inch headline, and set it aside. She resented the way the editors had emphasized the news. They were supposed to be focusing on her successes and the unity joining South America, not distracting the people with unimportant issues. "How does this matter to Chile?"

Once again, the military leaders shuffled tensely in their chairs. But this time no one spoke. China was a source of income to each of them as they sold the wealth from their conquests and pocketed the profits. In their opinions, commerce with China was an important element of Vergara's future economy for South America. For all of them, the loss of such a rich benefactor would be unthinkable.

"How did this happen to them? How could such a catastrophe befall such a prosperous nation?" The turmoil in the Middle East she understood; that was the hate of a thousand years. And the refugees in Europe were of no concern to her. Vergara saw no further than the continent she wanted to possess. But if there were a power capable of plunging the world's largest country into darkness, she wanted to know who wielded it. Not even the disk could accomplish such a thing, at least as far as she knew. She had never dreamed such dreams.

The general slapped her riding crop on the table. "The hell with them, all of them. A united South America will be able to defeat any adversary." She leaned on the table and made eye contact with each of the silent officers one by one. "I want to talk about the last pieces we must secure. We are here to finalize our conquest. Victory is within my grasp."

It had been a brilliant campaign; her staff was eager to review what they had accomplished. The smaller, poorer countries had sought to join Chile's union, falling over themselves to acquire the food and peace Vergara had offered. Paraguay was the most recent to proffer an offer of peace, and the general was mulling over the price such a peace should cost the corrupt politicos who cared only about saving their personal fortunes. And Bolivia, landlocked and surrounded by Vergara's minions, had formally agreed to her overture. The one standout was Peru, where not only the government but also the peasants were openly defiant in the face of Chile's incursions. The animosity between the two nations dated back centuries.

"It is the flow of tourists which gives Peru its courage." The same officer who had answered the general's initial question spoke up. "But with the people now panicked by what has happened in Pakistan and China, perhaps tourists will hesitate to come. It could be our opportunity to…"

"Yes. It is precisely that. We will seize the Altiplano and deny them their revenue." Vergara smiled though her eyes were cold. "By the end of this very week I want our soldiers in place in force. We will settle the issue once and for all. The spirits of our ancestors will be with us."

*

Strang propped the atlas on his desk opened to the page with the sine wave he had been so excited to discover what felt like months ago. He traced the two trails connecting the pairs of appositional sites: Easter Island to Mohenjo-daro and Nazca to Angkor Vihear. They had proven to be false trails, made all the worse because the team had read them left to right. Then they had rushed off without questioning their thin assumptions. It had been utterly unscientific, and Strang castigated himself for having wasted everyone's time. It was not a mistake he wanted to repeat.

And yet the time had not been completely wasted. The string of pearls, the aligned archeological sites, had eventually led him to what he believed to be the place they sought. A bright-red triangle was the proof. The triangle began on the upper of the two trails at Machu Picchu and then descended west three hundred and sixty miles to Nazca, southeast six hundred and twenty miles to Puma Punku, before returning three hundred and twenty miles to where it began. A pyramid of sorts pointing to the mysterious ruin of Puma Punku, which was almost exactly where the two oppositional lines crossed. Seeing how an *X* marked the spot, Strang chuckled.

The triangle was one hundred longitudinal degrees from where three other pyramids mimicked the arrangement of Orion's belt. Two beacons on two continents.

"Duality!" He thought of Artemis's pronouncement: duality was the principle of creation, explaining the struggle between the two collectives. Strang was exhausted. It was the way he always felt when a mystery was solved. The adrenaline of the investigation no longer needed, his mind and body relaxed. Yawning, he put away the atlas and went to speak with Willa. "I believe the answer has been found, my dear. All that is left is to reach it in time."

*

Keegan had a hypothesis concerning the question of when. The winter solstice marked the shortest day in Earth's northern hemisphere but the longest day in the southern hemisphere. Given the Earth's current axis tilt, that day was December 21 on any given year. The variance in the length of sunlight per day was the result of the Earth being tilted on its axis. The tilt occurred 4.5 billion years ago when the planet was hit by an object the size of Mars and nearly destroyed.

What intrigued Keegan was the oscillation of the tilt from 22.1 to 24.5 degrees in a forty-one-thousand-year cycle.

"What if..." He clattered a new algorithm into his computer. "What if" was a question Keegan disliked, but an idea had struck him, and he wanted to pursue it. If the continents had moved in the past hundred million years, perhaps the tilt had as well. And if it had, the solstice would not be December 21. There was nothing in the scientific literature to substantiate such an occurrence. Keegan combed back his hair with both hands. He'd have been laughed out of the room if he'd even suggested such a theory in the academic world he had once lived in. But things had changed. He had changed, and the impossible was now commonplace.

The answer to "what if" appeared on the screen. It sent a rush of excitement through him until he realized the full significance of what he saw. And a new question popped into his mind. What if they really did have only five days before the choice needed to be made?

*

Lin Tien tapped the side of his cell phone, attempting to make it obey his instructions. He had to know what Min and the children were doing. Would his gentle wife even know what to do? Rumors said the military had taken control of the cities. But what of the countryside where Tien's family lived? Min was in the country with few services available if she and the children needed help. And Tien was in a panic even darker than the streets he hurried down.

The city was strangely quiet. Candlelight shone from windows here and there though Tien knew most people were too frightened to draw attention to themselves. He could see a fire in the distance, its orange glow like a beacon in the darkness. Reaching the edge of the city, Tien worked to steady his breathing and find an inner peace. He must put away the panic and be present if he was to make it home.

He could hear the footfall of others moving nearby. If they were soldiers, he would be arrested for breaking curfew. If it were robbers, he would be beaten and stripped of his meager possessions. He waited for the sounds to fade and then read the stars to see which way he must go.

He fell in the wet soil and felt around him. He was in a field and hoped following the deep plowed ruts would take him to a road. Just before dawn, he realized he was hopelessly lost. He sat and waited for enough light to reveal the mountains. Then he would go toward them to where Min was waiting.

His thoughts filled with prayers for his family and for his country. Tien pondered the likelihood the world would come to China's aid. But he knew the world was wicked and feared their suffering would not be relieved for many months. If the sickness spread, one could only guess how many survivors would be left by then. The one bit of hope Tien could feel was connected to the man he had seen two days earlier leaving the Italian embassy. The tall man in his white robes had a face of sympathy. The memory of him gave Tien the strength to continue his journey home.

*

Ronan lay on his bed, sweat dripping from his body. He let the vision ease away. It was the fourth night it had come to him. He was on a stone platform with several others. They each held a disk to the sky, which swirled restless in shades of orange and red. His heart beat loudly in his ears, but he could hear the sound of soldiers marching and the roar of wind.

Angie mounted the steps to the platform and stood beside him, her hazel eyes blazing with affection as she took his face in her hands and kissed him. She was beautiful, and she was his, no longer the Angie who had pretended she didn't care for him. He could see it now. It had been a mask to hide her real feelings. The disk made everything clear to him. He lifted the disk above his head and saw the sky open.

Ronan awoke before the presence in the sky revealed itself. He felt afraid when he pressed his mind to look further. And lay there in his sweat wondering if the vision would come true. The kiss was fresh on his mouth. He imagined he could taste Angie still.

He loved her. He had from the moment he'd seen her in the hallway. But it wasn't merely because she was beautiful. Angie was smart and funny. Even when she seemed to be angry with him, he knew inside she was only trying to help him be a better man. The man she deserved to protect her in a world gone mad.

Ronan sat up and resolved to find the answers Angie was urging them toward. He would be the hero Artemis wanted. He would save the world if that's what was needed to win Angie's love. First, he had to get the disk. The vision told him the disk would make him strong.

*

Pele stood atop Mauna Kea and cast her mind to the west where the ocean churned with impatience, searching for its master. Pele cast herself into the past to find a bloodline long ascribed to myth. Eons before Ze'us had found this exquisite planet and made a claim on the primitive humans. To a time when the Others had buried their secrets and waited for the ones appointed to find them.

She saw the changes as the land masses formed and separated into continents. She saw the Earth covered in fire and then ice. Eventually, it warmed, and life emerged from the slime. And she saw the rise of a species destined eventually to dominate all the rest. Humans opened their eyes and lifted them to the stars.

A queen had emerged, using the stars to guide her subjects to the islands of the great ocean. The queen dreamed of an empire which became known as the Land of Mu. Her prodigy populated the bits of land and grew strong. Pele knew them well. They were beautiful and happy; they loved their home.

Pele let her mind wander across the islands, coming at last to Australia where the ancient queen's bloodline glistened, and she followed it to the one she sought. He was unaware of his heritage: a troubled young man innocent to the ways of men. Pele dove behind the pale façade and saw the royal blood coursing in his veins. He was the one for whom the disk was meant.

Pele folded her garment around her and laughed. "Use your gifts, Artemis. The fourth horseman is right before your eyes."

Hestia accepted the truth of the universe—it unfolded precisely as it should. The moment of choice had come. A fork in time was open, and for the first moment in her long existence, she could not see which path would be chosen.

*

The sound of screeching ripped Lucy from her work. She went to the window and saw the battle taking place at the back of the yard. Three feline forms were engaged in a vicious fight. Two larger animals were tearing at a third, who stood its ground despite the suffering being inflicted on it. Lucy recognized the thin, bedraggled victim as the animal she'd been trying to befriend for days. The little cat's cries of distress stabbed at her heart.

Lucy tore out of the door and raced to the animal's defense. By the time she reached it, the tormentors had fled, and Lucy found her cat curled on the grass. It clutched what was left of a bedraggled red ball in its paws and looked up at Lucy. Blood oozed from wounds at the animal's throat, and its tongue lolled from an open mouth, its breathing ragged.

Lucy cradled the cat in her hands and brought the ravaged little body to her breast. She petted its head gently and cooed to the injured animal as it gentled in her arms. Through the labored gasps for breath, Lucy could feel the poor creature purr. The little cat lifted its head and looked at her, gratitude in its dimmed green eyes. Then, releasing a final breath, the cat ceased its purring and slipped away.

Artemis knelt beside her just as the tears started to flow. Lucy cuddled the small, still body and felt her lover kiss the crown of her head.

"I don't think this little creature ever experienced being loved." Lucy whispered. "Look at her, Temmie. She's full grown, and she's so thin. I've been leaving food for her, but she would never come to me no matter how hard I tried. I'd have loved her."

"You did when it counted most." Artemis hugged her soulmate. "She found love, Lucy. She found you."

Chapter Seventeen

"It feels a little like fiddling while Rome burns," Lucy remarked as she made a final appraisal of the backyard. Tables and chairs were set up on both sides of the huge pool. The caterers had done a splendid job with the various trays of foods. There were Hawaiian dishes, all favorites of Strang. Estonia was represented as was Ireland and an abundant selection of exotic beers and wines.

The barbeque flared, and Lucy glanced to make sure Artemis still had her eyebrows. "Take it easy there, Temmie. I'd hate to have to throw you in the pool."

"What makes you think you could?" Artemis arched one of the singed brows.

"Well, I mean if you were on fire, you'd probably let me." Lucy grinned.

"Naw, I'd just jump in and drag you with me."

Lucy remembered exactly when such a moment had happened, without the fire part, shortly after she and Artemis had become friends and were on their way to being lovers. The good old days—she smiled at the memory—before the end of the world loomed on the horizon. Angie had suggested the party to brighten everyone's spirit. And even Artemis had agreed. Tomorrow they'd leave the analysis behind and head to Puma Punku, ready or not.

"Where is everyone?" Lucy asked, strolling to Artemis and gently rubbing her back. "It's time for the party to start."

Artemis closed the lid to let the brisket cook. "I think they are making a few phone calls. I told them to tell their families where we're going."

"Uh-huh." Lucy slipped her arm around her partner's waist. "You wanted them to talk to their families just in case we aren't coming back."

Artemis shrugged. "Better to cover all the bases."

"I prefer the expression 'load the bases.'" Strang stepped between the tables, gathering a handful of popcorn as he approached. He was dressed in chalky-white shorts and a bright-yellow flowered shirt. On his head was the semblance of a straw hat obviously older than most of the party's participants. In his free hand was a putter.

"I didn't know you played golf," Lucy said.

"I don't. Never could see the appeal of pursuing a small white orb when one could otherwise take a nice relaxing stroll." He presented the club, giving it a twirl. "I thought the club added a bit of savoir faire to my ensemble."

Artemis rolled her eyes. "Having a club around might come in handy if our three young geniuses can't bring themselves to bury the hatchet for an afternoon."

Angie slid open the patio doors and added a bucket of fresh ice to the cooler. She selected a beer and plunked herself at one of the tables. She wore a bikini top and crisp linen shorts, her blonde hair peeking out from beneath an enormous sun hat. Beer in hand, Stefan joined her at the table. He was stripped down to a pair of roomy basketball trunks for swimming. He cut an attractive figure, one Angie lowered her sunglasses to inspect. The couple clicked beer bottles and smiled. Their reaction to each other caused Lucy to reassess her choice of mate for her daughter. Artemis nudged Lucy's ribs with an elbow and nodded to someone emerging from the main house. Ronan stepped tentatively into hot sunlight. He was dressed in a long-sleeve shirt and jeans, his face slathered in sunscreen beneath a baseball cap.

Lucy glanced quizzically at Artemis.

"Redhead!"

*

The lush forest of Myanmar made forward progress slow. Minister Pindata wanted to reach the border before losing the light. He had raced from Manipur east to see for himself if the strange stories reaching him from Thailand and Laos could be true. A barrier had appeared along the southern edge of China. A dark rift in the ground as if the land itself was tearing away.

His vehicle crested a ridge, and Pindata instructed them to stop. In the distance he could see the enormous scar in the land. In the foreground the foliage was robust and verdant. Beyond the rift, a thick fog prevented curious eyes from seeing within.

Sin took the disk from his pocket and held it out toward the land. The disk spun, glinting in the sunlight, and hovered above his hand. A wave of warmth passed through him, and the ground trembled, the gorge widening while he watched. Pindata felt the truth of the action; his kingdom ended where the rift began. And he understood. This was the limit of what he possessed. He was to go no farther.

The caravan made its way west to the plane waiting to take the minister to Bangladesh, where a treaty giving Pindata complete control was ready for his signature.

President Chatterjee had requested his presence at his earliest opportunity. Nervous nations throughout the region were suing for inclusion in the pact between India and Pindata's peace accord. Pindata clicked them off in his mind. His range of influence extended from Southeast Asia to the Mediterranean. Africa was accepting his overtures with greedy eyes, and Pindata knew the northern countries from Egypt south were willing to follow his vision. There were pockets of independence, but he would destroy them at his leisure.

A damp wind buffeted his vehicle, and he tapped the disk in his jacket pocket. The wind stilled. The power was intoxicating. The council had suggested a statue of him be erected in each of the countries he had conquered. It was a sin of course to accept such objects of worship, and he had made a show of declining the suggestion.

The plane was fueled and ready. It would be a short flight, followed by a brief ceremony, and he would return home to oversee the packing. He was moving from the modest home in Cambodia to a more suitable domicile in Mumbai, India. Kamakrisha had selected it for him. The former UN official had proven a valuable resource though his motives were much too small-minded. Kamakrisha wanted peace for India. Pindata smiled. Such a modest request when a brotherhood of nations was available. Once Pindata was declared king, Kamakrisha would be retired like the useless Chatterjee to the countryside where accidents were an unfortunate fact of life.

Pindata boarded the plane and took a seat, anxious to get to Bangladesh and unaware it was a destination he was not going to reach.

*

"I may have been hasty in deciding which of the men is best suited to Angie," Lucy said, filling a glass with wine and handing it to her partner. She had watched her daughter and the well-muscled Stefan share looks and telling touches for nearly an hour. "Evidently, she has her own idea of what she likes."

"Even Wolf thinks Stefan and Angie make an ideal couple." Artemis took a sip of wine and let the tart liquid warm in her mouth before swallowing. "I never considered Ronan as a match. He's moody and insecure. Wolf thinks Stefan is the pick of the litter, but then he's got his hands full with our other delinquent. Given the three possibilities, I agree with Wolf." She shielded her eyes from the bright sun uninhibited in the clear summer sky.

"What does everyone have against Ronan anyway?" Lucy asked, her ego smarting slightly.

Artemis shook her head. "Want me to enumerate?"

"No." Lucy shifted in her chair and captured Artemis with a perplexed grin. "Ronan is smart and polite and wholesome-looking, don't you think? My mother would have adored him. I don't understand why Angie treats him like a house pet."

Artemis took a measured look at Stefan's physique as he walked over, switched the music to something with an upbeat tempo, and invited Angie to dance. Arching an eyebrow, she put her hand on Lucy's thigh and tickled the smooth, warm flesh. "Wholesome isn't everything."

Lucy reached down and stilled her partner's hand as she watched Angie and Stefan flirting back and forth. "No." She grinned mischievously. "It certainly isn't."

*

Keegan searched his dresser drawer for his phone. The noise from the garden party irritated his already overwrought nervous system. He'd shared with Artemis the timeline he'd discovered, and she had reacted oddly. Instead of praise or gratitude as he had expected, his dark-haired boss had seemed sad more than anything. And suddenly, the decision had been made that they would leave for Bolivia as soon as possible. Keegan bit his fingernails. He would never understand people's reactions. Artemis's response was just one more reminder of his failings.

He threw his trunks across the room and stifled a scream. He didn't want to attend a party. He wanted to punch someone. He just didn't know why.

Instead, Keegan sat on his bed and stuck the headset connector into the phone. *The whole fucking world is shit!* He pulled a T-shirt over his torso and ran his hand through his bedraggled hair. Another vision was trying to unravel in his mind. Keegan refused to let it. He stuck his earbuds in his ears and turned the music on. The melody washed through his brain, calming the angry thoughts. It was supposed to be their day off, he assured himself. They couldn't make him put his music away on his own time. He lay back on the bed and let the music fill him for a while.

Feeling calmer, he retrieved his trunks and exchanged them for the jeans he was going to wear. He slipped into a pair of flip-flops, tucked the phone and headset in a towel, and headed to the party. He wouldn't make an issue of it; this fix was enough to get him through the afternoon. A hamburger and a beer sounded pretty good too.

*

Strang leaned back, slid his hat forward, and closed his eyes. A decade after leaving, he continued to miss the trade winds; the cooling breezes had caressed many an evening spent with Willa in his arms. Setting aside a half-empty plate of pulled pork and cucumber salad, he watched the young people enjoying their day of frivolity. Although his thoughts were never far from the monumental decision the young ones were being called upon to make.

It beguiled him how novel such a moment would be. In the place of corporations and tyrants intent on maintaining their control of the world, the future was to be determined by fresh-faced representatives of a new generation. Strang considered that progress in the human condition. An era was passing. The wealthy and powerful would be swept aside by young prophets whether they were wise or not. Strang could only hope that wisdom would prevail and the proper choice would be made. Besides, he schooled himself when doubt emerged, without faith in the younger generation, the world would have no future at all. Ready or not, the youngsters would soon decide mankind's future.

A blur flew past him. Issuing a piercing rebel yell, Keegan cannonballed into the pool, dragging the fully dressed Ronan with him. A shock of cold water engulfed Strang, and he pushed back his soggy hat to find Ronan and Keegan engaged in a strenuous water splashing competition, the unintended victims of which were those who were peacefully relaxing too near the pool.

Stefan and Angie erupted into laughter. Artemis slid her chair back as the splashing grew more intense, and Lucy shook her head, chuckling at the two men. Stefan was decidedly the pick of the litter. Strang made his soggy way to his bungalow without uttering any of the curses echoing in his mind. Reaching his bungalow, he apologized for his thoughts as he passed Willa's urn and went to change.

Angie was sitting in the living room when he emerged dressed in a fresh shirt and slacks.

"Mom sent me to make sure you were okay," she explained, handing Strang a beer. "Temmie said to tell you Ronan and Keegan had drowned, but I thought that extreme."

Strang chuckled. "For Ronan, poor lad, most assuredly. For Keegan, not entirely inappropriate."

"The fireworks start as soon as it's dark enough. But first we're going to have a proper sit-down dinner in the main house and conclude the evening with a karaoke concert. How's your baritone, Wolf?"

Strang put his hand on his chest and hummed through a scale or two. "I have just the song, my dear girl."

Angie smiled and turned to leave.

"Wait. Please," Strang called before Angie reached the door. "I want to speak to Athena, if I may."

Angie's form straightened, the planes of her face taking on an imperious expression. Strang marveled again at the striking change.

"Thank you, Athena. Before we embark on the final act of this quest, there is something I wish to know. Do you, goddess of wisdom as you are, believe humankind is a species worthy of joining with your collective?" It was a question he could not answer even for himself.

Athena peered at him with dispassionate eyes. "It is not meant for me to decide the issue, Wolfgang. Artemis thinks you are. And I have loved your species more perhaps than any of the gods as you think of us."

"But we disappoint you."

Athena nodded. "Yes. You disappoint yourselves. Humans possess great promise. Their ability to love is great. Your history is filled with acts of self-sacrifice and generosity and redemption. But you have never managed to rise above the self where greed and ego influence your behaviors toward each other. It is my opinion humanity is not ready."

"And your species has risen, as you say, above ego?" The question was meant to be pointed. Strang had no desire to soften it.

"I do not hate humans, Wolfgang. I wish you no harm." Athena's demeanor gentled as she spoke. "Your species must determine your future just as mine did. Whether humans choose the collective who shaped and nurtured you or the collective seeking to possess you makes no difference in the end to me. You will become part of a collective consciousness which creates the universe, and you will progress in wisdom and responsibility. I wish you well."

"It matters enormously to Temmie," Strang replied, still digging to understand the difference between Artemis's profound concern and Athena's lack of it.

"It is your future." Artemis tuned her senses to the scientist, diving deeply into the emotions coursing through him. "But you are correct about Artemis. She is behaving foolishly. My sister knows we cannot escape the bounds of our collective. We cannot step beyond it. We cannot follow humans to the Others. We would not survive the turbulent void between us if we tried. But Artemis will persist until the last moment if she must."

"Lucy." Strang finally understood one mystery in the cauldron of ignorance into which the quest had thrust him. Artemis's love for Lucy placed his friend in great danger. "Then you and I share another common goal, Athena. I will do all I can to ensure Artemis survives whatever else may occur."

*

President Benjamin Hughes took a seat, leaving his visitor standing for a moment before gesturing to the other sofa. He had permitted the pope to enter the United States because he had to satisfy the rising voices in Congress. Media regurgitated the popular opinion the pope was doing a pious work in Europe. The refugee camps were clean and desperate people were being fed. There were, however, opposing views. Several prime ministers claimed privately the man was siphoning off their power and their economies. Hughes had no reason to disbelieve them.

The possibility a benevolent pontiff could accomplish a similar miracle for America, facing an influx of people intent on escaping the famine sweeping through its southern neighbors was a compelling idea. President Hughes smiled politely at the man seated across from him. All it would cost to accept Peter's proposal was America's constitutional right to freedom of religion. A price no leader would ever pay. Hughes was merely practicing politics seeing the pope at all.

Reading the deception behind the smile, Pope Peter folded his hands in the sleeves of his handsome white cassock. "Perhaps if you unburden yourself of your reservation, my son, we can agree on a future."

Benjamin resented being called son. Not that he was a faithless man. He was a weekly attendee to Saint John's, the presidents' church, two blocks from the White House. And he prayed never more than he had for past months while the world fell apart and impossible things continued to happen. But he was not a true member of the faithful and certainly not a believer in saints. Many people were ready to canonize the man staring at him. Hughes was not.

Peter repeated the terms of the agreement. It was a carbon copy of the one the European Union had accepted. He spoke of how the unrest once affecting Europe had been efficiently resolved once the Vatican began its charitable administrations.

For which you are richly compensated, the president thought. He knew all there was to know about the pope's tactics and overarching strategy. There would be no acquiescence to it. The US could handle its own problems without submitting to a religious charlatan.

"I'm curious." Benjamin had a few questions. "I would think your services were better used to assist China. I'm told you were among the last people to visit Beijing before the current difficulty. It's been nearly a week since the world has heard or seen what has happened. Surely your attention would be better spent there."

"Ah, China." Peter nodded. "All in good time. For the present China is the hands of Almighty God. Once you and I conclude our agreement, I will do what I can to aid them."

"Unfortunately, your eminence, we will not conclude this agreement or any other." The president was firm.

"Alas, *signore*, I believe you are correct." The pope sighed and closed his eyes. When he opened them again, there was a fury evident in his stare. He slid the disk from beneath the short cape covering his chest. Extending his arm, Peter revealed the object to his companion.

"Beautiful, isn't it?" Peter said, a smile of malice on his face.

The president stared at the object, incredulous as it rose from the pontiff's hand and stood upright as if aware of him. "What is this?" he asked, a jolt of alarm quivering in his voice.

"It is my destiny," the pope replied. "And yours."

The disk spun in midair, and Benjamin Hughes lost all ability to move. He struggled for breath, the muscles in his chest suddenly rigid. He tried to stand, but his legs failed to obey. Panic gripped him, and he felt his heart stop before all went black.

Peter called out for help. He was administering last rites to the president when his calls were answered by two secret service guards.

"That's not necessary, Holy Father," one of the guards said, recognizing the rite Peter was performing over the president's body. "President Hughes is not a Catholic."

The pope folded his hands in his sleeves and nodded, stepping back to permit the arriving medic to tend to the president. The medic checked for a pulse. Finding none, he looked over to where Peter had been standing and then about the large room. The pontiff was no longer there.

*

Stefan preferred the light in Angie's eyes to the fireworks exploding above them. He watched as flashes of color lit the contours of her face and smiled whenever she glanced at him. She was not going with them tomorrow. Artemis had asked Angie to stay behind until they sent her word all was in place. She would be the contact point since the three teams would not contact each other directly until they were certain their conversations were not being monitored.

Stefan had mixed feelings about leaving Angie. He'd had a vision of her lying on a stone floor with a terrible wind scouring the ground. If she remained behind, the vision could not come true, but neither could he protect her once he left. He wanted to take her in his arms and keep her safe.

"I liked the song you chose," Angie said, casually taking his hand. "You have a good voice."

Stefan grinned. "No so good. Wolfgang put us all to shame."

Thinking of Strang's boisterous rendition of "Battle Hymn of the Republic" made her snicker. The first round of songs was supposed to connect to the struggle ahead, and they did—vaguely. Angie had gone with "From a Distance," and Stefan had done a stand-up job with "War." The mood changed when Lucy had simply begun to sing "Con ti Partirò." Artemis rose to the challenge, and they completed the duet with "The Prayer."

Even Strang was emotional when they finished.

"Since we're on a Bocelli theme, I'd attempt 'Because We Believe' if I were younger," he said. "Or 'Nessun Dorma' if my Italian were better. Which regrettably it is not."

Keegan and Ronan stepped up to provide unintended but much-needed comic relief with a gyrating version of "We're Rocking the Planet" Angie doubted she would ever get out of her head.

The session concluded with Strang singing "Kalua," his late wife's favorite island song. He conjured images of Willa in his mind so vivid he could almost touch her.

The group grabbed another round of beverages and sauntered out into the yard for the pyrotechnic show Artemis had arranged.

"Do you think they'll be angry we left before the fireworks were completed?" Stefan asked, following Angie down the hall to her room. "I do not want them to think..."

Angie squeezed his hand. "Too late, they already think we're together, and no, they won't be angry. Mother knows how we feel, and Temmie gave me a wink when we left. It's our last night together."

Stefan smiled nervously. It was also their first.

Chapter Eighteen

Stefan set the uncooperative disk in its wooden box and slipped it into the carry-on he was packing. He and Keegan were the first to head south. The others would deploy via a sequence of complicated itineraries meant to keep them apart until the third and final day. Lucy had managed to find Stefan and Keegan a direct flight to Cusco so they could take the bulk of the equipment the team would need with them. The advance guard, as Keegan dubbed himself and Stefan, would make its way south to deposit certain items at designated points throughout the rambling Tiwanaku sites.

Strang and Ronan were scheduled to depart later in the day with an overnight in Dallas before arriving in La Paz. Artemis and Lucy were booked to fly out the next morning with a brief layover in Colombia before also landing in La Paz. Once the three teams were accounted for, Angie was expected to join them. With open hostility between Peru and Chile imminent, it was assumed local coordination would be inhibited by the heavy military presence. Artemis believed strongly the guise of being tourists was their best protection, and the group had agreed.

Angie would be the check-in point for the teams, who were to call in whenever possible and repeat a simple quote from Albert Einstein—"Fear exists only in the mind." The message could be modified if circumstances necessitated. If a team found itself in trouble, the message would include only the first two words. Once in place, they would do a dry run, walking through the ruins looking for the precise place the choice was to be communicated. From that point on, success depended solely on Ronan, Stefan, and Keegan and whatever the Harbinger ability enabled them to see.

"I thought you were going to leave the disk with Angie," Keegan said when he saw Stefan pack it away. He felt a sense of relief knowing the disk would be near but wondered what had changed Stefan's mind. "I thought you said taking it with us is sort of like having a spy in our midst."

Stefan shook his head. The idea of leaving Angie alone with the enemy's primary weapon had given him nightmares. "No. Well, maybe I did. But then I thought the disk is key to understanding our adversary." He twitched his mustache. "It talks to me. Like a woman, it tries to seduce me." He blushed. "Only I am not seduced."

Keegan glanced at Stefan. "You sure about that? I mean we all noticed you and Angie making a beeline for her room last night. And you're crimson as a beet right now. I'd say you got seduced real good. You might need the damn disk, given what Ronan is undoubtedly thinking about doing to you."

"Angie is not a seducer. Angie is a wonderful, beautiful, incredible woman." A grin appeared beneath his mustache. "I was talking about the disk."

Keegan understood exactly what the burly scientist meant. He remembered how the disk had reached out to possess him as well. He had kept it with him at all times, and it had carved a hole in his mind that still felt empty. He studied Stefan's face, looking for any indication of a change besides the romantic glow peeling off him.

"I'd be happy to take the disk off your hands, Stef."

Stefan closed his carry-on. "It comes with me." He reached out and gave Keegan a friendly pat on the shoulder. "I will protect your skinny butt from the evil disk. But if it wants to take a bite of Ronan, I will not interfere."

The man in question was waiting for them in the car. Ronan watched Keegan and Stefan load the trunk and take their seats. Then he started the engine without a word and headed to LAX. News of a declaration of war between Chile and Peru would beat them there.

*

"Have you ever been there, out there I mean, amid the stars?" Lucy put her arm around Artemis's waist. The night was warm, and the house was all theirs once again. The scientists had all departed, and Angie had gone to bed after a day of alternating between moony-eyed daydreaming and sporadic comments about how wonderful Stefan was. Artemis could hear Athena's contrary opinion in the background.

"Once." She answered Lucy's question. "Ze'us took me to the dark side of the moon when I was very little." She gave Lucy a hug as they walked. "I've always been mesmerized by the moon, you might say. The view of Earth is incredible."

"So, you were a moonstruck little alien. That's cute." Lucy tickled Artemis's ribs. "I wish I had known you back then. I know you said we've always been together, but I'd like to remember what you were like as a child, a teenager even." She paused and looked up at Artemis. "You never told me about the first time we met. How did we meet? How old were we?"

"You were about fifteen, the youngest daughter of a village elder. He was going to marry you off when you came running to me and begged me to intercede. You wanted me to take you into the Eed'en and teach you, what did you call it, ah, my magic."

Lucy paused and stared at Artemis. "Well, did you?"

Artemis laughed. "No, not at first. You were very young, and I was..." She ran her tongue along her lip. "Older."

"How old were you?"

There was no way around it now that Lucy had asked. "In Earth years? I was about a hundred and seventy-five. For my species that was barely out of my adolescence. Once I was bound to this planet, the physics changed."

Lucy had her mouth open and could only utter, "Uh-huh." She drew a deep breath and closed her mouth. "And exactly how long were you expected to live? Not on Earth I mean."

"Forever. No one in the collective had ever died the way mortals do here. Time is a quality of the physical realm."

Lucy could only stare. "You truly are a god! I don't think I've ever really understood what that means."

"Consciousness never dies, Lucy. It is the creative force; all the rest is just perception." Except for one immutable fact Artemis did not want to share. Duality kept the two consciousness collectives forever apart in an endless struggle. If mankind joined with the Others, she and Lucy would be separated for however long eternity lasted.

*

"There are several brain states, Wolf. What is it you want to know?" Ronan sat hunched in a plastic terminal chair, lazily observing the mechanics checking the plane he and Strang were about to board. They were taking an early flight out of Dallas. He was tired and restless and ready to get aboard where he could sleep out of reach of the aging scientist's constant peppering of questions.

Strang scratched his chin and pondered how to respond. Music flowed through the terminal just loud enough to be heard beneath his thoughts. He recognized the simple tune. It was an instrumental version of the dreadful song Keegan had been enamored with.

"Alpha, Theta, and Delta. I am aware of the various mental states." He nudged Ronan to make sure he was listening. "Explain the difference for me one more time. Include, please, their specific frequencies."

Ronan sighed and dragged a hand across his face. "Delta between zero and three hertz is deep sleep. Theta between four and eight hertz is associated with a meditative or blissful state sometimes referred to as the higher consciousness. Alpha between eight and twelve hertz is the woke, creative mental flow."

Strang nodded. "And these represent the frequencies with which neurons interact in the human brain?"

"Yes, yes. Brainwaves are produced by synchronized electrical pulses—neurons talking with each other, so to speak. It's harmonics. The slower waves make us sluggish or dreamy. The higher the frequency, the more alert we feel." Ronan finished with a loud yawn.

Strang gave Ronan a sympathetic glance. "I keep interrupting your frequency of choice, I see. There is another, you know. Infra-low brainwaves below point five hertz are assumed to be the cortical rhythms that underlie higher brain functions."

Ronan wanted to punch the man. "If you already know so goddamn much, why are you quizzing me?"

Strang shrugged and issued a low chuckle. "Just want to see if there was something new you might know. I am interested in brain timing and function. Artemis wants to understand more about it..." He stopped, not knowing quite how to describe what Artemis had in mind. "Based on what you've validated for me, I believe the Harbinger ability is most likely stimulated in the Theta state where intuition is most active."

"Thanks. I already considered that." Ronan leaned back in his chair and gripped the armrest. "You could have just asked that specific question and spared me this circular mental exercise."

Strang tugged the lapels of his traveling jacket and smirked. "Yes, I suppose I could. But then I'd have had nothing to do but listen to that detestable music."

A voice over the loudspeaker brought the men to attention. Boarding was beginning. Strang and Ronan grabbed their carry-ons and stepped into the line forming at the gate. They would arrive in La Paz midmorning. Strang was anxious to share a new theory with Artemis, one that might solve an issue he knew she still puzzled over.

*

Sacsayhuamán with its "living stones" was awash with military traffic. A mere two kilometers north of Cuzco's main square, Pachatusan's fortress offered an amazing view of the city Peruvian troops were preparing to defend. The zigzagged wall formed terraces where soldiers mustered and absorbed the spirits of their Incan ancestors to embolden them for battle.

"Armies make me nervous." Keegan eyed the military activity with apprehension as he wended his way through the heavy traffic. The large vehicles dominated the intersections. Frustrated motorists leaned on their horns. Keegan found the pandemonium mesmerizing and watched with an amused smile as one driver drove up on the sidewalk only to be halted by an armed soldier.

Stefan watched in silence and knew the presence of so many soldiers would make what he and Keegan had to do all the more difficult.

"Armies make you dead if you act like a fool," Stefan suggested as their hotel appeared in the distance. "Safer to be out of view. We should camp out of the city instead of getting a room at a hotel."

"We have a reservation." Keegan turned into the hotel parking lot. He reached back and covered their equipment bags with a tattered blanket someone had left in the rental car. "We're just tourists on holiday, remember?" he reminded his companion. "Pretend you're an American. Act oblivious."

Exiting the car, Stefan hiked his trousers and forced himself not to gaze around at the activity in the street. "I have an Estonian passport. American I am not."

"Then just smile a lot and let me do the talking," Keegan suggested. "No. Wait. On second thought give me your passport and I'll check us in. You stay here. In fact, just sit in the car. Do we want a double bed or twins?"

"Do you want to die crushed like a bug in your sleep?" Stefan asked, climbing back into the vehicle.

"No," Keegan called back, jogging to the hotel entrance.

Stefan watched the parade of military trucks and noted the concern on the faces of people scurrying about the busy streets. The sense of fear reminded him of his childhood when the elders used to speak of war and what they'd seen...and done...to survive. He wanted no part of it. Artemis had saved him, and he wondered if the magical, beautiful woman could do it again. The premonitions of the past few weeks did not suggest she could. Putting aside dark thoughts, Stefan conjured memories of Angie and their night together, a silly smile spreading beneath his mustache.

Stefan selected a map from the glove box and studied the route from Cusco across the border to Bolivia. There were half a dozen places around Lake Titicaca where they could stay. He traced a line from a dot labelled Puno to Tiwanaku. A Humvee rumbled past on the street, its cargo of troops reminding him how difficult it was going to be to get there.

Stefan leaned back in his seat and rubbed his chest. The altitude was going to be a problem as well. Cusco was eleven thousand feet above sea level, and they would be going higher yet to Puma Punku. He wasn't going to jog along the edge of the Andes like a stupid American; he was just going to breathe like a sensible Estonian tourist. And rescue the human race from a force he could feel bearing down on them all.

Chapter Nineteen

"Shit!"

Keegan saw the traffic slowing and knew it could only mean trouble. He checked to see if there was a turnoff he could take on either side and then cursed again. He slowed the big SUV to a crawl and followed the vehicle in front of them.

"Roadblock!" Keegan said to Stefan. "Just what we need."

Stefan smoothed his mustache, his eyes narrowing as he surveyed the road ahead. Men in tan uniforms were searching cars, turning some back and allowing very few of the others to pass. The border was closing in advance of the impending conflict.

"The Bolivian soldiers are not letting Peruvians through. We are not Peruvians," Stefan said calmly. "Us, they will let through."

Keegan was less certain of that. "Did your Harbinger sense come up with that?"

Stefan turned his head and frowned at Keegan in the driver's seat. "No! My superior Estonian reasoning did. It also tells me you should stop sweating, or the soldiers will be suspicious."

Keegan wiped his face. "You might be right."

The car in front of them was turned back. It performed a three-point turn, and Keegan caught the seriously anxious look on the driver's face as he drove off. A soldier peered into Keegan's open window and held out his hand while issuing clipped orders Keegan couldn't understand. Stefan handed the soldier a passport and a brochure about Puma Punku. Keegan dug his passport out of his vest pocket and held it up.

"Tourists?" the soldier asked in accented English.

"Yes," Keegan and Stefan responded in unison.

The soldier eyed the bags in the bag of the vehicle and motioned for them to open the rear. *Damn!* Keegan's nerves tingled. Stefan exited the vehicle and opened the hatch at the back. He indicated he wanted a cigarette from the soldier and then bummed a light. Smiling broadly, Stefan admired the badges on the man's uniform and feigned being impressed. He finished the cigarette, ground the butt into the pale soil, and thanked the man effusively. He moved his arm, inviting the soldier to examine the contents of the trunk. The soldier moved the bags around. Then he returned Stefan's grin and slammed the hatch shut.

"Okay," the soldier said, enunciating each syllable in a friendly voice. He twirled his hand in a circle, and the roadblock was cleared. "Go."

Keegan released a breath he'd been holding and eased the vehicle forward, counting eight more soldiers watching them leave. "Jesus H. Christ! That was terrifying."

Stefan issued a low, growling laugh. "Not so much. You just have to act like you are not going to cause trouble. Soldiers hate such a bad job as that. You act right, they care less who you are, where you go."

Sweat beaded on Keegan's brow. "You think there will be more of them? Roadblocks or soldiers, I mean."

Stefan looked across the flat, windswept terrain. "Yes, I think so." In his mind he could see the image of black-shirted men pouring across the Altiplano; the Harbinger had already revealed to him visions of what was to come.

"We don't have any weapons if there is trouble." Keegan noted, nervously checking the rearview mirror and the roadblock disappearing behind them. "Besides our stellar intellect."

"That leaves you completely unarmed." Stefan grunted. "I have the disk."

Keegan gunned the engine. Vulnerable was a feeling he disliked. He had built an irritating persona to hide behind, where insult or injury couldn't reach him. But being an asshole wouldn't protect him from men with guns. He thought of the disk now in Stefan's possession and dearly wished the object was still his. Like the music Strang had forbade Keegan from playing, the disk made him feel calm and, more importantly given his current situation, brave. He slid his eyes to the right and looked at Stefan. One way or another, Keegan resolved to possess the disk again.

*

The border between Peru and Bolivia passed invisibly through Lake Titicaca in the Altiplano—the high plateau of the central Andes. Arid and windswept, the vast mountain plateau was populated by farmers, descendants of a lost culture thought to have flourished as long as eleven thousand years ago, llamas, and alpacas. The large lake was anchored by numerous villages from which fishermen departed in boats woven from the tall reeds growing along the shore.

The main feature of Tiwanaku were the ruins of a central city constructed on an east-west axis and spanning four square kilometers. The site consisted of various ruined temples, walls, and the buried remains of a large pyramid. The puzzling massive blocks of Puma Punku lay a kilometer to the east. Between them, sharp angled stones emerged from the pale-pink dirt like wildflowers. Tiwanaku brought thousands of visitors to the twelve-thousand-foot-high plateau to marvel at its mysteries. An army had come for another reason.

General Maria Vergara steered the small boat through the cobalt water toward a narrow channel aside the Copacabana Peninsula. Dead reckoning where Bolivia ended and Peru began, she throttled down the engine and stared at the magnificent scene before her. The snow-capped peaks of Cordillera Real were to the east. To the west was Isla del Sol, where Viracocha was said to have descended from the sky and created the Incan race. But it was on the smaller Isla de la Luna that Vergara established her headquarters.

Her army would invade from the south and west. They would take the Altiplano with its rich tourist trade while Bolivian troops amassed along its northern border to present a Peruvian assault on the east. To Maria the final conquest would be retribution for the Wari defeat fifteen hundred years before. She could feel the presence of her ancestors everywhere, and once the holy ground of Tiwanaku was hers, Vergara knew the entire continent would kneel to the rightful leader.

Vergara tossed an offering of copihue into the blue water and watched the pink petals drift amid the gentle waves. She called upon the spirits of Incan warriors to grant her a quick victory over her enemies. Then she steered the boat through the narrow Strait of Tiquina to the small island which contained the Iñaq Uyu—the House of the Virgins of the Sun. A partially restored wall fronted a labyrinth of underground rooms. The complex was a sanctuary reachable only by boat and steeped in Incan culture.

Vergara cast her mind's eye north beyond the hundred miles of lake to the Peruvian cities her warriors were preparing to advance upon. The army was assembled from half a dozen countries, but they wore black uniforms uniting them in a common cause. Her cause. Peru could not stand alone against the inevitable. The disk in her pocket affirmed her belief, growing warm and emitting a low, comforting hum.

*

Stefan looked at the sun beginning its journey to the west. They were behind schedule by a least an hour. Keegan had refused to hurry, terrified they would draw the attention of the soldiers deployed along the narrow highway that led back to the border they had just crossed.

"We should call Temmie," Keegan announced.

"No way." Stefan eyed a pair of soldiers guarding a turnoff, presumably to one of the villages lining Lake Titicaca. "Angie was very clear about keeping our distance and not using our cell phones unless there was an emergency."

Stefan shuffled in his seat. "There is no time to stop and look for a hotel for the night. Just keep on going to the ruins." They could camp out on the Altiplano if necessary, he thought. That might even be safer.

"We don't have too much farther to go," Keegan told him, his head on a swivel as he scoured the countryside. Catching a sign pointing to the town of Desaguadero, he turned left toward the lake. "There's time."

The car rolled slowly into the outskirts of the small town, and Keegan realized his mistake. They were back at the border, surrounded by tan-clad Peruvian militia. He found a vacant area and started a three-point turn to reverse direction. A hand slapped the front bumper loudly enough to make both Keegan and Stefan jump. The soldier pointed his weapon at Keegan and yelled at the startled men.

Following hand motions from the impatient soldier, Keegan turned off the engine, and he and Stefan cautiously excited the vehicle. The soldier indicated a structure at the rear of the lot and pushed the men forward. Stefan hesitated, certain as bad as the situation looked, going inside a building could only make it worse. He glanced at Keegan, who looked pale as a ghost, and reluctantly started walking.

*

Artemis felt the plane swoop downward and glanced out of the window at the majestic landscape beneath them. To the west was Lake Titicaca, to the east the rugged Andes Mountains. In between lay the Altiplano or what Artemis feared was destined to be Armageddon. She folded her fingers around Lucy's hand, wanting the physical connection.

Lucy entwined their fingers. "Angie said she's booked two flights. One for tomorrow and one for the day after. We just have to let her know which one to take when we are ready. I can hardly wait for us to all be together."

Below, the Bolivian city of La Paz sparkled in the bright sunlight. As they descended, Artemis could pick out the Plaza Murillo and the Basilica of San Francisco. It had been decades since she had last visited the city, but she remembered strolling the Witches' Market and climbing the beginner friendly Huayna Potosi, which, as she recalled, was not all that friendly in the thin, high-altitude air.

Artemis turned from the window and twitched a smile at Lucy's excitement. *How beautiful she is.* She stared at Lucy's hazel eyes with their perpetual playfulness, her cute slightly upturned nose and full lips that always tasted of honey somehow. She felt the love binding her to Lucy and knew it was the only thing in her existence that truly mattered. *I will not leave her whatever the cost. I am tired of being afraid.* All she wanted at that moment was to be wrong, to say "I don't care" about the fate of a race or a planet in the vastness of time and space. *I only ask to remain with her.* She ran the backs of her fingers gently along Lucy's cheek.

"I choose to be with you," Artemis said, her voice choked with emotion.

Lucy cocked her head to one side and wondered at the hurt in Artemis's eyes. "And I choose to be with you," she replied, forming a slight, reassuring smile. "It's going to be okay, Temmie. If there's one thing I've learned, it always turns out okay."

The plane bounced once as its wheels hit the runway; then the engines roared as the big jet resisted the brakes slowing its forward motion. They gathered their things and made their way to customs. There were soldiers standing listlessly at the exits. Artemis felt eyes roaming over them as they claimed their bags and set off to rent a car. They planned to overnight in La Paz and wait for Strang and Ronan to arrive. Tomorrow, they would venture into Tiwanaku as two couples on a sightseeing excursion.

If all went well, Stefan and Keegan would show up during the day having secured accommodations in some nearby town. Then Lucy would send word to Athena to join them. The hardest part was out of Artemis's control. The wunderkinds, as Strang referred to the three young men, were to use their gifted abilities to select the precise point where the communication would occur.

Then only the choice itself remained to be made. *What if they fail?* Every muscle in Artemis's body tensed. She was standing on the edge of a cliff, and she could not sense the bottom. When she jumped, if she jumped, she had no way of controlling the fall.

Lucy steered the car according to the directions she'd been given at the rental stall. She let Artemis visit with her thoughts and concentrated on staying under the speed limit or what she assumed to be the speed limit; signs were infrequent and referred to kilometers. Lucy had never seen Artemis quite like this. She knew Artemis was afraid. It was obvious given the thin, pale lips and tension around her icy-blue eyes. There was no way to dispel her partner's fear, but Lucy did not accept the possibility of them being separated and told herself her faith would be enough to see them through whatever happened.

They arrived at Zona Sur five miles south of the city center and found a friendly hotel staff eager to assist them. Tourism was down with all the military activity and impending war with Peru. Given their pick from among the available rooms and suites, Artemis left the details to Lucy and stepped outside. It would take a while to acclimatize to the altitude. She wished they could afford to spend an extra day at the modest hotel. Strang might need the additional time, and she resolved to find coca leaves for him to chew to mitigate the effect of the thin, oxygen-poor air. They could wait for Athena to arrive. Artemis stared up into the brilliant Andean sky. *If Athena comes.* That was not at a certainty with time winding down. She felt Lucy's hand on her arm and followed the cheerful young man, who pushed a luggage cart with one arm and gestured wildly, talking about tours his brother could provide while guiding the women to their room.

*

Ronan noticed an odd cloud formation over the Andes. He pointed at the cloud with its weird saffron coloration and asked Strang if he could explain it.

Strang leaned past Ronan for a better view. "I believe that is a lenticular cloud formation. They form downwind when a strong air current meets an obstacle in its path. In this case the obstacle is the Andes."

"Looks like an orange flying saucer," Ronan observed.

"Yes, lenticular clouds are known to have such an appearance. I'm quite certain more than a few have made their way to the infamous Blue Book." Strang couldn't resist. "Expecting someone? A consciousness collective perhaps?"

Ronan ignored the sarcasm. He wondered who the hell could tell what to expect. A good argument could be made he was in the company of the insane, spinning wild theories of cosmic forces. Aliens were said to be violating human thought and competing for the affections of an insignificant group of humanoids somehow of great import to them. God! Ronan had abandoned the superstition of alien visitation years ago.

He shifted back to the window to watch the Altiplano passing by as the bus careened close to their waiting hotel. Belief in a decision meant to determine the future course of human life had never taken root in Ronan. Until the dreams had made him want to believe. And if it were true, Angie would see him for the hero he was. As for Artemis's desideratum, as far as Ronan was concerned, the world had already gone to hell. Except for Angie. She was waiting for him to step up. She deserved a hero. If his visions were accurate, he would have his chance to be one.

*

Pope Peter II had no memory of boarding the plane. The last thing he could recall was being in Washington, D.C. watching vain attempts to resuscitate the President of the United States. Peter rubbed his eyes, waiting for his mind to clear. He glanced to his right, looking for Cardinal Ritchars, who should have been with him if they were headed back to Rome. But Peter was alone on a private jet headed who knew where. He stood and steadied himself before making his way down the aisle to the cockpit door. The handle yielded unexpectedly, and Peter called out to the pilot.

A pleasant, middle-aged man looked back at him and nodded. "We are landing to take on fuel, your eminence. Please return to the cabin and make yourself comfortable. We have another four or five hours before we reach our destination. You will find an ample supply of food and drink in the cabinets at the rear."

Peter felt a headache beginning at the back of his neck. *How can this be real?* A score of questions fought for prominence in his mind. "Who are you?" was the one that made it to voice.

The pilot kept his attention on the rising landing strip. "Armistead," he said without glancing at the pope. "Clive Armistead."

The disk at Peter's chest vibrated, and the pope tightened his grasp on the doorframe as the plane slowed, thrusting him to one side.

"I must insist you return to the cabin, your eminence. And fasten your seat belt. We are about to land."

Clutching the backs of leather seats, Peter made his way back to his seat and fastened the belt around his hips. He stared out the window straining to see something to tell him where he was. The words *Cheddi Jagan International Airport* appeared in bright-red letters across the top of a building as the plane touched down and taxied to a small hangar.

The pilot concluded the landing protocol, and Peter was engulfed in silence. He watched the pilot exit the plane without a word and disappear inside the metal building. Moments later, two men emerged and pulled a fueling hose to the plane. What seemed a long time later, the pilot reappeared and made a slow walking inspection before returning to the cockpit. Peter felt the plane lurch down the runway and then tilt up and climb into the clouds.

He racked his brain, trying to place Cheddi Jagan Airport on a mental globe. South America? Or China, perhaps, he mused; he had intended to go to China after meeting with President Hughes. He studied the terrain as the plane rose higher into the sky and selected the first possibility, although he had no idea why he was where he was or how he had come to be there.

Chapter Twenty

Pindata Sin awoke to find he was alone in an unfamiliar room. He didn't remember the landing in Bangladesh or the signing ceremony he had expected to attend. Pindata felt his forehead to see if he was feverish. The jungle was a dangerous place full of germs and viruses, most of which were still waiting to be discovered. He wondered if he'd picked up a virus in Myanmar.

His head felt cool and dry. He sat up and stared at his surroundings. The rough stone walls made the chamber more cave-like than a hotel. Pindata could not remember ever having been in a cave before. There was a bed, a chair, and a small table where the disk glimmered in the low light.

Alarm yielding to curiosity, Pindata got up quickly and secured the disk. He suddenly knew where he was—Bolivia, though he did not know why. Hearing music coming from nearby, he ventured into a narrow passageway. He was thirsty and wished to bathe. Cleanliness was everything.

He found a basin in the next chamber and rinsed his face and forearms, saying ritual prayers as he did. He dried himself with a small white towel and continued through the passageway following the music.

"Minister Pindata Sin, I believe." A short, squat woman in a black military uniform greeted him when he entered a large chamber. The room was richly appointed with a tapestry and pre-Columbian pieces he somehow mysteriously recognized.

"General Maria Vergara." Pindata had no idea how the woman's name found his lips. "How pleasant to meet you."

The woman smiled. "Your Spanish is impeccable, Minister. But you seem unaware you are speaking in it."

He was. The woman was addressing him in Khmer, though the movement of her lips did not match the words he heard. He reached into his pocket. "Could it be our ability to converse is a consequence of this most beautiful object?"

"Or this." Maria displayed a disk of her own. "We have each been given a portion of the world to conquer. It is a big world, Pindata; another has already arrived. I feel certain we will be joined by more."

"How many? How long must we wait?"

Maria sat behind the polished cumaru desk she had brought with other furnishings to enhance the cave. "You must have visions of your own, Minister. While you find your answers, you must excuse me. I have work to do."

Pindata wandered out of the confining cave onto a large, manicured grassy area and filled his lungs with the thin Altiplano air. He had followed his visions thus far, and the power behind them must have brought him to this place. He held the disk between his hands and asked for an explanation. In his mind he saw a large platform made of gray stones. The sky was alive with color, and a field of black-clothed troops were audience to a wondrous event.

*

Tiwanaku was just under an hour from their accommodations in La Paz. Artemis woke before dawn and slipped out to buy coffee and cocadas. The sweet, caramel cookies laden with bits of coconut and macadamia nuts would make a perfect breakfast for Lucy's sweet tooth. She noted a bakery just down the street from their hotel and walked through the cool morning air. She enjoyed the stillness, knowing it would give way to the ceaseless wind once the sun rose above the mountains. Streaks of yellow and pink had begun to appear.

Shopkeepers were arriving to ready their establishments for business, and delivery trucks rumbled past with boxes of colorful items bouncing in their backs. Artemis stopped at a newsstand and purchased a copy of a three-day-old newspaper in English. The headlines full of violence and misery seemed to be from a much older moment in history. Humanity had not learned much in the last five thousand years, she mused. Finding the bakery open even at this early hour, Artemis selected several additional items, since Strang and Ronan had arrived in the middle of the night, and headed back to the hotel.

Hearing Lucy splashing in the shower, Artemis set the breakfast on a small table and sat on the bed to wait. She left the coded message for Angie and wanted to ask if Keegan or Stefan had been maintaining contact but decided to wait. Concern for the young men swirled like mosquitos in her thoughts. She knelt and focused her mind. The image of a door appeared, and she sensed Stefan pacing. Using her mind, she nudged Stefan to perform a specific action. Then she explored the scene around them and cleared their path.

"I smell coffee." Lucy stepped out of the shower and leaned her head into the main room. "I knew that was where you went. And what are those delicious-looking treats?" Wrapped in a towel, Lucy strolled into the room and popped a cookie into her mouth. Sunlight filtered in through the curtains and made the water on Lucy's shoulders sparkle.

"Ah, I don't know all the names. The one you just ate is called a cocada." Artemis's gaze traced the soft curves of her lover's body as Lucy licked her fingers and selected a second treat. Artemis beat the second cookie to Lucy's mouth and claimed the sugared lips with her own. The towel slipped to the floor.

*

A constant wind swept the Altiplano as Artemis, Lucy, Strang, and Ronan completed the brief drive to the pre-Columbian site of Tiwanaku. They made an obligatory stop at the small Museo and, leaving their vehicle in the parking lot, split into two teams with Artemis and Strang going west to view the Akapana pyramid or what was visible of it. The pyramid had not been reconstructed save for a few resurrected walls. The main body of the structure rested beneath an enormous mound of dirt; the only clue to its true appearance was an artistic sketch engraved on a plaque set up to give visitors an idea of what lay beneath the tall, shapeless mound.

Lucy and Ronan continued on to the Kalasasaya, which, unlike the pyramid, had been largely reconstructed. They strolled about the sunken plaza with its curious sculpture heads embedded in the walls and then climbed to the Kalasasaya's long platform and looked down at the outline of various unfinished buildings laid out in a grid around them. Tiwanaku was a feast for the imagination more than the eyes, yet to be returned to its ancient glory. There were few tourists milling about. Most had taken shelter from the wind and thin air at the museum complex where they bought drinks and strolled about under the watchful eyes of uniformed soldiers.

Climbing the ramp on the western entrance of the Akapana, Artemis and Strang had the better view of the ruins. The plane stretched out, seemingly endless before them. In the distance were the peaks of the Andes Mountains running like a spine down the length of the continent. Closer were the huge stones of Puma Punku, a kilometer to the east and clearly visible from the top of the buried pyramid rising sixty feet above the ground. Strang reviewed a printout of the artist's rendering of what the monumental structure was thought to have looked like. The pyramid's walls consisted of terraces and a grand staircase leading to a large platform with a sunken court in the center.

"The court is shaped like the Chakana," Strang remarked, showing the drawing to Artemis.

"That's not really surprising." She nodded. "The Akapana was the spiritual center of the ancient city."

Strang scratched his chin. "I wonder if Lucy and Ronan have found anything of interest. At least the Kalasasaya is identifiable compared to this hill of dirt." He lifted an eyebrow. On the surface there wasn't much to indicate a structure existed. Strang pushed back the worry he may have led them astray once again. "Of course, as we well know many things may lay beneath the surface. May I inquire as to what you see, my dear?"

"Right now, I'd be pleased just to find Keegan and Stefan." Artemis looked around, inspecting the handful of tourists for familiar faces. "They should be here by now."

"All in good time," Strang assured her with a hand on her back. "It's up to the wunderkinds to find the precise place they are meant to be. Remember, we are merely the observers."

He felt her muscles tighten. Lucy and Ronan were visible in the inner courtyard of the massive Kalasasaya reconstruction. Lucy was studying the impressive Gateway to the Sun which had been placed there like a gate, although its original location was lost to history. Strang shook his head at the haphazard manner in which the site had been assembled. Science had taken a backseat to tourism, much like the sterile ruins of Mohenjo-daro.

Artemis shared Strang's disappointment. Worse, she wondered if the site was capable of performing its purpose after being stripped of its original structure. She could sense Ronan's restlessness as he roamed along the interior walls glancing at the massive stones. The young scientist was not engaged, and there was nothing in the ruins to wake his interest. If their guess had been wrong, there would be no time to recover. The fear all was lost sent a chill down her spine. And Artemis was overwhelmed with the feeling this was to be her last day with Lucy. She clung to Strang's arm for a moment until the terror passed.

"Come, my dear," Strang said. "I beseech you, have faith in us."

The foursome met up at the Sunken Temple on the next block and spent time walking along the interior walls, noting the numerous stone heads depicting a variety of human features and animals. With the sun sinking in the cloudless western sky, Strang suggested a trek to the Puma Punku ruins. Given the effect of the altitude on them, they piled back into the car for the short trip.

Puma Punku, "the door of the puma," was yet another extensive platform in an unreconstructed condition laid out on a north-south axis. The site bespoke some ancient disaster that had scattered massive granite stones for hundreds of meters, leaving only a barren platform where a magnificent monument had once stood. The entire site had also been ravaged by looters. Many of the damaged and weathered granite stones lay in heaps around a rectangular, terraced earthen mound faced with megalithic blocks. Within the walls was the Plataforma Litica, the largest stone in the entire Tiwanaku archeological site. Most mysterious of all were the scores of H-shaped granite blocks with finely drilled lines and holes. Weighing hundreds of tons and towering up to twenty feet, these stones dotted the red clay soil like pieces of a puzzle no one had yet solved. There was no written record to explain how they were assembled or how the preciseness of the many holes and corners had been accomplished.

Ronan walked along a row of crudely placed H blocks, intrigued by the milling. He took out a small magnifying glass and examined the sharp edges that had somehow been expertly shaped. "This wasn't done with chicken bones or copper tools. This is truly amazing work."

"How was it done?" Lucy asked, taking a look for herself. "I mean what else did the people have to work with?"

Ronan shrugged.

"Maybe people didn't do it at all!" The unexpected voice startled them.

Keegan stepped around the end block and laughed at their stunned faces. "I mean, everyone knows this place was a landing platform for ETs about a million years ago."

"Uh-huh," Artemis said, coming up behind Keegan and tapping him on the shoulder. "I thought you didn't believe in extraterrestrials."

It was Keegan's turn to jump at an unexpected voice. He spun about and grinned. "I don't. Or I didn't. Now I have no idea. Nothing is as it seems."

"True that," Ronan agreed.

"And not a thing is as it will be." Stefan approached and sandwiched his bulk between Lucy and Strang.

Lucy saw Artemis roll her eyes and smiled to see relief on her partner's face. The plan had worked. They were all assembled at the very place Artemis had wanted them to be. Once Angie arrived, they would finally be ready. Lucy sent a text to her daughter. "Come."

Artemis ran her tongue along her lips. It was now or never, she knew. She had brought the Harbinger children to their destiny. It was up to them to fulfill it. "Gentlemen, I suggest you comb every inch of this site and determine if anything speaks to you. Open up those reticular activating systems and find the reason you are here."

"We are here, madam, because you sent us here. You and Wolf decided X marks this spot." Keegan looked at Strang. "Well, it's a rather large spot. Could you give a few hints of what we are expected to find?"

"It's not what you find, gentlemen. It's what you sense. This place is meant to speak to you. Try listening."

Ronan detected a buzzing sound coming from Stefan's backpack. "I don't know about all these rocks, but that pack is speaking to me. What the hell is that, Stef? Your alarm clock?"

The group assembled around Stefan and waited for him to rummage through his pack. He pulled out the wooden box, and all heard the disk within it buzzing. Stefan shook the box and then retrieved the disk. He tapped it against the palm of his free hand. "I'll be damned."

Both Keegan and Ronan reached for the disk, but the taller Stefan lifted it above his head. "Oh, no. This is with me until I finish my research."

"The time for research has passed." Artemis put out her hand, and Stefan reluctantly went to hand over the prize, but the disk escaped his grasp and rose into the air. They watched it drift toward the platform and lower itself on the center stone.

Artemis leaped onto the platform and retrieved the now-silent object. She returned the disk to its wooden container and tucked the item in her pack.

"That was creepy," Keegan said. "Guess this is the right place."

Artemis extended her arms and attempted to conjure a vision of the past. The outline of a massive structure appeared in the air around her, drawn by an unseen hand. Puma Punku outlined as it had once existed. Opening her eyes, she lowered her arms, and the image of the ancient structure faded away.

"Does anyone have an explanation for that?" Ronan asked, the first to find his voice.

*

The rest of the day proved less fruitful. Artemis stopped reading the thoughts of the wunderkinds when her efforts only fed the sense of dread growing exponentially on its own. They drifted back to the hotel and congregated in one of the rooms to speculate over sandwiches and coffee. Stefan informed Artemis about the troop movements. Their equipment had been confiscated, he confessed, but given the military presence, it was doubtful the materials would have been of any use.

Keegan explained how they had managed to outwit the soldiers who took them into custody. Strange as it might seem, he explained, Stefan had opened what was supposed to have been a locked door, and they had simply walked away. After spending the night in a filthy room with guards roaming about nearby, Stefan had felt an urge to try the door. Finding it unlocked, he and Keegan walked out and continued unchallenged to their vehicle. The car had been stripped of their bags, but their passports and wallets lay on the seats. Keegan had started the engine and they drove away without being noticed.

Lucy glanced at Artemis, who sat listening with a slight smirk on her face. "I left a message for Angie. She should let us know when she'll be arriving."

The look on Artemis's face changed from amused to concerned. It was not at all clear to her Athena would come. Time was short. Even if Angie was already on her way, it was highly possible she might not arrive in time. Dread continued to grip Artemis's heart, and she wondered if she were already abandoned.

Strang invited Keegan and Stefan to bunk with him and Ronan for the night. The men accepted the offer, not eager to spend another night on their own. Then the three younger men headed out to see if any nightlife existed in the sleepy town. Barring that, the trio would settle for a liquor shop and anything suitably alcoholic to calm their nerves.

Strang lingered a while with the two women. He felt intensely troubled, and his face showed how strenuous he had found the day, mentally and physically. He put his hand on Artemis's cheek and wanted to say what was in his heart but left his thoughts unspoken. She could read them, even if he could not bring himself to put what he felt into words.

Returning to his room, Strang sat at the small desk and opened his laptop. He entered his passwords and downloaded three files from the Keck. The laptop chimed, and Strang took a deep breath before opening the first file. A picture began to form on the screen. Pixel by pixel the familiar image of the Great Rift took shape, still bereft of its jewel. The object had not returned. It occurred to Strang he was most likely going to die without ever knowing what the object had been or the nature of dark matter. The major quests of his life would go unresolved.

Strang took off his glasses and looked up, expecting to see Willa's urn on the mantel, before remembering where he was. So far from home. "Willa, my love, I believe I have discovered the true source of pain. It is not failure as I once believed. I have failed to solve my mysteries. I failed to find a cure for you. It is not the failure upon us now that pains me. It is the potential of loss." He rubbed the moisture from his eyes. "The loss of our entire world, Willa. What we have been. What we are. And what we could have become."

Voices in the hall drew him from his gloomy musing. He saw shadowy figures moving beyond the room's window and went to the door.

"She isn't going to give it to any of us," Ronan insisted, weaving slightly as he walked.

"I can get it." Keegan's voice was a pitch higher than normal, but the braggadocio was familiar.

Stefan folded his arms across his chest. "You are like snowmen in Hades. Temmie thinks you useless. Angie and I..."

A fist bounced off Stefan's chin. Strang opened his door to find Stefan's huge hands around Ronan's neck.

"Gentlemen." Strang announced his presence. "The world requires so much more from you."

*

As soon as they were alone, Artemis took Lucy's advice and sought the solace of a warm bath. She let the water flow over her, washing away the pinkish dust and relaxing muscles she hadn't realized she held clenched.

Lucy tidied up the small room, clearing the table and disposing of empty sandwich wrappers and cola cans. She smoothed the bed, pressing wrinkles from the sheets and tucking the edges to keep them taut. The heavy blanket folded neatly at the foot of the bed, Lucy fluffed the pillows and arranged them along the headboard.

She took her carry-on from the closet and withdrew several items she had secreted away. Putting a silky red chemise on a hanger, Lucy smiled at what the garment would do for her lover's shapely body. Then she took a lacy black teddy she'd brought for herself and laid it on the bed. Artemis had admired both the garments in a catalog they'd browsed months ago when the world had been normal and there had been time to savor being soulmates. She reached into the bathroom and hung the chemise on the back of the door for Artemis to find.

Night on the Altiplano was cold. Lucy closed the window, leaving an inch for fresh air to circulate in the room. She retrieved two small candles from her bag and set them on the table. The scent of island blossoms drifted through the room. The mood cried out for wine, and Lucy had considered buying some until she understood Artemis would not want to dull her mind for the next day. *No!* Lucy sighed. They were not going to think about tomorrow if she could help it. This night was for them, and she was doing everything she could to keep tomorrow away.

"Wow!" Artemis called, appreciating the garment Lucy had put out for her. "It's a little short, but it feels wonderful."

Artemis stepped into the room, her damp dark hair loose about her shoulders and the chemise hugging every curve.

"Wow right back at ya." Lucy bit her lip. Artemis looked astonishing. She shook her head and grabbed her teddy. "Be right back," she said, heading in to take a very quick shower herself.

Artemis took a deep breath and savored the fragrant air. A bowl of chocolates caught her eye, and she selected a favorite. She munched it as she brushed her hair and waited for Lucy. Her soulmate had done all this for her...for them. Artemis felt their connection wrap itself around her, almost convincing her—a love that had lasted for millennia could not perish.

Lucy tiptoed into the room, cupped Artemis's chin in her hand, and bent to kiss her. Artemis enfolded Lucy at the waist and brought her into her lap. The kiss was followed with another, and Artemis's warm hands roamed Lucy's torso, lifting the teddy to reach the soft, familiar skin beneath.

"Wait." Lucy stood up and posed. "At least take a good look at it first. I was hoping you'd like it."

Artemis smiled. "I like it. I really like it. Now let me take it off."

Lucy dropped the straps from her shoulders and the silky garment slid slowly down her body, guided by her lover's hands. She climbed onto Artemis's lap facing her lover and saw a blush climbing Artemis's neck. She leaned in and kissed the pulse point, feeling it jump while Artemis's fingers found interesting places to trace with her fingers.

Shedding her chemise, Artemis scooted back onto the bed. She cradled Lucy tightly against her. They melted together, their limbs entwined. Desire raced through Artemis. She wanted to touch every part of her lover, consume her with hands and mouth. A hunger for Lucy banishing all thought, she lost herself in the softness of Lucy's skin.

Lucy moaned as heat swept through her, enflamed by her lover's practiced touch. She rolled on her back, and a long leg slipped between her thighs. Dark hair tickled her shoulders as Artemis teased a nipple and then encased it in warm lips. Lucy squirmed and pressed her center against Artemis's thigh, her body wanting more. Artemis planted a trail of kisses from well-tended breasts to a quivering navel. She felt the temperature of Lucy's skin grow warmer in reaction to her touch.

Lucy lost herself in the intensity as Artemis let the sensations build, and they were both helpless in its grasp. She gripped strands of dark hair in her hands and bid her lover move lower. Her body rocked at Artemis's intimate touch and steady rhythm driving her desire higher. Release engulfed them both, and their bodies arched, their souls touching for an instant, sending waves of pleasure through them.

Artemis cradled Lucy in her arms as they lingered in the sensation of being joined. Their breathing slowed, and their hearts resumed a steady beat. Lucy stirred, shifting slightly to nestle her head in the hollow of Artemis's shoulder. The world began to reappear around them.

"Whatever happens, Temmie," Lucy said softly. "I am yours. Only yours. No future can change that."

Artemis hugged her lover, kissing the crown of Lucy's head. Ignoring what her mind insisted, she spoke what her heart believed. "Wither thou goest, I will go."

Chapter Twenty-One

Artemis awoke with the knowledge the final day had come. Without getting out of bed or looking past the window, she knew. She felt Lucy curled around her and hugged her partner gently. *There is a moment just before the die is cast when all things are possible. When the choice is yet unmade.* It was a moment of clarity and peace, and Artemis found herself suspended in such a moment as she listened to the rain begin.

The Others were a consciousness unlike the one from which Artemis had come. The Others were the yin of creation. A force opposed to all she had ever known, the balance to the yang. The Others were hierarchy and fear. Artemis was the spawn of rhythm and love. The tension between the collectives was the progenitor of a universe created in duality—an omniscient ballet of light and dark. The mind of God.

Artemis resolved to trust in everything she knew about the universe. In all Ze'us had taught her. In Lucy. Hearing a soft moan, she found Lucy's bright-hazel eyes peering up at her and smiled.

"Good morning, sleepyhead. It's going to be a big day." Artemis kissed Lucy's forehead and pushed back the covers.

"Why is it you look beautiful in the morning?" Lucy yawned and retrieved the blanket, pulling it up to her chin. "It isn't time yet, is it?"

Time. Artemis felt her breath catch. There was no more time to give. "There is nothing I'd love more than spending the day in bed with you, my love," she said softly as she forced herself to leave the bed, refusing to accept it was for the final time. She stood and fought the fear trying once again to consume her.

"Oh, all right!" Lucy sighed. "I suppose we've come all this way to save the world. Might as well get it over with."

Artemis pulled the covers away and offered Lucy a hand up. Lucy stared at her. "Oh my God, Temmie, you're glowing!"

"Am I?"

"Yeah. Just a little, but you are glowing." Lucy sat up and rubbed her eyes. "No, wait. Now you're not."

Artemis took a deep breath. A number of conditions could cause her essence to spontaneously manifest. The one she profoundly hoped was that her collective was near.

Helping Lucy to her feet, Artemis forced a grin. "It's just my sunny disposition. Come on. Let's get dressed."

The plan was to attempt a practice run in the morning and wait for Angie to arrive later in the day. The three teams would go to the small restaurant near the museum for breakfast and then make their way on foot to Puma Punku. The poor weather was actually a blessing since it would keep the majority of tourists away, leaving them uninterrupted access to the place they agreed had to be the communication portal.

Artemis and Lucy dressed in tourists' slacks and light jackets. Lucy chatted about the weather, and Artemis interjected odd bits of information, pretending her thoughts were not elsewhere. The rooms were paid for a week. They should leave their things in the room except for one phone. The rain was unexpected this time of year. Lucy chalked up Artemis's disjointed dialog to nerves and merely smiled as if she understood. Given her own nerves were rioting, Lucy did.

Strang appeared at the door, damp hair matted to his head and a tray of adequate-smelling coffee in one hand. He told them about the scuffle the wunderkinds had indulged in the night before and shook his head, sending drops of water into the air.

"I recommend we each take one of them in hand and hope the rain dampens their combative humor." Strang punctuated the suggestion with a boxing gesture. "When I was procuring the coffee, I could hear the sound of guns in the distance. It portends an even more difficult day than we had anticipated." He glanced at Artemis and realized the inadequacy of his supposition.

"Were they that drunk?" Lucy asked, coaxing a brush through her hair.

Strang shook his head. "No, no. They were merely bumping chests, I think the saying goes. Each was interested in extracting the accursed disk from you, Temmie."

"It's staying with me today," Lucy announced, slipping the disk, sans box, into her jacket. "We can't let any of you fall under its influence. I on the other hand am a mere observer and of no real importance in this endeavor."

"You are the most important person of all, Lucy. You more than anyone are what humanity should be," Strang told her.

A blush tinted Lucy's cheeks. "Temmie. You are what we will become. The gods willing and the creek don't rise." She gave a little chuckle. "You are the choice we will make."

Strang set aside his coffee. "She's correct, my dear goddess. You are the essence of what we lesser mortals aspire to be. There is no better decision than to join with you. For whatever difference it makes, I choose you without a modicum of reservation. I am certain the wunderkinds will as well."

Artemis nodded, but the look in her eyes told him she did not share his confidence. He ran his fingers through his hair and glanced at Lucy, who sat leaning against her lover's shoulder. What a cruel result it would be if the decision went the other way, separating the two soulmates for eternity, he thought. It was easier to grasp the pain of loss between two lovers than to comprehend the catastrophe which could befall mankind.

*

Keegan, Stefan, and Strang selected the vehicle Stefan had rented in Cuzco. The others piled into the car Artemis had acquired in La Paz with Ronan volunteering to drive the short distance to the restaurant. The small café was empty due to the early hour and the inclement weather. They split up and selected tables as distant as possible in the tiny dining room. Appetites were modest, but they ate slowly, observing the flow of troop carriers on the road headed to the border with Peru. Keegan questioned if they shouldn't just return to the hotel. The idea didn't make it past Strang's stern frown.

A hand signal from Artemis indicated it was time to execute the next step. Stefan and Lucy left first. They paid their bill and then, bypassing the parking lot, began a leisurely stroll to the Puma Punku ruins. Strang and Keegan waited ten minutes before following them.

When it was time for Artemis and Ronan to leave, the intermittent flow of traffic in front of the café suddenly shifted. Trucks loaded with Chilean troops began returning from the border. Shouting in panic, the troops raced their vehicles through the Tiwanaku site, toppling pillars and plowing their armored vehicles into delicate excavations. The pyramid mound became a ramp for the trucks to challenge as they dug deep grooves into the rain-slicked soil.

Rockets shot overhead, exploding like fireworks above the ruins. Artemis saw Lucy take cover amid the andesite blocks at the edge of the huge stone platform. She took off at a run, her long legs giving her incredible speed, and soon left Ronan trailing behind. She bowled over soldiers in her way and catapulted over a row of H blocks.

Artemis reached Lucy as a rocket fell aside the restaurant, causing a wall to collapse and a groan to rise from the retreating soldiers. Lucy caught sight of Keegan waving from behind a line of H blocks twenty yards behind them. Somehow, Stefan and Ronan had made their way to Keegan despite the pandemonium. Artemis saw their position was precarious with more and more black uniforms heading to the cover of the platform.

She searched the field for a place to regroup. Strang waved from a low depression far to the left. Grabbing Lucy, Artemis motioned to the three stragglers and took off, using her strength to surmount a pile of H blocks with Lucy on her back. Explosions shot rocks and dirt into the air, making it difficult for Keegan, Ronan, and Stefan to cross the uneven field. They joined the women and Strang, gasping for air, their faces flecked with muddy uncertainty.

Peruvian troops, convinced of victory, poured into the ruins at Tiwanaku, shooting their rifles in the air and laughing as they amused themselves taking potshots at the carefully reconstructed walls of the Kalasasaya. The wind punished the land, sending debris raining throughout the sites and driving the routed Bolivian soldiers back to their vehicles.

"What in hell are we supposed to do now?" Ronan yelled above the roar of the wind. His cheeks were red from the exertion, and he fumbled through his pockets for his cell phone. "I don't suppose they have a 9-1-1 system here?"

"Not likely, boy-o." Stefan laughed. "We are in deep doodoo."

"Shit!" Keegan corrected him. "You can say shit. In fact, you should say shit. Real men say shit."

"Shit then," Stefan said, a toothy white smile spreading beneath his dark mustache.

Ronan crab-walked to the end of the depression they were huddled in. Artemis yanked him to his knees.

"What are you doing?" she snapped, her hand cinching his belt.

Seeing the fierceness in her darkened eyes made him catch his breath. "Looking for the good guys."

"We are the good guys." Strang relieved Artemis and took over restraining Ronan.

"Well, they are definitely not the good guys," Keegan said, settling back against one of the large, smooth stones strewn along the ravine. He had seen the soldiers in a vision. He clutched Artemis's arm and told her worse was to come if they didn't leave. Thus far the soldiers were not interested in pursuing them. And the troops continued to pour in from the north. A caravan appeared to the east, rounding the edge of Lake Titicaca, horns blaring and gunshots whistling through the air. The rain had ceased, but only Lucy noticed. She pointed to the sky. A translucent orange light radiated above the chaos. Streaks of red and purple shot across the horizon, and the clouds roiled, sending storm-force wind across the scene.

The caravan reached the entrance to Puma Punku. A limousine emerged from amid the military trucks. The limo drove forward a little way and stopped to let its occupants out at the base of the ruin. A woman was the first to emerge from the vehicle. She opened her hands, releasing a small disk which rose into the air and emitted a high-pitched tone. Artemis and her companions watched in horror as tan-clad Peruvian soldiers turned to dust in an instant.

"I'll be damned." Keegan whistled as he watched two men emerge from the limousine.

"Not if you perform the role you are meant to," Strang said, tightening his hold on the whimpering Ronan. He smiled at Artemis. "I believe we've found the remaining disks."

"Yes. I saw these people before in my mind." Stefan nodded. "They were dressed in white, red, and black. And they each have a disk. I saw them on the terrace holding the disks above their heads. They were..."

"...waiting for the fourth one." Artemis finished the sentence. "They know it's here."

A cheer rose across the Altiplano. Vergara shouted in victory. The pope gazed into the sky as streaks of silver slithered through the clouds, leaving dark trails in the vivid orange. Pindata felt a sense of power course through him. They were the new gods of a new world.

The ground trembled as huge andesite stones rose and assembled themselves, reconstructing the ancient ruin. The three disk owners climbed the freshly restructured stairway to the platform and called into the wind for all the soldiers to assemble. The command made its way through the celebrating army. Black-uniformed men stopped their rampaging and made their way to the Puma Punku.

"Give me the disk," Ronan demanded. "I must have the disk."

Stefan punched Ronan in the face, sending him sliding on his back in the red mud. Shaking his stinging hand, Stefan sank beside Lucy. "I'm glad Angie is not here. She will survive. That is enough for me to know now."

Strang sat back cross-legged and fought for breath in the thin air. He looked older than Lucy had ever seen him, and she patted his shoulder.

"We have known love, Lucinda. In that we are the lucky ones. It has been my great joy to call you and the goddess friend. Whatever happens, please know you both—and Angie of course—have given me purpose for which I am eternally grateful."

Lucy wrapped her arms around him and hugged with all her strength. Ronan moaned and came around, his head pounding viciously. He crawled over to Lucy and grabbed her arm.

"Give me the disk." Ronan coughed as he spoke. "If you don't, I'll play this, and they'll destroy you." He held his cell phone up and then tapped the screen, activating a few bars of the melody he had created. "It's the opposite of the tune Keegan used to listen to. Those people will react just like the disk."

Lucy felt her jacket pocket vibrate violently at the sound. Ronan turned up the volume only to have Artemis nearly break his arm and take the phone.

"Nah, nah." She waggled a finger and then slammed the phone against a rock. "The disk doesn't like your taste in music." She retrieved the disk from Lucy and held it fast in her hand.

"Can't say as I blame it," Keegan pointed out, turning to Ronan. "But you should know, it's the frequency, not the melody, stupid." They heard Strang erupt into laughter.

*

Angie waited for the soldiers to withdraw to Puma Punku before mounting the dirt slope to the top of the Akapana. She walked to the center of the mounded area where the sunken court lay partially exposed and then looked out over the Altiplano. She had expected to find Artemis and the rest at the pyramid, but the plateau was empty. Then she saw them huddled in a ravine halfway between the reconstructed platform and the pyramid. Three figures were staring at the strange sky. Bolts of lightning seared lines across the saffron-colored clouds, and the shadow in her head pushed forward.

"Artemis, you tenderhearted fool. Here. You are meant to be here." Athena felt the air quaver beside her, and a familiar figure materialized. "Hestia. They have come."

"As I predicted they would," the dark-haired goddess responded. She was aglow, resplendent in an earth-tone toga, her wavy hair blowing freely in the strong wind.

"It is time," Athena said, viewing the destruction all around. "Father wishes us to return."

Hestia cupped her sister's face in both hands. "Not yet, Athena. There is one more thing you can do."

Waving her hand, Athena caused the wind to calm and the sky to cease its turbulence. The army of soldiers froze in place; the three figures were halted at the top of the staircase.

*

Stillness. Artemis looked at the stalks of grass, once whipping in the wind, suddenly standing rigid. Strang sat motionless, one arm extended upward and his mouth open in silent laughter. Lucy's eyes stared at Artemis, but they were fixed, unseeing. Keegan, Ronan, and Stefan were stopped in midmotion. *Athena!*

Artemis drifted through space, passing undetected amid the frozen soldiers. She watched her companions gliding beside her, their bodies never changing their positions. This was not death, she knew. Death was liberating, freeing, and one was conscious of what is happening. This was different. Time had stopped its flow. They descended to a stone floor.

"Your aim went wrong, Ar'*tem*'is." Hestia embraced her. "This is the temple you sought."

Relief flooded through Artemis at the sight of her sisters. Radiant Hestia appeared exactly as the goddess had been before the Eed'en had abandoned Earth. Artemis's body reacted to their presence, sharing their energy, restoring every memory, every power she had once possessed. Athena stood tall and strong, but contained in Angie's body, the essence of the goddess radiated only a faint glow, looking almost dull next to the radiant Hestia. Artemis saw that her own body, too, glowed faintly. She was Ar'*tem*'is once again, and it felt glorious. She cast an appreciative look to Athena, a question in her bright-blue eyes.

"I couldn't leave you at their mercy, Artemis. The Others have no mercy," Athena explained. "Your friends are safer here, where you were meant to be. They will be absorbed with no further damage once I awaken them."

"It is not decided yet," Hestia chided Athena. "The collectives can wait a little longer for the choice," she reassured Artemis. She took the disk and traced the ancient map etched on its back. "This belongs to my islands, does it not?"

*

They awakened to see three luminous women staring at them. Strang surveyed their position and realized they were atop the Akapana mound inside a portion of the Chakana-shaped court. He shook Ronan, who looked around, stunned at the unfamiliar surroundings. Keegan studied the two women standing beside Artemis. One was Angie, although he could not explain the faint glow of her skin. His mind resisted, but he had no reason to deny what he saw.

Artemis offered her hand to Lucy, who was seated next to Strang. Lucy grinned, delighted to find Angie had joined them and wondering momentarily at her daughter's odd appearance.

"Everyone is glowing now," Lucy remarked. "How did you bring us here? You and your friend? Is she the one you asked me to find all those years ago?"

"No." There was no simple way to explain. Artemis bent and answered Lucy with a kiss.

Stefan completed the stride he'd been taking and stumbled on the stone floor. He found his footing only to have his knees go weak when he realized he was not where he had just been. "Well, shit!"

Keegan chuckled. "Now you say shit? We're saved! There's no cause to curse."

"You are not saved," Hestia told them. "It is time to make your choice."

"I choose you," Lucy said. "For however long infinity is, I choose to be with you."

Stefan moved to embrace Angie but was stopped by the harsh look he received. Athena narrowed her eyes at him, and he cocked his head, failing to understand. Folding his arms across his chest, he twerked his mustache from side to side and turned his gaze to the Altiplano below dotted with the frozen army. "I don't understand. This can't be real." He looked imploringly at Angie. "Are we real? I want for us to be real."

"And you?" Hestia held the disk out to Keegan. "This was meant to be yours. It has been waiting for you to accept its power. You are the scion of warriors, Keegan Montock. The pride of a people I have loved for thousands of years. You are the true son of Mu."

"Aw, no you don't. The disk is mine!" Ronan lunged at Hestia, dislodging the disk, which flew from the goddess's hand and impacted Angie on the side of her head. The blow caused her to collide with the stone wall. Her body slid limply to the floor, the disk landing beside her at Ronan's feet.

Lucy cried out, restrained from rushing to her daughter by Artemis's arm about her waist. Her eyes on the disk, Artemis tried to will the object to come to her.

"Let me go!" Lucy sobbed, beating her fist against Artemis's shoulder.

Strang ran his fingers through his hair and stared at the young woman who had called him father. He started to go to her, but his legs refused to move. He knew the soldiers would soon overwhelm them, felt the triumph of their masters ready to ascend the distant platform, and there was nothing he could do to change it. *Willa, my love, we have failed.*

Ronan knelt and touched the deep gash on Angie's head. He slumped to the floor and stretched out his legs. He gathered her into his arms, tears filling his eyes. He picked up the disk and held it up for all to see.

"The disk... It's meant for me, Ronan," Keegan stuttered, his own eyes wide with shock. He extended a shaky hand, asking for the object's return.

Artemis held Lucy firmly in place, preventing her from collapsing. She felt the agony surging through her. Her eyes met Hestia's, and she knew there was no more time.

Stefan's heart shattered at the sight of Angie pale and lifeless in Ronan's arms. It was just as he had feared. Just as his vision had predicted. He groaned. The Harbinger was a curse. Knowing had not been enough to prevent it from happening. He saw an apparition emerge from Angie's body. The ghostly shape drifted across the stone floor and took form beside Hestia.

Athena, clothed in aureate armor, stared across the field to Puma Punku. "I cannot hold this moment for much longer." Athena addressed Artemis. "You have mere moments. We must return to the collective before the choice is completed."

Hearing those words, Lucy looked up at Artemis, her face a mask of grief. "Must I lose you both?"

"Go!" Artemis shouted at her sisters. "Tell Father I love him, but I belong here with them." Her blue eyes focused tenderly on Lucy. "With her. Even if it's only for a moment more."

*

Athena and Hestia were gone. Artemis released Lucy and mounted the low rim of the sunken court and checked to see if the army remained in place. Sensing time inching forward, she returned to find Ronan gripping the disk at his chest. All he had to do was raise it, and the Others would acknowledge the choice. But his attention was centered on Angie's body.

Artemis ran to the center of the court. The pyramid was the key. It would amplify what Keegan and Stefan chose. Summoning all her strength, she raised her arms and called the stones forth. The dirt beneath them began to fall away. Stones rose from their resting places and reassembled into terraced walls. The pyramid of Akapana assembled beneath them, pristine and glorious, a sacred temple to the gods as it was meant to be. The air began to stir, growing into a wind that swept the dust of ages away. Below, across the Altiplano, the army awakened, and time resumed its agonizingly slow progress forward.

Artemis looked at the three young men who must make their choice. The army would be upon them soon. The three owners of the disks were about to speak, and the Others would hear them.

Stefan sank to his knees and gently touched Angie's cheek. He glared at Ronan. Stefan wanted to hate him. He wanted to beat the life from him, but he could not take his eyes from Angie. He flexed his fists at his sides. Artemis's voice reached out to him, filling his mind. *Do not give in to hate, Stefan. Think of the love you shared with Angie. Let yourself feel it. Your power is greater than theirs.*

Stefan clutched Ronan's shoulder. "It comes to this, boy-o. Which do you choose? Angie or the disk?"

"Are you all insane?" Ronan raged. "I know the human mind. I know what choice our species would make without the interference of these...these creatures." He glared at Artemis, the disk feeling hot in his hand. "It is in our blood, our history. We are conquerors. Can't you feel it? Join with me and we will rule in hell." He moved to raise the disk, but Keegan grabbed his arm.

"I never was much of a joiner," Keegan admitted with an awkward grin. "And I don't know the human mind. But you loved Angie. And I want to believe love is stronger than the army down there, stronger than fear or hate."

Ronan laid Angie gently on the stone floor. She looked so peaceful. He did love her, and he knew the disk could not bring her back. He stood and gazed across the field to Puma Punku, where three figures were lifting their disks to the angry sky. He winced as the disk in his own hands grew hot. Sighing, Ronan held the disk out to Keegan.

"Naw. It may have been meant for me, but I don't want it any longer. I'd make a dreadful king." Keegan shrugged and felt Strang's hand settle on his shoulder.

"What is your decision, gentlemen?" Strang asked.

The three young men looked up at the sky, each making a decision for the future they desired. Their decision was private, personal. They did not speak for their species or their planet. They were representatives by chance and ability, not appointed to their task. They understood where the two paths led, and each chose the future course humanity was destined to prefer. *When times are at their worst, human beings are at their best.*

A rumble traveled across the Altiplano. The sky opened; orange clouds rolled back before a blinding burst of light. The wind ceased. Then the sound of onrushing soldiers stilled into the silence.

"It appears the choice is made," Strang said to Artemis. "Which consciousness do you suppose was pleased?"

Lucy didn't care to know. She held Angie in her lap and caressed the girl's forehead. Taking hold of Angie's hand, she felt fingers react to her grasp. Artemis was beside them then, checking the wound and calling to Stefan. Artemis leaped to the ground and raced for the nearest vehicle.

Strang and Keegan watched as the soldiers pushed forward. Behind them, Pope Peter screamed as the disk exploded above his head, igniting his robes. A bolt of lightning struck the disk in Minister Sin's hands, instantly reducing both to ash. General Vergara hurled her disk into the fleeing soldiers. It spun and dove, piercing the ground. The Altiplano around the whole of Puma Punku opened and swallowed Vergara with her army.

"By the gods!" Strang stared at the clearing sky. "Willa, my love. I believe the good guys won."

*

"So, is everything supposed to be different now?" Keegan asked, slowly making his way down the resurrected staircase. His head swiveled to see what had changed other than the Akapana. Nothing appeared different. Even Puma Punku was as it had been before, granite rocks dotting the barren scrub around a low, destroyed platform.

Stefan swept past him, Angie's limp body in his arms. Lucy managed to keep up, her hand locked on her daughter's. Angie was barely alive, her fingers still curled about her mother's. Neither was willing to let go. Artemis pulled a Jeep to the bottom of the staircase, helped them load the stricken woman, and then sped off to the *centro de salud*. The one-story building was on the edge of Tiwanaku, a rustic medical center with none of the resources needed to assist them. Angie was given fluids by IV and placed on a gurney to await the helicopter Strang had summoned to transport them to La Paz.

Strang stood on the porch watching the sky and marveled at the crystal-blue color. The angry storm clouds had evaporated in an instant once the choice had been made. His mind alternated between visions of the moment Angie had fallen and images of the horrified reactions of each person as it happened. They had reacted with love, not fear. Strang stuck his hands in his pockets and shook his head. It could easily have gone the other way.

Ronan sat huddled in a corner of the sunken court. He couldn't reconcile what he'd done or the events he'd witnessed. He hugged his knees and pondered the Akapana rising at Artemis's command and the utter destruction of the charging army. The image of Athena emerging from Angie's body was the most difficult image for Ronan to comprehend. And the other goddess—had she thrown the disk intentionally to release Athena? They had glowed, he remembered, Artemis with them.

Ronan wiped the tears from his dirty face and got to his feet. He heard sirens in the distances and noted a group of locals approaching, no doubt drawn to see for themselves the enormous pyramid risen in their midst. He passed townspeople on the stairs, ignoring the questions and the astonishment on their faces.

What was there to say, he wondered. Who would believe the world had just been admitted to heaven?

Chapter Twenty-Two

They'd been waiting for Angie to be transported to a hospital in La Paz. Artemis stepped out on the porch of the small clinic to watch for the helicopter. Hearing it approaching, she opened the clinic door and stepped into a wide, illuminated passageway. The walls glowed with a subtle amber light, easy on the eyes but doing little to explain their sudden appearance. She dusted her hands and let the dizziness clear in her head. Her first thought was of Lucy, who would be frantic wondering where Artemis had gone. Steadying her focus, Artemis looked about and realized where she was. Eed'en. Her father's vessel!

"Athena!" she muttered, certain her sister had been involved in the unexpected abduction. "This is not the time!"

The last was issued in a full-throated growl that echoed down the metal walls, but there was no response. Artemis made her way to a door at the end of the hall where a familiar form was waiting.

Leto greeted her daughter with a radiant smile and closed the distance between them to wrap motherly arms around her in a warm embrace. The woman's joy overwhelmed Artemis as the sense of being cherished washed over her. Five thousand years dissolved into ether. She was home.

Loosening her hold, Leto stepped back to take in the vision before her. "How beautiful you are, Artemis!" There was an amused twinkle in Leto's gaze. "You have your father's eyes, my daughter. Yes, but the rest, the rest is me."

Artemis searched her mother's face, testing the sincerity of the embrace after all that had passed. "Is Ze'us here?" she asked, her emotions roiling between happiness and apprehension with a note of child-like chagrin. "I mean is this why I've been brought here? To answer for..."

"Can you not just accept a mother's joy at seeing her little girl again, Artemis?" Leto chided gently, taking her daughter's arm and moving them to the center of the translucent space surrounding them.

"I am pleased to see you, Mother. More than I can express." As she spoke, a smile emerged unprompted. "But I am needed somewhere else just now."

Leto issued a subtle laugh. "Your friends are quite fine, Artemis. They will survive a little while without you. I have been denied your company for more than two of Earth's cycles about its sun. Surely I am permitted to welcome my daughter back."

"Two...years?" Artemis was disoriented for a moment. "Ah, of course. Time is relative. The differential for you would have been far shorter than the passage of time on Earth." She looked up sheepishly at her mother. "I didn't even consider that. But it has been a very long time for me."

Leto settled on a long, padded bench in the center of the room and waited for Artemis to join her. "You have no idea how worried I have been. How much I've missed you. Hearing your struggles whenever your thoughts reached me was a torment like no other. I was not permitted to respond, but my heart shattered a thousand times. I felt you slipping further and further away." She gently touched Artemis's face with the tips of her slender fingers. "Even your father was concerned, not that he would ever admit it."

Artemis felt a jolt in her gut and lowered her head. "I assume he is still angry with me?"

Leto brushed a strand of dark hair from her daughter's brow. "He was never angry, child. You are Ze'us's daughter. He loves you." She paused, sensing Artemis's guilt. "Extraordinary how much you are like him."

Artemis looked down at her hands, lacing and unlacing her fingers. "But I went against his wishes! I defied him and stayed on Earth when he commanded everyone to leave. I have never even dared to hope he might forgive me."

A feathery laugh filled the air, and Leto took Artemis's hand between her own. "There was never anything to forgive, child. I assumed you would have realized by now. Ze'us intended for you to stay. It was part of his great conspiracy to reclaim the humans." Her voice was tinged with a fleck of anger. "I have never understood the appeal of this particular primitive race of beings. To my mind Earth is but a single bit of sand in an infinite universe. But your father loves it and its people." She flashed a rueful smile. "Ze'us is quite possessed of love, you know."

Artemis blinked at her mother's words and thought of Lucy. *Yes, love possesses one beyond explanation.* But that was not the issue foremost in her mind.

"What do you mean reclaim them?"

Leto's countenance darkened for a moment. Artemis needed to be given the truth if she was to be freed of a guilt she did not deserve to carry. Only then would the fractured family be repaired. Drawing a breath, Leto related the story of how an object had been found in one of the mining operations. A small metal disk buried deep in the ground waiting to be discovered. Not by Ze'us but by humans once they were advanced enough to join the Others. The object had taken Ze'us into a rage.

"It meant this planet and its pleasing—to him, at least—inhabitants had already been claimed by a consciousness powerful enough to rival ours. There had been ample evidence even before the disk appeared if your father had only looked. The physical violence of the planet, the fact species preyed upon each other in a hierarchical structuring so antithetical to our kind. There was only one way the Others could be thwarted."

Artemis's heart began to race. *Ze'us knew the Others had been first to discover Earth. That was the true reason he abandoned them so abruptly.* She closed her eyes as if to shield herself from further information she wasn't certain she wished to receive and turned pain-filled eyes to her mother.

Leto held tight to her daughter's hand, regretting the turmoil coursing through her. "Once the disk was discovered, your father knew there was only one course to be followed. One that would defy the nature the Others had instilled them."

"He gave the humans something to help them choose a different path," Artemis replied. "Ze'us gave them a tool—the Harbinger—enabling them to discern the consequences of that choice."

"He did more than that." The raw bitterness in Leto's voice stunned Artemis. "Ze'us could not bring himself to abandon the humans. So instead, he gave his daughter, our daughter, to prepare them. I objected. But Hera was only too pleased to see you sacrificed and my heart torn to shreds. At my pleading Hestia and Athena agreed to watch over you."

Memories of Ze'us's wife clawed forward in Artemis's head. Her mother's tormentor evidently had found a means to avenge a faithless husband's fondness for his concubine and their offspring. Earth, this insignificant bit of matter, had become a competition between more entities than she could have imagined. When she raised her eyes, Artemis found her mother composed and staring fondly at her.

"You did as your father wished, child. And in so doing you were victorious for us all." Leto stood and motioned to her daughter. "Come. Your father is eager to see you."

"Now?" Artemis asked, stunned at the prospect.

"Of course." Leto gave Artemis a smile that rivaled the one with which she had greeted her daughter. "Don't you remember how Ze'us loves a victory? Especially when he manages to take all the credit!"

Artemis simply nodded as she rose to follow. She remembered. She remembered everything now that the final pieces had been put in place. She was Artemis, daughter of Ze'us, child of a consciousness that created the universe. Goddess of the Hunt. Soulmate to Lucy. Heir to peace and love and immortality.

*

Doctor Wolfgang Strang spent the week following the events in Bolivia performing behaviors he had never previously been inclined to do. He cleared his office. Removing every file. Shredding every report collected in forty years, the research having become irrelevant to him. And when he had purged himself of every photo, every scrap of paper, every unsolved mystery and random speculation, Strang settled in a chair and wept tears of joy. He was free.

Transition was an emotional experience long before it registered in the left side of the human brain. Strang had stepped into heaven, leaving all else behind, save for Willa's urn. Willa, after all, was a part of him from which his heart would never be separated.

Drying his tears, Strang settled back in his chair and set his gaze on the silent urn.

"I think it was Keegan who observed nothing appeared at first to have changed. The lad saw the damage to the Altiplano and the towering pyramid Artemis had resurrected, and he expected more. I think he may have anticipated trumpeting angels or flying aliens in those first moments as the shock dissipated. He did confess the vibrance of the sky once the clouds withdrew and the keenness of his senses returned. But he attributed all that to his overwrought nervous system and residual adrenaline."

Strang lifted his arm and spun his hand. "Poor fellow. Miracles flowing all around him and he is too blind to detect them." He made a humming noise as he thought. "I see them, Willa. The miracles. Do you know what I see when I look up into the night sky now? Stars! Isn't that astonishing? Not spectrum analysis or an overlay of calculations. Neither distance nor composition. I see only stars, wondrous bits of light twinkling happily back at me. Precisely where I mean them to be. Within my reach at last."

He chuckled. "In short, my love. I see what you always saw. A universe ordered by a consciousness of which we are an eternal part."

Shaking his head, Strang admitted the transition was proceeding according to everyone's personal ability to accept it. Becoming attuned to the consciousness that created reality was not an instant happening. *One must get accustomed to heaven as it reveals itself.*

"Willa, my darling, I am going to skip supper this evening and go to bed." Perchance to dream, he thought, knowing he would find his Willa there. He hefted his body stiffly from the chair.

*

Pele went to the reef's edge and tossed a lei of flowers into the surf. The sea was calm, and the susurrus of the trade winds pleased her ears. She had embraced her brothers and feasted on the joy of their return. Paradise was saved. She thought of Artemis and the rest. Prophecy had eluded her at the end, but only made the decision all the more wondrous.

This was a fine world, a rare and precious island in the vast universe. Pele was grateful it had joined with them. She waded into the gentle surf and watched the wrasse dart around her legs. The water was as pure as she had seen it in thousands of years. It sparkled and played as she passed. A dolphin approached, emitting a string of clicks and whistles. Pele reached down and gently touched her visitor's head. A sensation passed through her. The intelligent creature was thanking her. It knew a choice had been made. It knew all the species of Earth had been saved.

Pele petted the dolphin. *"Aloha nui loa,"* she replied.

Life was all around her in a thousand forms experiencing the wonder of existence, linked atom by atom to the whole of what was. No longer bound to the single planet, Hestia stretched her essence, and the universe answered. All she saw was peace in an endless future.

Chapter Twenty-Three

"You know what, Temmie?" Lucy said, experiencing a wave of déjà vu watching Artemis drop a load of freshly dried laundry on the bed. "This is what we were doing this time last year when the whole thing started."

"The whole thing as in saving the world?" Artemis arched a dark eyebrow. "Life goes on."

Lucy shrugged. It was the simple, day-to-day activities of life that made it real. She went over and gave Artemis a hug.

"What's this for?" Artemis asked, setting aside a pair of shorts to return the embrace.

Lucy stroked her partner's cheek with the back of her hand and looked into her pale, mesmerizing eyes. She ran her fingers through the wisps of hair at Artemis's temple.

"I have some bad news," she said, feeling Artemis stiffen in response. "Your hair is turning gray."

"It is not." Artemis pulled away.

Lucy laughed. "Yes, it is. You're going to look like a proper grandmother. Good thing too. We wouldn't want Angie Junior to get confused when she tries to figure out who's in which generation."

"Angie Junior, huh. Are you so sure the baby is a girl?" Artemis teased. The baby wasn't due for another three months. Artemis knew precisely who the child would be, but she kept the knowledge to herself. Stefan and Angie wanted to be surprised.

"Yes. I am sure," Lucy said, returning to her laptop. "What do you think we should get Wolf for his birthday this year? And don't tell me to look for something useless. We know how that turned out."

Artemis folded a T-shirt and thought for a minute. "How about a new straw hat, although he seems irrationally dedicated to the ratty old thing he wears?"

"Too late," Lucy said, clicking a key. "I just ordered a telescope for him."

"A what?" Artemis was amazed. "Lucy, he's not interested in all that scientific stuff any longer. He's content to just be or something to that effect. Told me so just the other day. Besides, a backyard telescope won't show him much."

Lucy folded her arms. "Yes, it will. He stands out there staring at the moon and the stars all the time. Reminds me of what you used to do, only he doesn't assume the pose." She extended her arms and turned her palms up, imitating the way Artemis used to meditate.

"I think he's just talking with Willa when he does that." Artemis put the neat stack of clothes in the dresser drawer. She sighed. Strang had changed in the months following the choice. He was mellower and no longer on a perpetual search for meaning in the cosmos. To Artemis it seemed Strang's newfound peace presaged what was happening throughout the world. Hostilities, even ancient ones, were ending. Crops grew in abundance, and much of what had been destroyed by human arrogance was slowly being restored. The world was adorned in peace if not brotherhood. And Artemis could see her father's hand in all of it.

"I wonder if Wolf thought the gods would return," Lucy said a little sadly. "You know. He was always talking about the Greek gods like they were real to him. I harbored a few expectations of my own."

Artemis sat on the edge of bed and thought. "Like what?"

"Like that glowing thing you do." Lucy came over and sat beside her. "I read somewhere the ancients referred to the 'glowing ones.' That had to be you, right?"

"Ah yes. It's a protective reaction to the ultraviolet radiation from the sun," Artemis explained. "It is most pronounced when we are in proximity. Although we can display it when we want."

"When do I get to glow?"

Artemis nibbled Lucy's ear, and the two curled together. Hands traced familiar curves and tugged at clothes needing to be shed. Artemis cupped Lucy's chin and grinned in the way that made heat rush to sensitive body parts.

"Would you settle for an afterglow?" Artemis teased, laying Lucy on the bed.

Turned out Lucy would.

*

Deepak Kamakrisha stood at attention, his heart filled with joy. He watched President Chatterjee sign the treaty and hand the pen to the president of Pakistan. They shook hands and then faced the crowd of attendees and accepted the boisterous applause. Delegates from every country Pindata Sin had influenced rejoiced at the treaty. The wealthy nations had extended helping hands to the poorer ones. Refugees were returning to rebuild their homes. An air of celebration lifted hearts and minds throughout the Middle East.

Kamakrisha noticed a young man with blond hair standing off to one side. The man had been present at every signing as the once-hostile nations had found common ground. What was his name? Kamakrisha could not recall it, an odd name, difficult to pronounce. The man turned angelic-blue eyes at Deepak and smiled.

Pindata's vision was coming true in a way, Deepak thought. Nations were aligning, not under the dictates of an ambitious megalomaniac, but with decisions made by freer, wiser men and women. Deepak's own eyes had seen what his head had thought impossible. Humanity had found a common ground on which to stand. He would never know how. It occurred to him the mystery wasn't worth solving. Peace was a gift to be enjoyed, not questioned.

Kamakrisha walked into the afternoon sun and motioned for his driver. There was nothing more for him to do. India was going to prosper along with its neighbors. He was going home to his family after a lifetime of service. Putting politics aside left him with a sense of serenity rather than accomplishment. Deepak knew he had not brought about the changes. Neither had Pindata Sin, although reports of the man's inexplicable death in South America had been the starting point.

The blond man strolled by, granting Deepak a pleasant smile. There was a shine about him, Kamakrisha noted. Perhaps it was the sunlight. He watched the man disappear into a limo and drive off. Deepak felt a slight sense of loss as if an angel had touched his soul in passing.

*

"Tell me what the man is feeling," Dr. Ronan McAndrew quizzed his patient.

"Aw, he's feeling confused." Dr. Keegan Montock stared at the photograph and replied, "If he's not, I know I am."

Ronan shook his head. They had been spending Tuesday lunch hours on the drill for months and progress was occurring. "Come on, Keegan. You knew this one last week. Take a guess."

"Guess? Now that's scientific," the patient pointed out. But he couldn't argue with the transformation the sessions had accomplished. He was learning to read people better with Ronan's help. He studied the photograph and offered an answer. "Pleased. The guy looks pleased."

"Yes, he does." Ronan slapped Keegan's shoulder. "What do you say we run over and get a bite to eat? I have a lecture at two o'clock. And you deserve a reward. My treat today."

"At least you don't feed me dog treats whenever I get the answer right." Keegan smiled. "You're on. I'm due back for student conferences myself."

The University of Southern California had offered both men positions after accepting a generous donation from Choice LLC. Ronan was a natural teacher. His presentations had improved with practice, and a new sense of empathy made him particularly helpful to students who were struggling. He'd developed a theory about empathy for people like Keegan.

Applying Keegan's mathematical talent to his ability to read facial expressions was showing promise. Keegan could quickly determine the ratio between facial muscles. Assigning moods to specific ratios enabled him to determine the emotion being expressed. He literally calculated happiness, disgust, curiosity, and a score of other facial expressions. Keegan found conversation easier and no longer relied on quips or insults to protect himself. Next semester, he would branch out from research to co-instructor of a class on astronomy.

"Are you going to Strang's birthday party?" Keegan asked as he and Ronan sat at a cafeteria table.

"Yes. I'm looking forward to it. You?" Ronan added a packet of sugar to his iced tea.

"Wouldn't miss it." Keegan assembled lettuce and tomato the way he liked it on his burger. "Angie and Stef will be there. I can't wait to hear him call you 'boy-o' again."

Ronan chuckled. "Angie's about to pop. I want to see her all round and maternal and congratulate them on the kid." His happiness for them was genuine. Angie and Stefan were made for each other. Maybe not soulmates like Artemis and Lucy, but a compatible couple obviously very much in love. He munched on his sandwich and thought about bringing a gift for the baby.

"I saw you've still got the disk mounted on your desk. I've been meaning to ask you why?" Keegan asked.

Ronan grinned. "It reminds me how lucky I am. I didn't go to the dark side. I'm not such an asshole after all. That realization changed my life."

"Changed the world according to Artemis." Keegan wiped his mouth. He could read the expression on his friend's face. Contentment. "I know what you mean. Life has gotten a whole lot easier for me since the, ah, event. I thought everything would change like a kaleidoscope, but it didn't. Things just started getting better. Gradual like. It will be good to see Artemis and Lucy again."

"You're going to wow them, Keegan. I can't wait to see Strang's reaction." Ronan smiled. It was not just the change in Keegan's disposition. Dr. Montock finally looked the part of a college professor. His hair was trimmed if a little long at the edges, his clothes were presentable, and the trademark slouch was long gone. "You are a new man."

Keegan straightened in his chair. "Think they'll be surprised?"

"Oh, yeah." Ronan slid his tray to the side and looked at the time. "All except Artemis. I'm sure she already knows."

*

Paolo walked through the small wheat field, his hands roaming over the tips of the healthy plants. His village was going to have a surplus of food for the winter, much better than the crop a year ago. He remembered the hunger pangs and the terrible things famine had driven him to do. He had made his peace with it. Amnesty had been given to everyone, and he told himself if the world forgave him, he could forgive himself.

His wife and children were waiting in the car. They were off to Santiago to shop for the week. There was money enough for food and more. Paolo was going to buy his two little girls new dresses and get a pair of boots for his growing boy. He planned to insist his wife select an item for herself. A new scarf or perhaps some utensil to make her daily chores easier. He patted the coins in his pocket and grinned.

A tiny girl came running to him. Paolo picked her up and gave the child a hug.

"What is it, Rosa?"

The child smiled shyly. "Juan wants to go now. He says you will get us ice cream, Papa. Will you? I want pink."

Paolo kissed her cheek and carried her back to the car. There was even enough for ice cream too. He looked up at the clear blue sky and thanked the gods. The car rumbled to a start, and he steered it back to the main road. He glanced at his wife in the seat beside him. She had never looked so beautiful, he thought, not even when they'd first met before the years of trying to survive had stolen her youth. She took his hand and smiled shyly. Paolo grinned back, feeling his heart skip at the sight of her.

*

Strang patted his stomach, unable to consider taking another bit of cake. Ronan and Keegan waved goodbye from the door, and Strang waved back. It had been a grand party. He walked over to the mantel and put his hand on Willa's urn.

"Sixty-one, my dear." He chuckled. "I didn't expect to achieve that milestone. There were moments when all seemed lost. But my conclusion was premature. I must be getting old."

Angie came over to give him a hug, and Stefan shook his hand. He saw the joy in their eyes. They would be good parents. And Angie had made it official. Strang was to be known as Grandpa once the baby came. It was a title he cherished more than any other, save for Father. He went to the door and watched Artemis and Lucy setting up the telescope in the back of the yard. He chuckled. It was a symbol of his previous life and more. It was a gesture of respect and love. That had pleased him most of all.

Once the sky grew dark enough, Strange wandered over to try out the new device. Pointing the scope to Orion first and then to the Great Rift. He smiled at the image so different from the sterile numeric representation provided by the Keck.

"Hello, Phaeton, my dear fellow," Strang said, referring to the Greek mythology of how the Milky Way was formed.

"Alas, Phaeton is busy just now," a deep male voice answered. "Perhaps I may be of service to you."

Strang turned to see who was speaking. An imposing figure stood in the center of the yard. He was exceedingly tall with dark hair crowned silver in the moonlight flowing abundantly to his shoulders. The man drew nearer, and Strang smiled when he saw the pale-blue eyes, so like they were to Temmie's.

The stranger set his hand on the telescope. "Do you still yearn to understand the cosmos, Wolfgang?" he asked, his voice so deep it seemed to rumble directly from his massive chest.

"Dark matter was what I sought to comprehend," Strang said with a self-deprecating grin. "But I have it on good authority I am not meant to possess such knowledge in this life."

"All in good time. When you are ready. May I suggest you look within rather than without? You may find what you are looking for. There is more to encounter in dreams than those we've lost."

Strang took a deep breath. The man's presence overwhelmed his senses, powerful, wise, commanding, like no one Strang had ever encountered. The visitor offered his hand to the amazed scientist, who was too astonished to take it.

"I understand from my daughter today is the anniversary of your birth." The voice resonated like a wave, nearly pushing Strang back a step. "You have been of great assistance to your species, Wolfgang, and by so doing to mine."

The men stood and observed the canopy of stars in silence for what seemed to Strang like hours. As the time passed, he felt answers slipping into place where once his mind had been filled with questions. There were no words spoken between them. No long explanations for mysteries the astrophysicist had spent many decades pondering. Strang simply knew with elegant simplicity that which he had longed to understand.

Eventually, the stranger bid him goodbye, and Strang watched him walk away into the shadows. A chilly breeze made him shiver, and he headed to his bungalow. He felt airily light. A sense of happiness rose from deep within him and something else—a sense of anticipation he could not place.

He opened the door slowly as if uncertain what awaited inside and stepped into the living room.

She was lovely, Polynesian features in the bloom of youth, smiling eyes just as Strang remembered.

"Willa!" Strang whispered, barely able to speak. His wife stood before him precisely as she had looked on their wedding day. He held out his arms, and she embraced him, nestling her head in the hollow of his shoulder. She smelled of the islands and sunshine and happiness. And despite all the scientist thought he knew of the laws that governed time and space and matter, Willa was real.

A slight smile formed on Ze'us's lips. "It doesn't hurt to accelerate the process from time to time," he told himself as he savored the love the couple shared. "They'd have figured it out eventually anyway. Everyone does. Speaking of love..." He paused at the edge of the huge yard and cast an ear to the main house.

*

"That's your father?" Lucy asked, fascinated by the figures in the yard. She watched as Strang and a large, imposing man stood side by side and silently observed the night sky. Then the stranger simply walked away.

Artemis pulled her from the window. "Um-hum."

"He's...he's..." Lucy stuttered. She had no words to describe the man, a rare foible for a reporter. All she could do was look up helpless to find Artemis's amused blue eyes.

"Yes, he is, but I'm sure he still can't pronounce your ancient name." Artemis grinned.

"Lucilambereemah!" The name echoed in the room followed by a low, fading chuckle.

Artemis sighed. "I stand corrected."

Lucy stared at Artemis. She felt intoxicated, even giddy. Artemis put her arm around Lucy's waist and walked them to the sofa. It was going to be fun watching the world adjust to its new environment. The collective was all around them, walking among them. And bit by bit the humans were beginning to perceive it. She tousled Lucy's hair.

"I don't think we'll suggest that particular name to Angie and Stefan." Lucy composed herself. "I'm sure we can come up with something better."

Artemis stretched out on the sofa and put her hands behind her head. She had seen the soul seeking rebirth and was delighted with what the future held. Turning to Lucy, she formed a knowing smile. "How about Claire?"

About the Author

Mary Eicher lives with her two daughters in Southern California. With degrees in Psychology and English from the University of California, she left an executive position in Silicon Valley to pursue a career in creative writing. Mary has traveled extensively in Europe and worked with the Pacific Whale Foundation in Australia and dolphin research facilities in Hawaii. Recipient of a Silver Pen award and other acclaim for her short stories, Mary is a frequent contributor to fandom sites and anthologies. *The Harbinger*, the first book in the Artemis series trilogy, is an Award-Winning Finalist in the Fiction: LGBTQ category of the 2020 Best Book Awards sponsored by American Book Fest.

Email
maryeic@aol.com

Facebook
www.facebook.com/MaryEicher

Website
www.OfficialMaryEicher.com

Twitter
@MaryEicher19

Other NineStar books by this author

The Artemis series
The Harbinger
Perceptions

Also Available from NineStar Press

Connect with NineStar Press

www.ninestarpress.com

www.facebook.com/ninestarpress

www.facebook.com/groups/NineStarNiche

www.twitter.com/ninestarpress